ALABAMA

OFFICIAL STATS

NAME: T. J. (Thomas Jefferson) Swift

VITALS: Age: Early 30s
Height: 6 feet plus
Eye Color: Golden-brown (like a cat's)
Hair: Rusty-brown

OCCUPATION: Ex-cop

OBJECTIVE: Figure out what to do with the rest of his life.

ADDITIONAL INFO: T.J. is a dedicated protector who believes he is no longer worthy because of a mistake he made that cost his wife and child their lives. He has an angry scar that angles from his right eyebrow and plows a furrow across his brow and ends in his thick hair.

DANGEROUS
TO
LOVE

DANGEROUS
TO
LOVE
USA

BONNIE GARDNER
STRANGER IN HER BED

Silhouette Books

Published by Silhouette Books
America's Publisher of Contemporary Romance

To Mud, who always encouraged me to be creative,
even if it meant crayons on the wall.
To Brenda, who knows a good idea when she hears one.
To Marg, who knows Tuscaloosa.
To Ava, who reads, and Kathie, who proofreads.

SILHOUETTE BOOKS

ISBN 0-373-82299-5

STRANGER IN HER BED

Copyright © 1997 by Bonnie Gardner

Visit Silhouette at www.eHarlequin.com

Printed in U.S.A.

BONNIE GARDNER

has finally figured out what she wants to do when she grows up. After a varied career that included such jobs as switchboard operator, draftsman and exercise instructor, she went back to college and became an English teacher. As a teacher, she took a course on how to teach writing to high school students and caught the bug herself.

She lives in northern Alabama with her husband of over thirty years, her own military hero. After following him around from air force base to air force base, she has finally gotten to settle down. They have two grown sons, one of whom is now serving in the air force. She loves to read, cook, garden and, of course, write.

She would love hear from her readers. You can write to her at P.O. Box 442, Meridianville, AL 35759.

Books by Bonnie Gardner

Silhouette Intimate Moments

Stranger in Her Bed #798
Montoya's Heart #846

Harlequin American Romance

Uncle Sarge #876
Sgt. Billy's Bride #911

Dear Reader,

Imagine coming home from a trip and discovering that people think you're dead. That's what happened to Robin Digby in *Stranger in Her Bed*. Not only did she find her apartment occupied by a strange man, but she discovered her bank account closed, her friends in mourning and a killer looking for her. Not exactly a warm welcome.

Think that could happen only in a book? Something similar actually happened to me. I came home from a conference to find a newspaper article about a woman with my name being found dead. And not an hour later a former neighbor called to inquire about funeral arrangements. The coincidence got my imagination going, and *Stranger in Her Bed* was born.

Enjoy.

Bonnie Gardner

Please address questions and book requests to:
Silhouette Reader Service
U.S.: 3010 Walden Ave., P.O. Box 1325, Buffalo, NY 14269
Canadian: P.O. Box 609, Fort Erie, Ont. L2A 5X3

Chapter 1

Robin Leigh Digby shifted her backpack to her other shoulder as she climbed out of the taxicab in front of her apartment in Tuscaloosa, Alabama. She pulled a crumpled wad of bills from her pocket and paid her fare. "Damn, only a couple of dollars left," she muttered as she jammed her change back into her pocket. If Cheryl had come to pick her up at the bus station, she wouldn't be squandering her last few bucks on an extravagance like a cab.

She probably could have walked the few blocks from the bus station to Reed Street, but it had been late and she was dog tired. And Tuscaloosa might not be as dangerous as New York City, or even busy Birmingham, for that matter, but Robin knew better than to walk even such a short distance all alone at such a late hour. So when a Druid cab materialized in front of the station with a sympathetic-looking *female* driver, Robin had taken it as a sign and climbed in.

Besides, she could always get more cash from an automatic teller machine in the morning. It could certainly wait until after she'd been to bed.

Her carryall slung over one shoulder, Robin gazed up at the weathered old building and yawned. She had been too tired to be annoyed when Cheryl didn't appear at the appointed time. And when she called to remind her roommate to pick her up at the bus station, she'd gotten a phone-company recording. She shouldn't have been surprised. Cheryl must have forgotten to pay the bill again.

The old-style apartment house looked beautiful, even in the early-morning dark. Robin hurried up the entry stairs and pushed open the common front door, smiling as it creaked in protest, just as it always had in the year she'd lived there. It was good to be back. The summer internship in Cacaxtla, Mexico, had been a dream come true, allowing her to check off real progress in her five-year plan to get on with her life since her divorce. But now, after months away, Robin was eager to return to her old routine.

Just a few more minutes, she told herself as she trudged up the flight of stairs that led to her second-floor apartment. Just a few more steps, and she'd be home. Home to a solid roof and a real bed. After two months of camping out at the isolated archaeological dig in the jungle, she longed for the luxury of a hot shower, a soft bed and American junk food. Not necessarily in that order.

Though Robin had promised herself a real shower, the notion of sleeping in her own bed was much more appealing. Her day had begun over thirty-six hours and several time zones earlier, and she was dead tired. Cacaxtla might be only a half day away as the crow flies, but her budget ticket had taken her on the scenic route. She had zigzagged from Mexico City to Los Angeles then east to New Orleans and even farther east to Atlanta before she had finally arrived back in Birmingham. And then there had still been the two-hour bus ride. It was all she could do to stay on her feet. The shower could wait, she decided. She needed a good night's sleep. Or two.

As Robin shoved her key into the lock of apartment 2-B, she noticed something vaguely different about the door. She hadn't been away long enough to forget what had been there before she left. Someone had removed the straw wreath that doubled as a decoration and nameplate. Robin shrugged. She was too tired and too happy to be home to worry about sticky-fingered wreath filchers now.

The lock mechanism clicked, and Robin picked up her bag and shouldered her way in. She was home.

The warm feeling lasted only a fleeting second. It fled as Robin registered a change in the appearance of her living room. All the homey touches she had put there were gone, and the room looked as inviting as a cheap motel. Only the VCR sitting atop the portable TV and the ten-speed bicycle propped up against the wall showed any personality.

And they weren't hers.

Robin and her roommate hadn't had either of those things when she left. Had Cheryl gotten a new VCR and a bicycle? No, they couldn't be hers; Cheryl was just as broke as she was. Unless she'd won one of those sweepstakes she was always wasting stamps on. The ones she could have used to mail the phone bill with.

Robin chuckled. They should be that lucky.

Then she noticed a light coming from the kitchen. Was Cheryl at home after all?

Dropping her bags by the door, Robin detoured from her course toward the bedroom to flip off the light. As she reached for the switch, she stopped short.

There at the kitchen table, sprawled across a pile of books, was an extremely healthy-looking man. And he was wearing only enough to cover him and retain the technicality of being dressed.

Robin didn't have the energy to scream, and probably wouldn't have if she had; it wasn't her style. She stared at the man as a handful of questions flew to mind and stopped before they came out of her mouth.

Did Cheryl have a new boyfriend? If so, where was Cheryl? And hadn't they agreed about not bringing home strays? The man shifted positions and groaned slightly, bringing Robin back to the situation at hand. She looked at him closely, trying to gauge the situation as best she could in her exhausted frame of mind.

He was asleep. That was in her favor. At least the slow, rhythmic motion of his slumped body suggested that he was sleeping. Judging from the way he was lying across the clutter of books and papers, he had tried to pull an all-nighter. And judging by the lack of movement and closed eyes, he hadn't succeeded.

The man looked older than the average student in this college town. The thickness of the books pillowed beneath his head, and the size of the pile, led Robin to think he was a graduate student. But this guy was no academic nerd. His tanned skin stretched tightly over well-developed muscles. His hair was a rusty brown, and much shorter than the average grad-student cut. It was thick and unruly—whether from his uncomfortable sleeping position or by nature, Robin couldn't tell.

She stared for a moment longer, then cleared her heart out of her throat. As she tried to speak, Robin was surprised to discover that her voice was cracked and tired. "Hello?" she asked. Somehow, "Who are you?" and "What are you doing in my apartment?" didn't seem appropriate. And hadn't she read somewhere that it was dangerous to wake sleeping people? Or was that sleepwalkers?

The man stirred and pushed his head up from the pillow of books. He rubbed his temple with the heel of his hand and sleepily focused golden brown eyes on Robin. Eyes like a cat's, Robin noticed, just before she saw the angry scar that angled from his right eyebrow and plowed a furrow across his brow and hid in his thick hair.

T. J. Swift tried to shake the sleep from his eyes. He squeezed them shut and forced them open again, hoping the action would clear the fog from his mind. He thought he saw someone standing in the entryway, but that couldn't be right; he lived alone—by choice. He squinted at his watch. Damn, two-thirty already. He still had three more pages to write before he could go to bed, and he was no closer to completing his quota than he'd been four hours ago. Maybe another pot of coffee would do it. He started to shove out of the chair, but stopped midway.

She hadn't been a figment of his tired imagination. Standing in the kitchen doorway was a woman he had never seen before, and she looked just as surprised to see him as he was to see her. T.J. was too groggy to react quickly, and too stunned by her unexpected appearance to say anything. But his eyes still worked. Barely.

She was wearing grubby sneakers and faded khaki trousers, with a similar work shirt over a light blue top. Years of training still had him cataloging descriptions as if he would need the information to make a case, T.J. realized as he continued to look. Her clothes looked as if she had slept in them, yet they skimmed over a firm, well-shaped body that had curves in all the right places. She was tanned brown, and her hair was a tangled, short golden mop that glinted with silver. Her face was dirty and streaked and completely devoid of makeup, yet her clear blue eyes shone from beneath thick, arched brows. She wasn't model-beautiful; her hands were sturdy and strong, with blunt, snubbed fingernails that looked like they were used to work. But she would get any man's attention.

But she doesn't belong here in my apartment, T.J. reminded himself as he rose from the chair. His body was cramped and stiff from his catnap, and he couldn't stay in the half-up position forever. He needed to stretch.

T.J. yawned, raising his arms high above his head. He

was surprised to see the woman flinch and shrink back from him. Had he done something to frighten her?

He found his voice. "Hey. I'm not going to hurt you." He tried to sound nonthreatening, but sleep had made his voice thick and raspy. He hadn't succeeded in calming her, he guessed, because his words came out more like a growl than like reassurance.

She edged back a little farther.

"Look. I'm not holding a weapon." T.J. held his hands open in front of him, hoping to assure her that he was harmless. For now. But he knew that his six-foot-plus frame could be just as intimidating as a gun.

The woman stopped retreating and watched T.J. warily, her blue eyes following each move he made.

T.J. rubbed his eyes again and looked across the room to her. He was finally awake enough to ask questions. "Now, tell me what you're doing in my apartment in the middle of the night."

The wary look flew from her eyes, replaced with...what? Surprise? Then...suspicion?

"*Your* apartment?" Robin wasn't sure she'd heard right. "This is 2-B. It's *my* apartment. And I'd appreciate an explanation of why you're in it." But she was afraid she already knew.

Since she and Cheryl had both planned to be elsewhere over summer vacation and couldn't afford to continue the rent payments, they had temporarily sublet the apartment, using the referral service provided by the campus housing office. The tenant had been told to be out before today. This shouldn't be him, but something told Robin it was. Her aching weariness forgotten, she shot him what she hoped was a dangerous look.

"Wait a minute, lady. I don't know who you are, but I've got a signed lease."

"I've got one, too," Robin insisted stubbornly. "I'll

prove it to you.'' She pivoted and headed toward the hall closet.

But when she opened the door, nothing was right. The lidded cardboard box that she used to store her important papers was gone. In fact, all of her stuff was gone! Hanging neatly on the hangers were a couple of jackets and a raincoat. And the shelf above was bare.

Robin whirled around, nearly colliding with the man, who had sneaked up behind her. She was so startled, her breath caught in her throat.

It took her a moment to recover and get the words out. ''What have you done with my things?

''My roommate and I sublet this apartment before we left for the summer. But the agreement specifically stated that our stuff was to remain here while we were gone.''

Suddenly Robin remembered that she had no idea who this man standing so close to her was. He could be the tenant they'd sublet to, but she had only his word for it. She stepped back. ''Who are you, anyway?''

''My name is T. J. Swift,'' he replied, giving her a level look.

The name sounded familiar, Robin thought. And he sure didn't look like he had anything to hide. As if he could, in his half-dressed state. Robin fervently wished that she had the sublet agreement in her hands. Was he the one she and Cheryl had agreed to temporarily rent the apartment to? If only she could remember his name.

She wished she'd had time to meet the person who'd taken the apartment. But as an alternate for the summer archaeological internship in Mexico, she'd had such short notice of the opening that she left the details up to Cheryl. If only the guy she'd replaced had broken his leg a week sooner.

''Do you have a copy of your lease?'' Robin finally managed to ask.

He didn't say anything, but turned and walked with catlike grace into Cheryl's bedroom. He returned with two documents.

The fatigue from nearly two days without sleep was beginning to catch up with Robin again. "Do you think we could sit in the living room while we settle this?" Robin asked as she felt herself sway.

"Sure." He turned and led the way to the old brown sofa.

Robin sank wearily onto the familiar frayed cushions and looked at the man expectantly. She held out her hand, and he passed her the papers.

The first was a one-year lease dated the first of July of that year. It was made out in the name of T. J. Swift and bore the familiar signature of Mr. Edwards, the elderly apartment manager.

"But this supersedes our lease! How could Mr. Edwards do that? I thought he was my friend," Robin blurted.

Robin looked at the second document. It was a copy of the sublet agreement. It had her roommate's name and T.J.'s name and their signatures on it. It specifically stated August 9—yesterday, or rather two days ago by now, she figured fuzzily—as the termination date. And, Robin realized with a sinking feeling, it made no mention of her. She and Cheryl had agreed to share the apartment after Cheryl signed the original lease. She wondered if she even had a legal leg to stand on. Maybe T.J. *was* the rightful tenant.

Robin waved the papers in the air, hoping to bluff her way through. "See, this is the agreement Cheryl signed, and it states specifically that we're to reclaim possession today." She shook hair from her eyes. "I mean yesterday."

T.J. sat up straight on his end of the sofa. He looked at her for a long moment, then his eyes narrowed. "I don't know what your scam is, lady. But I do know that the situation changed drastically after Cheryl Rodgers's roommate was found murdered the day I moved in last June."

"But Cheryl wouldn't give up our apartment without

consulting me. I had as much invested in this place as she did—'' Robin stopped abruptly and considered what she had heard. Maybe it was the jet lag, but Robin was positive that the man had just said that Cheryl's roommate had been killed.

"I guess she just didn't have the heart to stay here after that," the man went on.

Boy, she really did need some sleep. He couldn't possibly have just said what she thought he did. "Excuse me? Did you say her roommate? What roommate?" Had Cheryl taken in another one?

T.J. looked at her for a moment. "The woman she shared the apartment with until they both had summer jobs somewhere else." He thought for a moment. "I think her name was Robin. Yeah, that's it. Robin Digby was found murdered sometime in the middle of June. Mr. Edwards told me."

"Murdered? Died? As in dead?" Robin's heart chugged on in slow motion, then slowly ground to a halt. She went cold all over. "This can't be happening," she muttered.

The room closed in on her, and Robin saw him from inside a long, dark tunnel. Her feet and her arms went numb. Then everything went blank.

Chapter 2

T.J. stared at the woman as she sagged over onto the cushions of the couch. He groaned. The last thing he needed right now was a hysterical, unconscious woman on his hands. He had a research paper to finish and give to the typist by Friday. Not only was he already two days behind schedule, but he was damned certain to be held up even more now.

He didn't know who the hell this woman was. Had Cheryl Rodgers had another roommate he didn't know about? All he was sure of was that this couldn't possibly be Robin Digby. The police had a corpse that they'd identified with fingerprints, and they couldn't be wrong. They were certain the body they had found was Robin Digby's, and that was good enough for him.

He'd been questioned by the police at the time of their investigation of the death of Cheryl Rodgers's roommate, but he'd been excused when he told them he'd never met her. And he was positive he'd never seen this woman before, either.

He would certainly remember her if he had.

He had met Cheryl, the person who'd had the apartment before him, and this was definitely not her.

If T.J. was ever going to get back to his paper, he was going to have to straighten this out—and fast. He left the mystery woman on the couch with her feet raised and headed for the kitchen. He needed coffee and a damp cloth. Coffee to clear his head, and the cloth to clear hers.

She had already begun to stir by the time he had put the coffeepot on and returned with the dripping washcloth. He laid it gently on her head and was relieved to see her struggle against its cool wetness. Her eyes slowly opened. She had the frightened look of a wounded animal as she watched him remove the cloth.

T.J. wasn't good at apologies, but he guessed he'd have to make one. "I could have handled the news about Robin Digby's death more delicately. I assume you hadn't heard. Were you a good friend of hers?"

The woman shook her head slowly. "No. Not a friend." She still sounded confused. "Not a friend," she mumbled as she pushed herself up on one elbow. "I'm Robin," she said very clearly, "and, as you can plainly see, I'm not dead."

For a second, he looked as if he were going to keel over, just the way she had, but he quickly regained his composure. Robin was less worried about his predicament, however, than about hers. And it was a predicament. There was a very-much-alive man in her apartment, claiming that it was his. And he was insisting that she was dead. She wasn't going to take that lying down.

Robin pushed herself slowly to a sitting position and looked at him. He was still crouching at the side of the couch. He'd acquired a T-shirt, she noticed, vaguely disappointed that his broad chest had been covered. Then she reminded herself to stop looking at the scenery, interesting as it was. They had something important to settle.

As Robin opened her mouth to speak, he beat her to the first question. "Do you have any identification that proves who you are?"

How did he manage to look confused, apologetic and so damned commanding all at the same time? Robin wondered as she tried to remember where she'd left her luggage, such as it was.

"I guess I should have expected that. My wallet is in my backpack." Robin swung her legs over the edge of the sofa and started to get up. Still feeling light-headed, she swayed, then sank back to the cushions. "My legs don't seem to want to hold me up," she murmured. "Would you bring my bag to me? I left it by the door."

He pushed himself up from the crouching position beside her and went to get the bag. Robin watched his lionlike movements as he veered into the kitchen to toss the rag. She shouldn't be so fascinated, she reminded herself. He was a perfect stranger. She remembered his well-honed muscles, now covered by that scrap of a shirt. Perfect was right. But Robin had other, more pressing things to be thinking about.

Now she understood why Cheryl hadn't come to pick her up at the bus station, although it wasn't very comforting. And this probably explained the phone company recording when she had called. The phone hadn't been disconnected for nonpayment, but because Cheryl had moved out. But why would she give up the apartment? The rent was very reasonable, even for one, and Cheryl still had another year of graduate school to go.

T.J.—was that his name?—came back with the backpack and handed it to her as he lowered his length onto the couch beside her.

Robin poked around in the bag for her wallet. She found it and passed it over to him. "It's in here."

"Remove it from the wallet, please." T.J. sounded just like a TV cop she used to watch.

"You sounded like a policeman for a minute there," Robin commented as she flipped through the plastic card protectors and located her driver's license and student ID card. She remembered her passport and dug for it.

"Used to be one," he muttered.

Robin handed her identification to him. "Oh." Maybe that was how he'd gotten the scar.

"Did you get that scar in the line of duty?" Robin's curiosity overruled her manners.

T.J. clamped his teeth together, and his jaw set firmly, making the muscles twitch as it tightened. His silence told Robin that she'd better drop the subject. There was probably some better time than this to make polite conversation.

Robin watched expectantly as he examined the two plastic-covered scraps of paper and opened the passport. He flipped through the pages and double-checked the entry and exit stamps. He was taking a ridiculous amount of time to check. Then he looked up at her, scrutinizing her face. Robin squirmed under his careful gaze and was relieved when he turned back to her identification.

Then T.J. looked back up and stared at Robin as though he were looking through her. "I don't know what you're trying to pull, lady," he said carefully. "This may be Robin Digby's ID, but there's no way you can be her. There's a slight resemblance here, but except for the eyes, the size and coloring are all wrong."

Robin felt as though she had been slapped. He was all but calling her a liar. She snatched her cards back from him and stared at them. He *was* calling her a liar. And she was actually going to have to prove to this man that she really was Robin Leigh Digby if she was ever going to get him out of her apartment.

T.J. didn't know what he expected her to do, but he didn't expect her to stare at him as if he had suddenly grown horns. He'd never been in a situation like this before, but his cop instincts told him to throw her out. Or turn her in. There was no way he would believe she was Robin Digby, come back from the dead.

She still hadn't said anything. Not in anger, nor in her defense. T.J. wished she would do something. Anything.

The silent minutes ticked away as T.J. watched a series of emotions flit across her face. She tentatively raised a hand. Was she going to strike at him? No. She put it to her face, slowly running her sturdy fingers across the planes of her cheekbones, the curve of her jaw.

"Do you have a mirror?" Her question surprised him. What a time to be thinking about what she looked like.

"In the bathroom. It's the second door on the—"

She cut him off before he could finish. "I know where the bathroom is in my own apartment," she replied coldly. She got up and went straight to it.

T.J. didn't know why, but he followed her down the hall and watched as she turned on the light. They both blinked in the fluorescent brightness.

She stared into the mirror as if she'd never seen herself before that moment. The woman abruptly turned on the water and splashed her face, making muddy rivulets through the grime there. She lathered up some soap and scrubbed and splashed again until her face was clean. Then she stared at the image in the mirror as she blinked water droplets from her feathery eyelashes. The drops rolled down her face and off her chin and spotted the khaki shirt, but she couldn't seem to tear her gaze away.

"Wow!" was all she said.

"Lady? Is there some point to this?"

She looked at his reflection in the mirror in front of her. "Robin. My name is Robin Leigh Digby," she told him carefully, as if she weren't certain he would understand. "I'm twenty-eight years old. I'm in my second year of graduate school in the anthropology department at the university, and I've been away at an archaeological dig in Mexico all summer. I had some kind of Latin American bug while I was there, and lost some weight. Apparently a lot more than I thought. My hair is bleached by the sun, and my skin is tanned from so much time outside. And this is my bathroom we're standing in.'' She paused for a moment, then added, ''And my apartment.''

''Okay, okay.'' T.J. held up his hands in exasperation. ''We'll have to settle all this in the morning.''

''Fine with me,'' she said. ''I'm exhausted.''

''Do you have someplace to stay tonight?'' T.J. had to get her out of the way. He still had that paper to finish.

She—Robin—looked at him as if he were absolutely stupid. ''Of course I do. I intend to sleep here, in my own apartment and my own bed.'' She stared at him defiantly, her arms folded across her chest.

Of course! T.J. groaned. Why was this happening to him?

''No way, lady. Or Robin. Or whoever you are. You go find yourself a motel room and come back in the morning.''

''You can't throw me out of my own apartment. See, I have my own key.'' She held it up.

The key did look like the one he had. And she had gotten in somehow. But just having a key wasn't sufficient evidence for him to let her stay. He shook his head vehemently. ''No. You go get a room somewhere. Anywhere but here.''

''No. You go.''

If she weren't such a damned nuisance, T.J. would have admired her tenacity. But she had to go. He tried to reason with her, but no logical arguments came to his fatigued mind.

He stared at her, waiting, watching for her next move. She looked for a moment as if she were going to cry. But she didn't. Instead, she dug in her pockets and dragged out two crumpled ones and a handful of change and held it in her palm. "I can't afford a motel. Even if I intended to go to one." Her eyes dared him.

In spite of her defiance, T.J. knew that if he wanted to, it would be no problem for him to overpower her and remove her bodily. He stepped forward. Then he stopped.

Defiance or no, he could see that Robin, or whoever she was, could barely stand. Her muscles trembled as she maintained her stubborn stance. Then she began to sway. T.J. reached out to steady her, but she flinched, and her knees buckled.

He caught her. "Look, I'm not going to hurt you," he said, as patiently as he could manage, as she struggled from his grip. He let go and watched as she backed up against the wall and eyed him.

"Oh, hell." He knew he shouldn't do it, but he couldn't turn her out. Especially if she really did belong in the apartment by some strange coincidence. And she didn't have any money to go anywhere else. He shut his eyes and sucked in a long breath.

"Okay. You can stay," he finally told her. "But only for tonight," he added. "I can see that we're both too beat to discuss this rationally now.

"We'll get Mr. Edwards to come up here first thing in the morning. Maybe he can help straighten out this misunderstanding."

She shot him a triumphant look and turned. At least she didn't head for his bedroom. He was too tired to argue any more tonight. And he was way too tired to work on that blasted research paper.

T.J. ran his fingers through his hair and waited until he figured she was safely out of sight. He listened for a moment and smiled as he heard the lock mechanism on her door snap firmly shut. Then he turned off the kitchen light and headed for his own room. It was obvious he wouldn't be getting any more work done tonight.

Something told T.J. that nothing would be solved in the morning, but as beat as he was, he could hope. He did have a valid lease. Why wasn't he sure he'd win?

Robin woke from blissful, dreamless sleep to the sound of falling water. She rolled over and covered her head with the pillow and tried to will away the noise. Rain at the site could set the schedule back days, she thought groggily.

It wasn't rain, but running water, she realized as she became fully awake. And she wasn't at the site anymore. She was finally home. Then she remembered. *Him.*

It took Robin a few minutes to orient herself to her familiar but unaccustomed surroundings. She had slept too soundly in the soft bed and woken muddled and confused, instead of refreshed, as she had expected. Slowly, the events of the night before came back to her.

She had been too tired to think clearly last night, but she couldn't forget that he'd said people thought she had died. But why? Her friends all knew that she had gone to the dig in Cacaxtla. This morning the questions she should have asked last night finally began to form in her mind. T.J. had told her that stuff about her being dead, but how did she know she could believe him? How did she know that he hadn't fabricated the entire story just to get his hands on her apartment?

Even in her early-morning fuzziness, Robin realized how stupid that idea was. "Get a grip, Digby. Safe, cheap apartments may be hard to come by around here this time of year, but that's a little extreme," she muttered as she flung the covers off and stepped into the chilly, air-conditioned room. After two months in the jungle, the artificial cooling seemed much too cold.

Robin chafed the gooseflesh on her arms and hurried over to her dresser to find something clean—and warm— to wear. She had been so tired the night before that she kicked off her grubby shoes and tossed aside the work shirt and trousers and slept in her tank top.

Now she needed that shower she'd promised herself, as well as a change of clothes. Robin reached for the drawer pull and stopped as she caught a glimpse of her reflection in the mirror. It really didn't look like her, or at least not like the woman she had gotten used to seeing in the past few years. She traced the newfound hollows beneath her cheekbones lightly with her finger. After the first few days in the primitive conditions of the camp, Robin had given up trying to keep up appearances, and she hadn't bothered with a mirror for the rest of the time. No wonder he didn't believe her. She looked different even to herself.

The case of Montezuma's revenge she'd had was a severe one, nearly getting her sent home. But she had finally recovered and had continued with the strenuous and tedious program at the site. She'd known she had lost weight; the looseness of her clothes had told her that even before she left Mexico. But she hadn't realized how much. She looked very different. And very good. Even without makeup.

Robin looked like the woman who had smiled brightly at the world from her college yearbook picture. That slim and confident woman had been poised at the beginning of an adventure. But that had been before her ex-husband, Dub. She shook the memory of Dub Doubleday out of her mind and focused on her image in the mirror.

It looked almost as though those four painful years hadn't happened at all. Maybe with the new look, her old insecurity would be replaced by confidence. God, she hoped so.

Robin stopped her introspection and tugged to open the drawer, fighting against the warped runners. The Alabama humidity had done a number on the old dresser, and being unused for a couple of months hadn't helped. She yanked until it came free, and she ended up with an empty drawer in her hand. Robin snatched open the rest of the drawers. They were empty, too.

She rushed over to the closet. Even it had been stripped bare. There were a few boxes, apparently his, but none of her things were there. Where were they?

The sounds in the bathroom stopped, and Robin remembered the person who had the answers. She yanked on the khaki trousers. Full of righteous indignation, she went to find out, once and for all, what had happened.

T.J. squinted and tried to see around the fog on the mirror. Normally, he'd open the door and let the steam out and the cool air in so that he could see to shave. Though not overly modest, he still didn't relish the idea of *her* walking in on him. He stretched the skin on his cheek tight and started to scrape the razor over his face.

He was almost finished when somebody pounded loudly on the door. The noise came so unexpectedly that he jumped and nicked himself. The angry voice of the woman who called herself Robin Digby came clearly through the heavy wood.

"What have you done with my stuff? My clothes?" she demanded loudly. The question was followed by another barrage of knocks.

Jaw clenched, T.J. counted to ten, then twenty, before he answered. "I'll be out in about five minutes. I'm in the middle of shaving."

"Okay." The voice sounded contrite. "But hurry up."

"I'll be out when I'm done," T.J. replied. Damn, that woman rubbed him the wrong way.

He found himself taking his time just to irritate her. Besides, it was her fault he'd nicked himself, and it was going to take some time to fix that up, too. T.J. tried to finish shaving as slowly and as carefully as possible. Swabbing at the trickle of blood slowed him down.

Finally, he was done. She had been quiet while he fin-

ished, but just knowing that she was lurking outside the
door was enough to unsettle him. He wiped the remaining
lather off his face and splashed on an ample amount of
aftershave. The nick near his jawbone protested the alco-
holic dousing and made him wince.

"Are you finished in there?"

T.J. tried to ignore her and rummaged in the medicine
cabinet for a styptic pencil. He couldn't find one, and the
wound was still seeping. He swabbed it with a wad of toilet
paper and shrugged. What did he care if he bled a little bit?
He wasn't going anywhere. He tore off a triangular wedge
of tissue and stuck it over the nick. It wasn't attractive, but
it did the trick.

She smacked the door three times. "T.J., are you finished? It's awfully quiet in there."

T.J. sighed. There wasn't much sense in delaying. He
squirted on some deodorant, readjusted the towel around
his middle and opened the door.

Robin had just raised her hand to bang on the door again
when he opened it. With a surprised look and an upraised
fist, she stepped back, out of his way.

Her anger had brought color to her cheeks that hadn't
been there before, and her golden hair was wild and tousled
from sleep. It was hard to believe that she could look even
more beautiful in the morning light. Why couldn't she be
ugly? T.J. lamented. It would make it a lot easier for him
to play the heavy in all this. If she looked like the woman
on her identification cards, it would be much easier to throw
her out. But then, if she looked like Robin Digby's picture,
they wouldn't be having this argument.

She'd shed the khaki shirt, but the blue tank top did
nothing to conceal the curves it was supposed to cover. And
the hardened nipples thrusting against the knit fabric did
nothing to encourage his objectivity.

"It took you long enough," she stated icily.

Her combative tone helped bring him back to earth.

T.J.'s police training had kept his temper in check so far; he hoped it would continue to work. "If you hadn't surprised the hell out of me, I might have finished quicker. I cut myself." He fingered the clotted spot on his jaw.

"I'm so sorry." Her tone was anything but apologetic. "Perhaps I could help you with a tourniquet."

That did it. He wasn't going to listen to this. He was going to have to leave, or say something he would probably regret. He turned.

"Where are you going? You still haven't told me what happened to all my stuff."

T.J. straightened his shoulders and stiffened his neck and walked to his room.

"Come back here!" she yelled after him.

He turned back to look at her. "You'll have to ask Mr. Edwards what he did with your belongings. I called him this morning. He'll be here at eleven." T.J. closed the door firmly between them.

Chapter 3

He'd actually slammed the door on her. Okay, he'd closed it, but still… Robin stared at the door for a few minutes, until her anger subsided.

Would he be coming out soon, or had T.J. decided to stay in there? She'd wait. T.J. didn't look like the type to hide, and she wasn't going anywhere.

Once her anger was spent, Robin began to think. Propped up against the wall in the short hallway, she began to realize that he was probably as confused about the whole situation as she was. He seemed like a nice guy, or would have if they'd met under other circumstances.

Wait a minute, Digby, she warned herself. Can't you see where this line of thinking is going? Remember what happened with Dub. You've just come out of a bad marriage; the last thing you need is to be making goo-goo eyes at some hunk that you've only seen wearing less than the average Chippendale's dancer.

But what she'd seen was too good to forget. His muscles indicated that he was a man of action, as well as letters, and she wondered what kind of activity he did to keep his muscles so toned and his chest so broad. Of course, the bike. That accounted for his fitness, but what was responsible for that massive chest? She thought of the dark thatch of hair at the top of his head. Though it had a definite chestnut cast, it was still dark enough to put him in the tall-dark-and-handsome category. And his amber eyes had a red glint that hinted at banked fires.

Too bad he was such a hard case about her apartment. Imagine him not believing her. Why would she lie?

Chuckling softly, Robin thought about the absurdity of the situation. If I were going to impersonate somebody and take her apartment, she told herself, I'd certainly pick somebody from a higher income bracket.

Robin listened to the faint sounds coming from behind the closed door and tried to imagine what he was doing. T.J. She had to remember his name. He'd been in there long enough to dress. Was he going to hole up until Mr. Edwards arrived?

The sound of approaching footsteps and the doorknob turning answered that question. He flung the door open and stopped short when he found her still standing in the hall.

He was fully dressed, Robin noted with relief. And regret. His strong, broad chest was covered by a teal polo shirt, and he wore faded jeans that clung to his thighs like skin. Robin caught the look in his eye. Even with his clothes on, he still looked sexy—and the scar made him look just a little dangerous.

"Don't you have something to do?" T.J. demanded as his eyes scanned the lithe figure lounging against the wall outside his door. Her arms were crossed against her chest, but did nothing to hide the feminine swell of her breast against her shirt. If anything, it emphasized her soft curves.

"I have all sorts of things I could be doing," Robin

retorted. "But somebody is holding all my belongings hostage and is squatting in my apartment."

"Look." T.J. tried counting to ten again. "I'm as upset as you are about this situation, but there's nothing I can do until we get it straightened out. Until you can establish who you are and what you're doing here, this is my apartment. If you can prove your prior claim, then we'll deal with that."

He watched her. It was obvious she was struggling as much as he was to keep cool. But she didn't say anything. She had a mouth on her, but at least this time she wasn't using it.

Neither of them said anything for a long moment.

What if it was true? What if she really is who she says she is? Where would that leave him? T.J. tried to ignore the doubts. He looked at her. Was she going to wear those same dirty clothes forever?

He decided to change his tactics. It was obvious that she didn't respond well to the approach he'd taken before. They'd done nothing but snipe at each other since she materialized in his kitchen doorway in the middle of the night. Maybe if he apologized...

"Look." He couldn't bring himself to call her Robin, at least not until he was sure she really *was* Robin. "I know this is a difficult situation, and I don't have a clue how to deal with it. But until we get things squared away, we're going to have to be civil. I'm sorry I upset you."

She looked at him as if that were the last thing she'd expected. He hadn't meant to throw her for a loop, but it gave T.J. a small measure of satisfaction to see that he had unsettled her. After all, she'd already done a number on him.

"It's okay," Robin finally said. "I don't guess it's your fault, but I sure would like to get to the bottom of this. Not just the apartment business. You can't imagine how weird it is to have somebody tell you you're dead."

He could have told her he understood, but she wouldn't have believed him. Hell, sometimes he didn't really comprehend it himself. T.J. had watched himself from above that battlefield casualty collection point in Saudi as a medic declared him dead. He still had a hard time dealing with it. But the two situations were different. Entirely different.

T.J. swallowed a lump in his throat and answered huskily, "Yeah. I guess it must be rough."

Change the subject, Swift, he told himself. This is way too heavy for now. Or any time. He looked at her. Robin. In those incredibly grubby, sexy clothes, with streaks of dirt running down her arms.

"Do you want to change or shower or something?" The image of her naked in the shower flashed into his mind. That had obviously been the wrong thing to say.

The angry glint returned to her green eyes. Weren't they blue yesterday? Robin started to say something, then stopped, apparently composing herself.

"Nothing would make me happier, but until somebody produces my belongings," she finally said, "all I have are the clothes that I'm wearing. And I'd dearly love to wash off this Mexican topsoil."

"Don't you have some clothes in the other bag?" T.J. was certain he had seen a carryall parked near the door.

"Just a change of underwear in my backpack. I wanted to travel light, so I trashed the rest of my clothes. They weren't worth keeping after all that dirty work. This was the most decent of all the stuff, if you can believe it." Robin held her arms out, as if to model what she was wearing. "I expected to have clean clothes to change into when I got here." She looked down at her arms, as if she had just noticed the dirt and grime, and tried to rub away some of the top layer.

Almost as an afterthought, Robin continued. "I have all my research notes, a camera and a portable tape recorder in the other bag. I wasn't about to let them out of my sight and worry about them through baggage claim.''

''I see.'' What was he supposed to do with her until Mr. Edwards arrived? Maybe, if he'd told him why he wanted him to come here, Mr. Edwards might have agreed to come sooner. But T.J. hadn't wanted to plant any ideas in the man's mind, and Edwards had already had something else planned that morning.

''Is that coffee I smell?'' Robin pushed herself off from her spot against the wall.

''Yeah. I made it before I got in the shower. Want some?''

''Thank you. I don't think I've had anything to eat since about this time yesterday. You don't suppose you could scare up a Pop-Tart or something?''

T.J. laughed. The notion of her eating Pop-Tarts struck him as funny. ''I'll do you one better. I'll make breakfast.'' It was probably the worst thing he could do. Everyone knew you shouldn't feed strays unless you wanted them to stay. But it would help kill time until Mr. Edwards showed up to break the stalemate.

Robin had long since passed the point where she could stand herself, so she decided to take a shower while T.J. made breakfast. There was still the matter of what to wear once she was through, but at least she would be clean. Robin shuddered as she slipped out of her pants and stood in the familiar white-tiled bathroom, wearing only her blue tank top and her panties.

It took a minute for the water to run warm, just as it always had, Robin noted with satisfaction. But when she slipped behind the curtain and into the tub, she noticed something was different. The showerhead was shiny and new. Had old Mr. Edwards finally put in new fixtures? When the first stinging spray hit her, she knew he hadn't. Mr. Edwards would never have sprung for a showerhead that sported a massager. Obviously, T.J. had done it him-self.

Well, she didn't care who had done it; after two months with nothing but a tepid, jury-rigged camp shower, this felt like heaven. Robin stood still for several wonderful minutes and luxuriated under the steamy, pulsing spray. Eventually her stomach rumbled and reminded her that breakfast was waiting. Robin hurriedly finished washing her travel-stained body.

The soap felt good against her neglected and grimy skin. Robin felt a tingle of awareness as she realized that this same bar had probably run over T.J.'s very male parts only a short time before, but Robin's desire to get clean overrode the awkward thoughts.

She soaped herself all over and rinsed and then did it again. Robin wanted to remove all traces of the camp, but most of all, she wanted to feel like herself again. She reached for his shampoo and quickly lathered it into her hair. It was wonderful to have even bargain-brand shampoo again.

Finally, as clean as she could be, Robin stepped outside the shower. She stood in the chilly, conditioned air, tow-eling herself dry, and wondered about her clothing situa-tion. She finally decided to wear the trousers again, and the khaki shirt; she did, at least, have clean underpants. The tank top was just too filthy to wear again. She rinsed the top and her underwear out in the sink, using bar soap, and hung them over the shower rod to dry.

Robin sprayed on some of T.J.'s deodorant and wrapped her towel tightly around her. She picked up the trousers and peeked out the door to see if the coast was clear, then scurried to her room.

Somewhere in her backpack were a comb and a brush and her few remaining articles of makeup. Robin rum-maged through the jumble and found the items she needed, making a little pile on the bed. The inventory was pathetically small: her hairbrush and comb, one stubby tube of lipstick, mascara, and a crumbly cake of blush. But it was enough.

Robin pulled the comb through the tangles of her hair until it was reasonably free of snarls. Thank goodness she had cut it during her stay in the wild. Even the do-it-yourself haircut was easier to manage than the long, thick, overpermed hair she'd taken with her. She shook the excess water droplets out of the limp strands and unwound the towel from around her chest. She quickly donned the shirt and buttoned it. What was she rushing for? Did she expect him to burst in on her at any moment? Robin forced her fingers to slow. Though it felt odd to have a man in her apartment—or was it his?—she didn't think he was the kind to break down doors.

She hardly looked like much of a catch right then, anyway. Robin surveyed her reflection in the mirror. She still couldn't get over the change in her appearance, and she could definitely see how different she looked from her ID pictures. No wonder he hadn't believed her. Robin grimaced as she remembered how fat and unhappy she'd been when the pictures were made. She'd lost the first ten of those twenty pounds in the past year, and the other ten had melted away quickly from illness. Hard work in the tropical heat had toned and firmed her.

Robin looked ruefully at her scarred and callused fingers. Every chipped or broken nail proclaimed her months of hard work. She wondered how long it would take before her hands looked like hers again.

Her complaining stomach reminded Robin to hurry. She collected her small cache of cosmetics from the bed and did what she could to her face. Satisfied that she'd done her best, she tugged on her pants, tucked in the shirt and checked herself one last time in the mirror. She was no fashion plate, but she would do.

Barefoot, she flung open the bedroom door and followed her nose to the kitchen.

T.J. looked up from the skillet of bacon he was tending when Robin came in. She was still in the same clothes, but she looked clean. Her hair hung damp and loose around her face, and her cheeks and arms were scrubbed pink. Just a trace of makeup brightened her face. Any more would have been too much.

But she still didn't look like the woman in the pictures, his suspicious cop's mind reminded him. He decided to remain cautious.

"Bacon's done. As soon as I scramble the eggs, we can eat." He speared several slices of bacon and laid them on a folded paper towel. Then he got the rest.

"It really smells good. Is there anything I can do to help? I feel funny standing and watching you cook in my own kitchen." Robin looked at him and didn't so much as blink.

Her own kitchen? She was either telling the truth or the most accomplished liar he'd ever seen, T.J. told himself. He forced himself not to bristle at the remark. "You could scramble the eggs while I finish with the bacon."

Robin got the carton of eggs from the refrigerator and put it on the counter, then opened a couple of cabinets, looking for a bowl. "You've rearranged the cupboards, I see."

T.J. stiffened at her comment about rearranging, but reminded himself to keep cool. "Yeah."

Robin cracked eggs into a bowl she'd finally located and began to beat them as the timer on the stove dinged.

T.J. bent to retrieve a pan of biscuits from the oven.

"Biscuits." Robin arched an eyebrow, obviously surprised. "I'm impressed."

"Just canned." He didn't know why he felt he had to explain. He liked biscuits for breakfast.

"I'm not complaining. You want me to get juice or something?"

"Sure."

Robin got juice and glasses and set them on the table. By the time she had done that, T.J. was ready to do the eggs. He poured the beaten eggs into the skillet, introducing them to the hot, greased pan. In minutes they were ready.

"Sit. Eat. It'll get cold if you don't," T.J. said as he put the plate of eggs down.

"You don't have to ask me twice," Robin replied as she scampered around the table and sat. "This smells great."

"Yeah." T.J. scooped up a forkful of eggs and chewed as he watched Robin smear a generous supply of butter on a biscuit. She ate as if she hadn't seen food in weeks.

Thankful that she seemed too hungry to make conversation, T.J. ate his breakfast slowly and watched her wolf down the majority of what he'd prepared. He was intrigued by this woman, who claimed to be the former occupant of his apartment, who had apparently risen from the dead. He wasn't sure whether he wanted her to be who she said she was or not. But one thing was certain; he would have liked it better if she had stayed gone.

Or dead.

The doorbell rang. Robin stopped eating, a forkful of food poised in midair.

"That's Mr. Edwards," she said, and glanced at the clock on the stove. "He's early."

"You finish eating. I'll let him in." T.J. pushed himself out of his chair and went to get the situation straightened out once and for all.

Torn between finishing her food and dashing out to greet Mr. Edwards, Robin finally settled on the food. She hadn't eaten in almost twenty-four hours, and a few more seconds wouldn't make that much difference in straightening the mess. Besides, she was pretty miffed at Mr. Edwards. Renting out her apartment to somebody else, indeed.

She polished off the rest of her eggs while straining to hear what was going on in the other room. All she could hear was a low masculine rumble. Curiosity getting the better of her, she downed the rest of her juice and shoved her chair away from the table.

As she got up, Robin recognized T.J.'s voice, loud and clear, amid the grumbling coming from the next room.

"The problem is out in the kitchen, Mr. Edwards. Why don't you come take a look at it." T.J.'s strong, sure footsteps led the way.

He entered the room first, shadowed by Adam Edwards, whom Robin had called Mr. E. Some referred to him as Mr. Ed because of his long, horselike head. But never to his face.

"It would help a bunch if you would tell me what I'm supposed to be looking fer."

"Over there." T.J. stepped aside and gestured in the direction of the table.

"Is something wrong with the table?" Mr. Edwards asked, barely looking at Robin.

"You don't see anything strange?"

Mr. Edwards shook his head. "No." He finally noticed her. "Do you know what this man is talking about, Robin?"

Chapter 4

The old man looked at T.J. then swung his head back to Robin in a classic double take. He stared at her, his eyes widening with surprise.

Mr. Edwards paled and sagged slightly, but quickly regained his composure. "Good God in heaven. Is that really you, little Robin? They told me you was dead." His voice was husky, and his eyes were misted. He swayed, then grabbed the back of the nearest chair to steady himself.

"You know who she is?" T.J. looked incredulous.

"Of course I do. But you could have given me some warning. My ticker's not as young as it used to be."

"Tell me, girl. How is it everybody in Tuscaloosa thinks you're dead?" Mr. Edwards pulled out the chair he clutched and sank heavily onto the seat.

"I was hoping you could tell *me* that. It wasn't exactly a picnic arriving here last night and finding out about my demise." That was an understatement, Robin thought. "And where is all my stuff?"

"It's downstairs in the storage room. When Cheryl

moved out, she cleared out her stuff and packed yours away, too. We couldn't get in touch with your folks."

"Why did Cheryl move out?" Then Robin's eyes flew open with alarm. "My folks! Do they think I'm dead, too?"

"I don't think so. They wasn't in town when I tried to contact them. I got ahold of your husband, and he said they done went on a cruise," the old man explained. "He said he would try to get up with them."

For the first time since her parents had announced their plan to go around the world, Robin was glad they'd gone. And she was more than grateful for Dub's inability to follow through with anything. Dub hadn't known where her parents had gone, and he hadn't had the slightest idea how to go about finding them. At least they had been spared the anguish of finding that their only daughter was dead, even if it was a mistake. She had worried about them gallivanting to all parts of the world and not being in touch. But now it had turned out to be a blessing. They were due back in two weeks, and by then it would be all cleared up. They might even get a good laugh out of it.

"I'm glad you couldn't reach them, Mr. E."

"Me, too, girl. Me, too."

T.J. cleared his throat. "About the apartment—" He didn't get to finish the statement.

Mr. Edwards interrupted. "I can't get over how the police could be so sure you was dead. They told me they had your fingerprints to identify the body." He shook his head sadly.

"You mean there really was a body? What made them think it was me?"

"Your husband," T.J. and Mr. Edwards answered together.

"Dub? Dub Doubleday, my ex-husband? He identified the body as me?" Robin shuddered. The notion of somebody looking at a dead body and thinking it was her gave her the creeps. "Are you sure it was Dub?"

"Right sure," Mr. Edwards replied. "I reckon'ized his name. Used to play for the Miami Dolphins or something." He thought for a moment. "There was something in the paper about him just this morning."

"Let me see it," Robin demanded.

"I don't get the paper," T.J. replied.

"I got one downstairs. I'll go fetch it and bring it back up." Mr. Edwards started to leave, then turned back to Robin. "It sure is good to see you here, alive and all," he told her, patting her hand.

"It's good to be here, Mr. E."

Robin turned to T.J. "Now do you believe me?" she asked defiantly.

"I guess I have to," T.J. grudgingly acknowledged. "But that still doesn't settle the issue about who has the right to this apartment."

"Of course it does. First come, first served. I was here first—the apartment is mine," Robin fired back.

"I don't think that phrasing would hold up in a court of law," T.J. replied wearily.

"First you act like a cop, now a lawyer. What next? A doctor?" Robin paused. "Are you seriously considering taking this to court?"

The thought hadn't crossed T.J.'s mind, but now that she mentioned it, it wasn't a bad idea. He'd really hoped to settle this amicably, but Robin's combative attitude was making that impossible. "I do have a little legal expertise, and I probably could present a case in small claims court." If she hadn't been so damned feisty, he probably wouldn't have said that. But she wouldn't quit rubbing him the wrong way.

"Save all that legal-eagle stuff for somebody who'll be impressed. You have to let me have the apartment back. It's next to impossible to find a decent, safe apartment around here at this time of year. Cheryl waited a year to get this one.''

Listening to Robin's diatribe just made T.J. dig his heels in deeper. Damn, she was irritating. Hadn't anybody ever taught her how to negotiate? "And you think it would be easier for me to find someplace to live?" he questioned archly.

"Well, yes. Your…"

"…standards must be lower?" T.J. finished for her.

"Yes," she replied softly.

"Thanks a lot. I'd like to live in a cheap, quiet apartment just as much as you."

"That's fine. Just as long as it isn't this one." Robin's aquamarine eyes flashed.

"Possession is nine-tenths of the law," T.J. countered stubbornly. "I'm in—you're out."

"I look pretty in to me. You'll have to remove me bodily." Robin crossed her arms and stood with her legs planted firmly on the linoleum.

Just for a moment, T.J. considered forcibly removing her from this apartment. But the doorbell saved him, and her, from that indignity.

Mr. Edwards had barely stepped into the room before Robin took the newspaper from his hands. She unfolded the *Tuscaloosa News* and stared at Dub's face, which was featured prominently on the front page. The headline announced: Former Dolphins Player Arrested In Local Murder.

Robin barely glanced at the picture; she was more interested in the facts behind the arrest. Dub had been arrested just the day before and was being held because he couldn't make bail. Robin wasn't surprised that he hadn't been able to secure his freedom—until she read on, her anger growing as she did. She was so engrossed in the content of the story that she didn't notice T.J. coming up behind her and leaning over her shoulder.

"Well, I had finally come to the conclusion that Dub was slime, but this spells it with capital letters," Robin announced with conviction when she finally finished reading.

"How does this prove he's slime?" T.J.'s voice was so close behind her that Robin jumped. "Obviously, he didn't kill you. You're still alive."

"That's just the point. It says here that what led them to Dub was that he cashed in a hundred-thousand-dollar life insurance policy on me that would have expired five days after my alleged death. That would look pretty suspicious to anybody."

"So? You had a policy." T.J. pointed out reasonably.

"He told me he would cancel it when I finally wised up and got out of the marriage." How could T.J. be so obtuse? "The point is that Dub had to know darn well that the dead woman was not me, yet he claimed the insurance. He didn't have my permission to have a policy on me anymore, and what right did he have to use my dead body for financial gain? Especially since it wasn't even really me." Robin paced the room as her agitation grew.

"It says here…" T.J. held up the paper. "It says here that the woman was shot in the face with a shotgun, so they couldn't use her facial features for making an identification. They had already identified her by her fingerprints. They probably just called Dub in as a formality."

"Well, their thoroughness sure has made a mess out of things. But I still don't see how Dub could think it was me once he looked. Sure, the general coloring and body size matched my description," Robin agreed coldly. "But Dub knew me well enough to recognize other parts of my body."

Mr. Edwards coughed and looked down. And Robin

blushed when she realized what her comment had suggested. It was true, but something she'd just as soon forget.

"So there's a distinctive mark in an area that doesn't normally see the light of day that Dub knew about," T.J. stated flatly. His tone might have been level, but Robin thought there was a glint in his catlike eyes.

"Something like that." Suddenly, Robin wasn't thrilled with the direction the conversation was leading in. "And an appendix scar..." She didn't know why she added that. Yes, she did; it didn't sound quite as lurid as the location of her birthmark.

"Wait a minute." Something just occurred to her. "I don't have a criminal record. I've never been printed. How can they say they were my fingerprints?"

T.J. looked surprised. "You don't have to be a criminal to be fingerprinted. You could have applied for a job that required a security clearance. Lots of jobs these days require background checks," he explained.

Robin snorted with disgust. "Oh, right. I needed a security clearance to teach social studies in Demopolis, Alabama. I only lived there all my life. I hardly think so."

Rubbing his chin thoughtfully, T.J. offered another option. "I suppose there could have been another Robin Digby around here who had been fingerprinted some time in her life."

"Don't you think I would have heard about it if there was somebody else lurking around here using my name?"

"She wasn't using your name. It was hers."

"Maybe, but I don't think so. Robin Digby isn't exactly as exotic as Marigold Faberg-Eckstein or something like that, but it isn't Mary Smith, either," Robin reminded him.

"Yeah, maybe," T.J. agreed. "But I wouldn't rule out the possibility of there being two of you, either."

"Then you think Dub Doubleday lied about her being you, just to get the insurance money?" Mr. Edwards interjected, looking as if he had been punched in the stomach.

"That's exactly what I think." Then, remembering that Mr. Edwards was a football fan, Robin tried to smooth it over. "I'm sorry, Mr. E., but sometimes sports figures do have feet of clay. Playing the game doesn't always build character; it feeds the ego and encourages greed. It was hard for Dub to handle it when the applause went away. I don't think Dub would ever intentionally hurt anybody, but I doubt that he would hesitate to take advantage of an opportunity to make a profit. Especially if it were dropped in his lap."

The cheering had ended far too soon for Dub Doubleday, and he had spent the past four years living in the past and wallowing in self-pity. That was why Robin had finally let go of her own hopes for a happy life with him and started over.

"It could have been an honest mistake," Mr. Edwards suggested hopefully.

"I've watched people identify bodies. They don't always look real close. Considering the reported condition, I doubt that Doubleday made a thorough examination," T.J. volunteered.

Robin made a face. "You would be on his side," she replied. "I wonder what he wanted the money for."

"It said in the story that he'd ordered a new sports car. That's what tipped them off," Mr. Edwards remarked.

"Hardly the action of somebody overcome with grief. I wonder if he gave me a nice funeral with the insurance money." Robin smacked the folded newspaper against her open palm, then thrust the paper at T.J. "Here, you read between the lines some more. Maybe if you read it long enough, you can see clear to nominate Dub Doubleday to the nice-guy hall of fame."

She headed toward her room and her backpack. "I'm going to the jail and have it out with him."

"Wait!" She couldn't run out now. T.J. would rather have let her go, but they hadn't settled anything about the apartment. It might seem trivial in comparison with a murder investigation, but he still had that paper due in a week. He didn't have time to look for new accommodations.

"What?" Robin looked more irritated than curious.

"We've got to settle this apartment problem."

Robin turned, her impatience evident on her face. "Look, T.J. In the last twenty-four hours, I've traveled a zillion miles, been told I'm dead and my body used to scam some insurance company out of a small fortune. And you're still going on about the apartment. Give me a break."

Mr. Edwards chuckled. "So this is the problem you wanted me to fix. I see you have yourselves in quite a pickle."

"It isn't funny," T.J. pointed out sourly. "Robin and I have to get this apartment situation squared away." T.J. was afraid he knew how it would be settled, and he didn't like it. She'd be in, and he'd be out.

Mr. Edwards rubbed his horsey, stubbled chin. "Now this is a tough one. I don't think I've ever ran into this partic'lar problem before in all my years of landlordin'. I might have to study on it for a while."

"You don't have to think about it, Mr. Edwards. I had the earlier claim. The apartment's mine." Robin's eyes flashed.

She is one stubborn woman, thought T.J. in response to her mulish reply. The old cliché about being beautiful when angry certainly applied to her. "But everybody thought you were dead."

"That's true. It was an honest mistake, with you bein' dead and all." Mr. Edwards glanced from Robin to T.J. and back to Robin again.

"But I'm not dead!" Robin wailed. "I have the prior claim!"

T.J. interjected. "But your roommate relinquished the apartment." He was glad he'd remembered that. Cheryl

Rodgers had waived her claim when she had given up the lease. That should be a mark in his favor. "Since she was the actual leaseholder, she had every right to relinquish the apartment."

"But I'm not dead!" Robin insisted.

"We didn't know that, sugar," Mr. Edwards said gently. "Cheryl was pretty broke up about it, too. She thought she was doing the best thing with her not needing it no more."

"But why did Cheryl give up the apartment? She could have found someone else to share it with her. She wasn't finished working on her degree yet; she would have still needed a place to live."

"You'll have to ask her that." T.J. thought he had a solution. "We could get mediation from an impartial source. Maybe somebody in the University Law Department could help."

Instead of satisfying her, the suggestion only seemed to agitate her more. Robin's eyes narrowed. "I don't want mediation. I just want my apartment back. I just want to find my stuff and get out of these filthy clothes." Her voice quavered and her eyes brimmed with tears. "All I want is to have my life go back to the way it was before. I wish I'd never gone to Cacaxtla."

Tears began to trickle down Robin's cheeks. T.J. watched her struggle to contain them and wondered how they were going to get out of this mess. When it was obvious that the salty drops were winning, Robin covered her eyes and started for the bathroom.

Instead of letting her go, T.J. grabbed her arm and pulled her to him as she tried to go past. He folded her into his arms. Damn, he hated to see a woman cry. He hated it even more now, because it was his fault. And damned if he knew what to do about it.

It felt good in his arms, thought Robin, even as she struggled out of T.J.'s strong embrace. It embarrassed her that she'd fallen apart. It didn't say much about her progress with the five-year plan she'd devised to get her master's degree, establish her career, and generally prove she could provide for herself. Maybe it was jet lag that was keeping her from thinking clearly.

Why hadn't Dub made her feel like that? Dub! Oh, no. She had promised herself that she wouldn't get involved with another man so soon. Maybe not ever.

What was the old saying? Once bitten, twice shy. She had no business feeling this good wrapped up in T.J.'s arms.

Robin pushed herself away. Why was she sniveling? She'd spent the past few months proving to herself that she could handle anything that man or nature could dish out. Why was she falling apart now?

"I'm sorry." Robin wiped at her eyes with the back of her hand. "I don't usually do this. I guess I'm still tired from all my traveling. And this business about being declared dead has been very unsettling."

T.J. looked across the distance Robin had made between them. "I suppose so. Will you be all right?"

"I'll live. 'I am woman, hear me roar,' and all that jazz."

This was one of those days when Robin really wished she hadn't vowed to devote five years to getting her life on track. When she ended her marriage to Dub Doubleday, the five-year-plan had seemed like the thing to do. In the past eighteen months of trying to prove how strong she could be, she had almost forgotten how good it felt to be in a man's arms. Until now.

It was different in T.J.'s arms. For all Dub's muscles and physical training, he had not been a strong man. Not where it really mattered. Robin had known T.J. for less than a day, but she sensed real integrity within him. She had known Dub for half of her life, and had never really been able to trust him.

T.J.'s strength almost seemed dangerous. Not to her

physical being, but to her emotional weaknesses. It wasn't anything he'd said or done. In fact, Robin realized, he'd shown remarkable restraint, considering the way she'd spoken to him. Maybe that was why she sensed she could trust him.

Robin stepped back another couple of steps and almost collided with Mr. Edwards. She stopped, remembering the dilemma at hand. She faced the elderly man.

"Have you had time to think about the problem, Mr. E.?" she asked hopefully.

"Well, Robin sugar. I think I still need a bit more time." Mr. Edwards stroked the scraggly beard on his long chin and looked thoughtful.

"I think we need to sit down together and talk this out," the old man finally said. "Park yourselves down here and let's talk about it like men." He looked at Robin. "And woman."

T.J. was glad to have something to think about besides her. He'd gone so long without holding a woman in his arms, he'd thought he'd gotten used to the emptiness. But feeling Robin's small, firm body crushed against his had rekindled all the yearnings that he had tried so hard to suppress. That he hadn't deserved to feel since that awful day years ago.

He watched as Robin took a spot on the end of the faded old sofa. Edwards sat at the other end. Good, there wasn't room for him. He couldn't take another assault to his senses from being so close to her.

There was a rickety cane-backed chair propped up against the wall across the room. T.J. got it and carried it back to the sofa. He turned the chair so that the back faced the old man and Robin and straddled it, sitting with his arms resting on the back of the chair.

Mr. Edwards cleared his throat. "The way I see it is this. We got one apartment and two folks who want to have it."

"We know that, Mr. E. What do we do about it?"

"Now wait just a minute, sugar. You want to live here because it's close to your classes." He looked at Robin.

"Yes."

"And T.J. wants it because it's quiet and cheap," he continued.

"Right." T.J. stiffened in his chair. They'd already been over this territory.

Mr. Edwards went on. "And Robin here wants it because it's cheap and safe."

Robin nodded.

"So far, so good." Edwards looked evenly at both of them, swiveling his head from one to the other. "You with me so far?"

T.J. and Robin nodded, almost in tandem.

"Okay. T.J., you're a quiet, decent fella. Wouldn't you say so, Robin?"

"I guess."

"Good. And T.J., you can see that Robin is a good woman. Quiet, neat, and smart as a whip."

Quiet he wasn't so sure about, but he'd go with the other two. "Okay. But what's all this leading up to?"

Mr. Edwards looked at them, his long face breaking into a horsey grin. "You got two bedrooms here. They's two of you. I reckon you could share!"

Chapter 5

The silence stretched out, long and shocked. Robin stared at Mr. Edwards as if he had recently grown a second head. Then she looked at T.J. He was staring at her as if his hot-coal eyes wanted to burn through her.

Robin finally broke the stunned silence. "Absolutely not."

"I concur. There's no way that we could live under the same roof." T.J. echoed Robin's sentiments.

"Then I wash my hands of it," Mr. Edwards said quietly. "You two settle it. I don't rightly know who should get the place. Cheryl and I made a honest mistake, and I don't want either of you to suffer because of it. You decide." He got up and headed for the door. "When you're done fightin' over it, tell me who won." With that remark, he opened the door and stepped outside.

Robin wanted to call him back, but something told her that nothing would sway her landlord from his decision now that it had been made. She also knew she wasn't about to give up the apartment. That would mean conceding defeat, something she'd vowed never to do again. There had to be a way she could coexist with this man she barely knew.

Then again, she thought, as she groped for just the right words to say she would accept Mr. Edwards's proposition, maybe she could pretend to agree. Then begin a campaign to drive T. J. Swift crazy and out of her hair. No, she reminded herself. That wouldn't be fair. She might be angry about this turn of events, but she couldn't do that.

Robin looked over to where T.J. was lounging on the cane-backed chair. She still hadn't found the right words, the perfect speech. Maybe if she gave him enough time, he'd do it himself.

But T.J. just sat on the chair leaning his arms against the back, chin propped on his hands, and gazed at her. Or through her. His amber eyes didn't seem to be focusing on anything at all.

Finally, Robin couldn't stand the silence. "I can see the wheels turning in your head a mile a minute. What are you thinking?" Robin congratulated herself for being able to maintain a conversational tone.

"I was just running through the pros and cons," T.J. replied slowly. "Do you cook?"

Was he trying to run her off? Surely he didn't think she would agree to cook and clean just so she could stay. "I haven't killed anybody yet." She didn't add *But I'm thinking about it.*

"I know this is going to sound sexist, but my dinner menu has consisted mainly of Lean Cuisine. I wouldn't mind a decent hot meal now and then." He looked as though he thought Robin might challenge him.

"Are you good at getting up early?" That one ought to get his attention, Robin thought smugly.

"As long as there is an alarm clock," he admitted.

"Good. I think mornings are the devil's own invention, but I love a good hot breakfast." Would he agree to get up and make breakfast? Robin wasn't really that bad at getting up, but she wouldn't turn down an extra half hour's sleep, either.

"I'll help with the cleaning."

Had T.J. really said that? It would be worth putting up with him for that alone. Robin knit her brows. "Clarify that. Does that mean that you actually know how to operate a vacuum and a dustcloth, or are you just planning not to leave your socks and newspapers on the floor?"

"I don't get the newspaper, remember?" T.J. looked evenly across to Robin. "I mean that I'm checked out on all cleaning devices." He looked almost indignant. Then he added, "I'm a compulsive thrower-awayer."

Robin groaned. "It'll never work. I'm a compulsive saver." This was really kind of fun. What else could she come up with to ask him?

"I take morning showers," she ventured.

"To help wake up, I suppose." T.J. filled in the rest. He chuckled. "I do, too, but I get up earlier. It shouldn't be a problem."

"Do you study with sound effects?" Robin was beginning to run out of questions. At least the kind that were acceptable and polite to ask. She had plenty more.

T.J. laughed. He had a rich, deep laugh, Robin noticed as she heard it. It was much nicer than the measured tones he'd used with her earlier. His stiff, formal way of speaking seemed to be relaxing now, too.

"Do you mean do I like to listen to car crashes and wolves howling?" T.J. was obviously teasing. "I don't mind a little background music when I study."

"Heavy metal?" *Please say no.* Robin crossed her fingers.

"No. Light rock."

Robin breathed a relieved sigh. "Good. I think we could try it. Platonically, of course."

"Of course." T.J. hadn't even thought to question what

sort of arrangement it would be. He'd spent the past three years alone, but never become accustomed to it. Eight years of marriage had made him used to sharing his life with somebody. And his nights. It had been comforting to know that there was somebody waiting for him at the end of the day.

He realized that he hadn't liked being alone, though he had refused any kind of company at all for the past three years. The thought of having someone to come home to, even platonically, was not unpleasant.

"I guess we could give it a shot," T.J. added after a moment of reflection. "Platonically."

"Good." Robin clapped her hands together with the gleeful abandon of a schoolgirl.

"Do you want to go tell Mr. Edwards?"

"No. What I want to do is get my stuff out of storage and get out of these clothes."

"Okay. We'll go tell Mr. E. together and get the key to the storage room. Then I'll help you carry up some things."

"Once I'm dressed properly, I'll go to the jail to see Dub."

"Good, I could use the quiet. I've got a research paper to turn in to the typist on Friday. I've already wasted half of today."

"Okay, I'll get out of your hair. I just realized that it might be a little weird going there. Do you think there'll be a problem with my identity if I go?"

Robin had a point, T.J. realized. He hadn't believed her about who she was. Why would they? "I don't know. But let's not worry about that right now." T.J. was already thinking about problems Robin probably hadn't even thought of yet. "Mr. E. is waiting for an answer. You need to get your stuff, and I need to get back to work on my paper."

She must still have been pretty slow on the uptake, Robin thought. Because of jet lag or lack of sleep or something.

It occurred to Robin as she followed T.J. down the stairs that she knew very little about him. She had just agreed to set up housekeeping—okay, share an apartment—with a man she barely knew. Didn't know at all, really. A virtual stranger. Hadn't her mother warned her about this?

Yet some instinct had told her that T.J. was one of the good guys. Robin certainly couldn't have explained how she had reached that conclusion, especially considering her track record with Dub. But she had. Maybe it was because her guard had been down. Two days with little sleep and even less food could be wearing on a body and a mind. Then finding out that most of her friends and acquaintances believed she was dead would certainly kick a person where it hurts. The fact that Dub Doubleday, ex-husband and current pond scum, had been the one to announce her demise to the world had been enough to set her head spinning. Maybe that was why she was so ready to believe in T.J.

In the past twenty-four hours, Robin had been subjected to more emotional upheaval than most people experienced in their lifetimes. Either she was too shell-shocked to think clearly, or her exhaustion had made it possible for her to cut through to the real man. Maybe it was a bit of both.

He used to be a cop, she reminded herself as she watched T.J. knock on Mr. Edwards's door.

How do you know he was? Robin's rational mind reminded her. You're just taking his word for it. And why isn't he still a cop?

Robin didn't have an answer for that question, but she suspected the scar on his forehead had something to do with it.

The scar, at first intimidating, now seemed reassuring. She wondered if he would ever tell her about it.

Mr. Edwards opened the door. "Well. You're both still breathing. Who won?"

"Both of us," T.J. answered.

"Good." Mr. Edwards looked much too pleased. "I'm glad to see you come to your senses."

"It seemed like the logical thing to do." Robin wasn't so certain about logic having anything to do with it; it had been more like a gut reaction.

"Now that that's all settled, I reckon you want to get your hands on some of that stuff I got stored," Mr. Edwards said, reminding them of why they had come downstairs together.

"Yes. All I'm interested in right now are my clothes. I can get the other stuff some other time."

Mr. Edwards ducked back into his apartment and came back with a ring of keys. He selected one and held it out, leaving the others dangling. "This is the one. Now, you be sure to prop the door open with something. If you don't, it could slam shut and lock you in."

"Okay." T.J. took the key and headed toward the storage area downstairs.

Robin stayed a moment to chat with Mr. Edwards, eventually working the conversation around to T.J. "What do you know about T.J.? Am I going to be all right with him?"

"Sugar, you couldn't be in better hands. T.J. used to be a policeman in Birmingham. Then his reserve unit got called up to the Persian Gulf. That's where he got the scar. He can't be a cop anymore, so he's back in school to learn another trade."

Robin laughed. "I'd hardly call graduate school learning a trade. Thanks, Mr. E. You've made me feel better." She turned and hurried after T.J.

"I hope it works out for you two," the old man called after her.

Robin turned back in time to catch a merry twinkle in Mr. Edwards's eye as he stepped back inside.

What could he mean by that? If she didn't know better, she'd think he was matchmaking.

He wouldn't do that. Would he?

* * *

The storage room was dark and musty. T.J. groped inside the doorway, trying to find a light switch. There didn't seem to be one. All he'd found were cobwebs.

"There's a chain hanging from the light fixture." Robin had come up behind him. God, he'd nearly jumped out of his skin.

"Oh." He tried to slow his racing pulse. "Do you know where it is?"

"Yes. You hold the door wide so I can see not to trip over anything, and I'll give it a yank." Robin stepped gingerly into the room and waded slowly through stacks of boxes and piles of junk, waving one hand in front of her. "Here it is!" Robin's comment was punctuated by the light coming on.

The room wasn't much brighter. But at least the bare sixty-watt bulb made it possible to see what was lumped together in organized chaos.

"Mr. E. said that Cheryl had put most of my clothes in suitcases. That should simplify our search." She walked around in the dim light. "There." She pointed to a small stack of green plaid cloth luggage.

"You want to check to see if everything you need is in there before we carry it up?"

"Good idea." Robin unzipped the largest of the three cases. "This one is fine."

T.J. grabbed it and carried it to the door. He used the bag to prop it open. As he did, he began to realize what he had just agreed to. He was going to let that woman into his life. A woman he didn't know. A woman who had been mostly disagreeable. How was this ever going to work?

"Most everything is in these three suitcases." Robin's voice intruded on T.J.'s introspection. "I'm hoping my makeup is in this overnight case." She popped the clasp and looked inside. "Good. It's all here."

"I'll take these two," T.J. said, hefting the biggest cases. "You get the other two and lock up."

"Okay." Robin carried the overnight case to the door and used it to replace the big suitcase T.J. had just taken. She went back for the other.

T.J. didn't know why, but he felt obligated to wait for her. Suppose she locked herself in. He chuckled. He'd never have such good luck. Robin yanked on the light chain as she passed with the other suitcase in her hands. She shoved the two small cases out the door and pulled it shut behind her.

"I guess this is it," T.J. announced, more to himself than to Robin.

"That's all for this trip," Robin replied.

"You mean there's more?"

Robin looked puzzled. "Well, yes. All we have here are my clothes. We still have to bring up my household goods."

"Household goods?"

"You know, pots and pans, decorating touches."

T.J. thought about the cluttered room. "Just how much of that stuff is yours?" he asked with a sinking feeling.

Robin considered. "I'd say most of it is mine. Remember, I'm a compulsive saver."

"And you really need it all?"

"Well, yes. I don't see how you've managed with three jelly glasses and two chipped plates." She turned to head up the stairs.

T.J. groaned and followed her up. There was no turning back now. He hoped she was going to be easier to get along with in the future than she had been up to this point.

The contents of the three suitcases were as precious as buried treasure, as far as Robin was concerned. She rummaged through the kaleidoscope of colors, rediscovering each item as if it were new. After months in serviceable tropical khaki, after days in the same clothing, she was more than ready for a change.

Robin poked around until she found what she wanted, a cool summer shift in powder blue. She'd always liked that dress; Dub hadn't. Maybe that was why she chose it today. If she was going to see Dub in jail, she just might want to turn the screws a little bit tighter. She held the dress up to her.

It was a good thing that the wrinkled look was popular campus chic; after being folded and jammed into the suitcase, it looked as if she'd slept in it. Robin could have asked T.J. for an iron, she supposed, but she didn't want to take the time. She smoothed out the wrinkles as best she could with her palm and laid the dress out on the bed. After ten minutes in the August humidity, the wrinkles wouldn't make a difference, anyway. Yes, it was going to be wonderful to get into something that didn't look like third-world militaria.

After repairing her makeup with the supply from her overnight case, she slipped into her dress. Robin felt like a new woman. The blue in the dress always made her complexion come alive. Alive, she thought with a smile. After all, today is the first day of my rebirth. And the new Robin is going to be very different.

Robin checked once more in the mirror, making an ineffectual attempt at smoothing the wrinkles. She declared herself passable, and shrugged. She rummaged through the case one last time and came up with a serviceable purse and a pair of scuffed sandals. After transferring most of the contents of her backpack into the purse, she slipped into the shoes. With the purse slung over her shoulder, she hopped toward the door, tugging the straps over her heels.

She almost lost her balance as she tugged on the second shoe. For there in the hall stood T.J. just coming from his room.

"Oh, you—you startled me," Robin stammered, for lack of anything original to say.

T.J. didn't say anything; he just stared. Then he whistled, long and low. A wolf whistle.

Robin stared back.

"You clean up pretty good," T.J. finally said.

A light, bubbly giggle escaped from somewhere in the vicinity of Robin's throat. Then she laughed gaily. "Where did that come from?"

"What? The whistle? I was just paying you a compliment."

"Yes, you did, if somewhat backhanded. But thank you anyway." Robin giggled again. "Actually, I meant this. The giggle. Where did that come from?"

T.J. looked confused. "From you. Certainly not from me."

"That's just it," Robin tried to explain. "I don't giggle."

"I see. Well, I distinctly heard you not giggling just now."

"Guess being dead does strange things to you." Robin turned quickly, her purse swinging behind her and smacking her on the bottom. She all but skipped to the door.

She called over her shoulder as she tugged on the handle. "I'm off to the jail. Hope you can get some work done on your paper."

She did clean up well, T.J. concluded as he stared after her. Even in that wrinkled, shapeless dress, she looked fine. But he hoped she'd stay away for a while. He had much too much work to do to be bothered with her. By her.

T.J. wished she had not made the reference to being dead. It was something that he didn't take lightly. Something he did not like to think about. After his experience in the desert, he had more questions than answers, and there were few people to ask about it. He'd tried the chaplain while he was still in the hospital, but hadn't gotten the answers he needed. And he didn't have time to get metaphysical right now. He didn't want to.

War drums were pounding in his head. T.J. rubbed his temples. There was a headache coming. Damn. That was all he needed. He went to the bathroom and dug through the bottles in the medicine cabinet until he found the aspirin. He groaned. Only one left.

Day two of the Robin Digby hostage crisis. And things were not going well at all.

Chapter 6

It wasn't as hard as Robin had expected it would be to get in to see Dub. She had to log herself in, but nobody looked very closely at her name or noticed the significance. Now she waited in the dimly lit visiting room for Dub to appear.

Robin was so absorbed in surveying the squalid room that she didn't hear him come in. She was reading one of the posters that were supposed to disguise the block wall behind her when a voice interrupted her inspection of the surroundings.

"Somebody said you wanted to see me, Miss—?"

"Digby," Robin said, with as much dignity as she could manage. She turned. It was obvious that nobody had told Dub who was waiting. Robin watched the expression on his face change from polite indifference to shock as she faced him squarely.

His surprised silence didn't tell Robin as much as she'd hoped, because he shouldn't have been shocked to see her. Unless he really had believed that it was her body he identified. His eyes were as wide as pale blue saucers.

Robin settled onto the wooden chair across the grille from where Dub stood and waited for him to sit down. His mouth opened and shut as he tried to form words. To Robin, he resembled a fish gasping for air.

"I... Robin?" Dub looked carefully at her, then collapsed into the chair. "I almost didn't recognize you."

"Considering I've been dead for two months or so, that's understandable."

"Robin...I..." At least he had the grace not to mess it up with a lot of phony explanations. And it was nice seeing him without a ready answer; Dub had never been at a loss for words in the past.

"What? You're shocked that I'm alive? Overcome with joy?" Robin couldn't believe that she'd once thought that Dub was the epitome of manhood. She supposed she had been seduced by the dashing figure in the football uniform. Now he seemed a pathetic caricature of what she'd loved.

"I'm glad you came to see me," Dub finally said. He even managed to sound a little humble.

"Why? Because I can prove you didn't kill me? I might have happily done it if it weren't for the little matter of that insurance claim you made. First, you told me you had canceled it. Then, you had to have known that it wasn't me on that slab." Robin stared into Dub's eyes, as if daring him to contradict her.

Dub ran nervous fingers through his thatch of straw-colored hair. He looked pale, or had the fluorescent lighting given his skin that pasty, unhealthy look? He closed his eyes. "That's not fair. They told me they'd already proved it was you by your fingerprints." He shuddered.

Robin wanted to reach through the grille and shake the rest of his explanation from him, but the iron bars protected them both.

"I knew you were gone on that archaeology trip, so I hoped it wasn't you. But, damn it, they had your fingerprints. And with your folks off on that cruise and nobody knowing how to get in touch with 'em, the police needed somebody to confirm the identification. So they looked me up. At first I was gonna tell 'em it couldn't be you, but…

"They said they had your fingerprints, Robbie."

"You can't spend four years with a woman and not recognize her, face or no face," Robin countered coldly.

Dub covered his face with his hands. "The body had been out in the hot sun for a couple of days or so." He pulled his hands away and shuddered again. "It didn't look like you. Hell, it didn't look like anything I'd ever seen before. It didn't look real. They had your fingerprints," he repeated lamely.

Robin had to grudgingly accept that Dub probably had believed it was she he saw on that morgue table. She had to admit something else, too. The tone Dub had so often used in the past to persuade her into doing what he wanted now only sounded whiny. And he wasn't fooling anybody with that phoney good-ol'-boy accent. What had once seemed endearing to Robin's lovestruck ears now sounded dumber than dirt. What had she ever seen in him?

"I thought I was doin' right. And I gave her a nice funeral."

"Where? Not in my family plot in Demopolis?"

"No. I bought a plot at Palm Ridge."

"Oh, how convenient. Just walking distance from my apartment. I can stop by and visit anytime I want."

"Now, Robbie, don't be like that. I did what I thought was best, considering I wasn't one-hundred-percent sure it was you."

Robin wanted to scream. "Do you realize that because of you, for all practical purposes, I really *am* dead? If you weren't sure, you should have told them so. It would have been better for everyone if she'd just stayed unclaimed. I don't have the vaguest idea how much work it will take to reestablish my identity, but you can bet it won't be as easy as it was for you to make me dead. What did you think it would do to my parents if they heard?

"And what about the insurance? Why didn't you cancel it like you said you would?"

Dub floundered for a moment. "At first I hoped you would come back to me. When it finally sunk in that you weren't goin' to, I just kept putting it off."

"You'll have to give it back, you know."

Dub blanched. "It's all gone."

"No wonder you couldn't make bail. What happened to the money, Dub?" Robin didn't need to ask. Another get-rich-quick scheme. She should have known. "You couldn't possibly have spent it all on the Turbo-Roadmaster."

"No. I invested it."

"I suppose it'd be too much to expect that it went into blue-chip stocks," Robin responded dryly.

"I met this guy who had this really great deal. He wanted to open a chain of sports bars that sold sporting goods on the side. He needed a celebrity to endorse it."

She should have known it. The con man, whoever he was, had known exactly how to get to Dub, by bolstering his fragile ego. "Was this before or after I 'died'?"

Dub looked puzzled. "Before," he finally answered.

His answer told Robin a lot. Maybe Dub would not have been so eager to believe that the body was hers and to cash in on the insurance policy if that opportunity hadn't already been on the table.

"He said he'd double my money," Dub offered.

"Did you check him out?"

"I didn't think I needed to. He looked like a nice guy."

Robin rolled her eyes. "You didn't think. So now you're in a whole lot of trouble." She sighed heavily. "I suppose you expect me to get you off the hook."

He answered quietly. "I haven't said anything in my defense, except that I didn't kill you. What are you gonna do?"

"Surely you didn't expect me to cheerfully waltz into the district attorney's office and announce, 'Oh, it's all a mistake. I'm not dead at all. Never mind.'

"I don't think I could flutter my eyelashes fast enough and play that dumb. You're on your own, Buster." Robin slid her purse off the ledge in front of her and turned.

"Robin," he called after her. "I wish you'd help me out. For old times' sake?"

She turned back. "I hardly think it was wise to ask me to do anything for old times' sake. Our old times weren't all that good, Dub." But she relented a little. "I'm not doing anything until I've seen a lawyer."

"Fair enough," Dub said softly. "And, Robbie, you look real pretty. That weight you took off looks real good on you."

The compliment almost cut through Robin's anger and resolve. Almost. But then she remembered all the lies he'd told her and all the empty promises he'd made through the years. That might've worked then, but it wouldn't now. She stood straighter and pressed the button that summoned the guard.

It was another of those migraines. T.J. used to brag that he had never had a headache in his life. Until Saudi. His doctors told him that they'd diminish in intensity and frequency as time went by. But so far, they kept occurring with alarming regularity, completely sidelining him when they did. Until the incapacitating headaches stopped, there was no way he could do any kind of work where someone else's life depended on him. If there ever came a day when he could be certain they were gone. He'd like to blame Robin's sudden appearance on them, but he knew that the late-night work session had more likely been the cause. He'd gotten overtired without her help.

The aspirin hadn't worked. There was no way he'd be able to get anything done in his present state, and there was no sense in trying. T.J. stumbled back to the bathroom and found a prescription bottle and tapped one tiny yellow tablet into his hand. He popped it into his mouth and washed it down with water straight from the tap.

He stayed there, hunched down under the water, and let it run over his face for a moment. The cold seemed to help. Then he turned it off and groped his way to his room.

He collapsed onto the bed and, mercifully, sleep soon claimed him.

It was quiet in the apartment when Robin arrived. Almost too quiet. She was excited about her meeting with Dub and eager to tell T.J. what she had learned. She wondered where he was. He had said that he wanted her out of the way so that it would be quiet and he could work, but this tomblike silence was eerie. Hadn't he said that he liked to play music when he worked? It was almost as if he weren't there. Had he gone to the library? But the lights were on and the coffeepot was plugged in and full in the kitchen.

For the first time since she'd returned to the apartment from Mexico, Robin looked around. Really looked. There was nothing there. All the warm and homey touches Cheryl and she had put there were gone. Apparently Cheryl had taken her things home and packed Robin's away, but why hadn't T.J. done anything to the apartment? There were no personal items to tell her about the man who lived there. Except for the portable TV and the bicycle in the living room, there was nothing there but the shabby, mismatched furniture that had come with the place. She wondered how a man his age—he had to be in his thirties—who had done as much living as he must have done, could manage not to accumulate more belongings.

What was it he'd said? Oh, yeah. He'd said that he was a "compulsive thrower-awayer." Why? What was he trying to forget?

Robin shrugged. It wasn't her business, and she didn't

know him well enough to ask him, as much as she wanted to. Maybe when they knew each other better, he'd open up to her. Something told her getting him to do that would be about as easy as trying to light a fire in a windstorm. She remembered how he'd shut down when she asked him about the scar. He was obviously a very private person. But why?

After resolving to do something about the impersonal decor, Robin headed for her own room to unpack. It would be easier to continue with the wrinkled look, but Robin needed to do something while she wrestled with the Dub dilemma.

She supposed she should try to call Cheryl, but in all this confusion, she hadn't had time to think clearly. She turned back and picked up the phone and dialed. No answer. She placed the receiver back on the cradle and bustled on to her room.

A low sound reached Robin's ears as she passed by T.J.'s room on the way to her own. She stopped. The door was closed, yet she was sure she had heard something. She didn't hear anything now, but she was certain that she had heard it. She listened intently. There it was again. It was definitely a groan. Or a moan.

He wouldn't have anybody in there? No. It sounded more like pain than pleasure. Robin listened again. T.J. was definitely in discomfort. Robin tapped on the door.

"T.J., are you all right?"

No answer.

Robin knocked again, a little louder. "T.J., if you don't answer me, I'm coming in."

Still no answer. Unless you counted the feeble sounds that were coming from behind the door. Something was wrong. Suppose he was in trouble? Maybe he needed help. Robin turned the knob and pushed gently against the door.

The room was situated on the dark side of the building, and though the shades were open, it was dim. T.J. lay sprawled across the bed on his back, with one arm across his eyes; the other was flung out to the side.

His face was the color of library paste. As Robin moved closer, she could detect a damp sheen of perspiration on his brow. Was he sick? She reached out to feel his forehead. It was damp and clammy, but there was no fever.

T.J. stirred, and Robin moved back. Maybe she should leave. He was obviously unwell, but not sick enough to need her help. He would live without her acting as nurse-maid.

Robin started to leave, but noticed a small, framed picture on the nightstand facing the bed. Curious, she turned it toward her. It was of a smiling blond woman and a small carrot-topped boy with a gap-toothed grin. She picked up the picture for a closer look.

Somebody was in his room, T.J. realized groggily. He forced his eyes open and blinked. It was Robin. What was she doing here? he thought. Looking at his stuff? Why wouldn't she leave him alone? Though still only half-awake, he registered that he was, at least, free of pain. But not of her. He rubbed his eyes to clear them.

"What are you doing in here?" T.J. asked, his voice hoarse from sleep.

Robin jumped slightly. He'd startled her. He hadn't meant to make her jump. She almost dropped what she was holding. Then T.J. realized what it was.

"Put that down," he ordered, much too sharply. "Keep out of here and away from my belongings."

He watched as Robin quickly put the picture of Ginger and Rusty down. She carefully placed it where it had been and backed away from the nightstand. "I'm sorry. I didn't come in here to pry. I heard you groaning, and I thought you might need my help."

T.J. pushed himself up on one elbow. His arms felt heavy, and he was still lethargic, but at least the headache

was gone. It occurred to him that he had jumped to con-
clusions and an apology would probably be in line.
"Thanks," he murmured. "I'm still used to being alone."

"Okay. I thought you might be sick or something. Or
hurt. If you're okay, I'll leave." She left the room.

Massaging his temple with one hand, T.J. shoved himself
up to a sitting position with the other. Damn! He hated the
woozy feeling he got after one of those headaches. He
flexed his shoulders, rotated his head and looked up. She
was back, holding a glass of clear liquid. Water?

"I vaguely remember making coffee before I lay down.
Is there any left?"

Robin looked genuinely concerned about him, T.J. realized. It was nice having somebody like her looking after
him, even if he didn't deserve it. She offered him the water.
"The pot was on when I came in, but it's probably strong
enough to eat through a mug. Maybe this will help."

"Thanks." T.J. took the glass and drained it. "That does
help. And I like my coffee that strong. Maybe now I can
get my day back on track." He managed a weak grin.
"Pour me a cup of mud while I get myself together? I'll
be there in a minute."

The absence of the blinding pain made T.J. feel good.
The fact that Robin had willingly trotted out to get his
coffee made him feel better.

Acrid steam wafted into the air as Robin poured two cups
of the coffee that T.J. had brewed. She wrinkled her nose.
The dark brown liquid even smelled strong. She gingerly
took a sip from hers, grimaced and poured it into the sink.
T.J. could have his strong coffee. She'd find something
else.

The cabinets and the refrigerator seemed empty, but
Robin repeated her search, in case she'd missed something
the first time. "Guess it'll be water," she muttered.

"Sorry. I haven't been to the store lately."

Robin stood up straight and banged her head on an open cabinet door. "Ouch. I didn't realize that you were here." She turned around quickly, rubbing her head.

T.J. took a gulp of his hot, strong coffee and made a satisfied sound. Then he drained the cup.

"Keep drinking that stuff and you'll be up till Christmas," Robin said dryly, still massaging the tender spot on her head.

"I may need to be, if I'm going to finish my paper."

"Maybe I can help. When is it due?" Robin ran cold tap water into a glass.

"Friday."

"Tomorrow?"

"No, Friday week," T.J. clarified.

Robin made an exasperated face. "No sweat. What's the rush?"

"I was planning to get it to the typist tomorrow."

"Why? I'll bet it'll sit all weekend and collect dust on the desk until Monday. Can't you get it to her or him first thing on Monday? We're between semesters—there can't be that much typing business right now." Robin took a swallow of water.

"I just wanted her to be able to start first thing on Monday." T.J. poured another cup of coffee.

"Okay, if you get it to her early on Monday, you'll still be first in line. You'll have the whole weekend to work on it." Robin put her glass down and folded her arms across her chest. "Now. Tell me what all that moaning and groaning was about. If I'm going to be staying here, I need to know what to expect from you. Am I going to be tripping over your inert body on a regular basis?"

T.J. looked as if he were going to shut her out again. What was it that kept him so guarded all the time? And who were the people in the picture?

Fingering the red scar on his brow, T.J. finally explained. "I've had excruciating headaches ever since this. Sometimes they're so bad that I have to drug myself to sleep to get past them." He paused. "It hasn't been happening as much lately. Only when I get tired."

"And I didn't help much last night or this morning," Robin concluded. "I'll just have to see that you don't overdo it."

"I try not to." T.J. shrugged his broad shoulders. "But I keep giving myself deadlines that I can't seem to meet."

"Well, you'll just have to learn to set more realistic goals." Robin clasped her hands together with a loud slap. "Tell me what you need to do, and I'll help get you back on schedule."

T.J. grimaced. It galled him to have to accept her help. Or admit that he needed it. But he did. He looked over at Robin. Maybe it wasn't going to be so bad having her around. But he had no intention of taking advantage of her generosity without giving something in return. "Whoa! Hold on, lady. We can wait a few more minutes. Tell me what Doubleday had to say."

Robin narrowed her eyes and made a wry face. "He claims he thought it was me. So I guess I'll have to believe him for now."

"What about the insurance?"

"Says he never got around to canceling it. He hoped I'd go back to him."

"And the sports car?"

"That took only a small part of the settlement." Robin laughed. "He probably felt he needed it to keep up with his personal appearances. He expected to be making celebrity endorsements."

"For what?"

"That has to do with the rest of the insurance settlement. He invested it in a chain of sports bars. Of course, the partner in the scheme has departed for parts unknown with the money."

Robin laughed again. "It never occurred to him that what

he'd done would look suspicious to anyone with half a lick of sense. And, of course, he hadn't counted on being arrested for my murder.'' Robin laughed bitterly. ''Now he's begging me to get him out of it.''

''Will you?''

''Probably. But first I want to talk with a lawyer. In fact, I probably should have seen one before I went to see Dub. You don't think anybody will think I'm involved in Dub's scheme, do you?'' Robin's blue-green eyes were wide. And scared?

T.J. hadn't thought of that. He'd been more concerned about the technicalities of being declared undead. ''I don't think so. But getting a lawyer is a good idea. I can recommend one.''

Robin's face brightened. ''I couldn't help noticing the books you were working with. Are you a law student?''

''Criminal justice.'' Robin was pretty observant to have noticed what books he'd been working from, T.J. realized.

''Like being a district attorney?''

''No, more like jailhouse management. To put it simply, I'd be qualified to be a warden,'' T.J. said. ''But I am taking a concentration in law, too.'' He laughed. ''I still can't decide what I want to be when I grow up.''

''Cute. Tell me about this lawyer you know. Can I afford him? I have a feeling that I probably won't be able to get my hands on my own money for a while.''

T.J. almost missed the last statement. He was too distracted by her clear blue eyes looking earnestly into his. ''You can afford him. Campus legal aid.''

''Great!'' Robin grinned. She had a beautiful smile, T.J. noticed. ''Now that that's all settled, tell me about that picture.''

''What picture?'' T.J. asked, though he knew exactly what Robin was talking about. He'd do anything to postpone the pain.

''The one I was holding when you nearly snapped my head off. That one. Who are they?''

Chapter 7

T.J. looked as if he weren't going to answer. Then he took a long, deep breath, and his answer came out like a sigh. "My wife and son."

The thought that T.J. might be married hadn't occurred to Robin. She glanced at his left hand. No ring. Divorced, then. The awkward silence between them grew deafening. Finally, Robin felt she had to speak.

"He's a fine-looking boy. Does he live with his mother?"

"No."

Robin wanted to scream. No? Does the man have to say everything in monosyllables? What does he mean, no? The thick silence hung heavy with questions that Robin didn't dare ask, fearing the answers.

T.J.'s face bore a haunted, sad expression. He closed his eyes and took a deep breath. "They're dead," he told her in a flat monotone. He put down his coffee mug with a heavy thud and left the kitchen.

The jolt she got from T.J.'s unexpected answer left Robin

speechless. She had never felt so awful in all her life. Yet, curious at the same time. Instead of helping her to understand T.J. better, the answer to her innocent question had only created more mystery. Was his hurt still fresh?

For lack of anything else to do, Robin picked up T.J.'s empty mug and carried it to the sink. She sensed that he didn't need her nosing around him right then, and she needed to do something to fill the interval until he was ready to work. She squirted some dishwashing liquid into a sponge and wiped out both mugs. Then she rinsed them and placed them on the counter to dry.

He was in the living room, sitting on the sofa, staring out the window, though Robin doubted he was seeing anything. She walked quietly over and touched him lightly on the shoulder. "I'm sorry. I didn't know," she whispered.

It took T.J. a moment to respond. When he did, it wasn't with words. Instead, he reached back and placed his hand on top of hers. Somehow the warmth from his hand, radiating into her cool one, showed Robin that he had forgiven her.

At last, T.J. said something. "Me, too," he said in a voice raw with emotion.

Robin's response caught in her throat. She swallowed. "I understand. I'll try not to ask you so many questions."

T.J. turned and looked at Robin, locking his brown eyes with hers. "I know you will," he said softly. The moment grew longer.

"I'm ready to change the subject now," Robin said after what seemed like an eternity and then some. "Are you ready to get to work?"

Smiling a sad sort of smile, T.J. got up and moved her hand from his shoulder to his warm grasp. "Not really, but let's do it anyway."

She didn't want to let go, but she knew she had to. Robin pulled herself gently from T.J.'s grip. "Get your notes and manuscript, and we'll get started."

* * *

After two hours, T.J. was amazed at how easily Robin had organized his notes. Now he was putting together his outline. He couldn't guess how many hours he'd wasted writing in circles before getting this much done. At this rate, he'd have the paper written with time to spare.

As much as he appreciated Robin's help, he was at the point now where he could finish himself. And in much less time than he had originally estimated. Robin had tried to stay out of his way, but even her tiptoeing around had been distracting. Exasperated at still not being able to concentrate, T.J. had extracted two twenties from his pocket and told her to go shopping. He chuckled as he remembered her comment about him sending her to do women's work. But she'd busied herself in the kitchen, making a list, and then gone.

Now the apartment was mercifully quiet. And empty. It was strange how she had already settled in as if she belonged there. T.J. shrugged. She did, he reminded himself. It had been her apartment first. He straightened his pile of notes and clicked his pen open. After a moment to collect his thoughts, he started to write.

Robin had known she was in his way, and she had tried to keep from getting underfoot. She'd called campus legal aid, but nobody could talk to her until the next morning. She was too restless to stay still, so when T.J. suggested that she make a grocery run, it had come as a welcome relief.

She studied the aisles of the grocery store, feasting her eyes on all the choices. After months of filling but plain camp food, she was ready to cook and eat. And gain back all the weight she had lost, she reminded herself. Steeling herself to withstand the siren call of the junk-food aisle, Robin resolutely set out to buy the ingredients for well-balanced, nutritional and economical meals.

When she guessed she'd put enough food in the basket

to exhaust T.J.'s forty dollars, Robin trundled the shopping cart to the checkout stand. She had hoped to have more money to shop with, but T.J.'s money would have to do. She had been unable to make her card work at the neighborhood ATM, so she had not been able to contribute to the kitty. She surveyed what she had in the cart. It would do for a few days.

Robin started piling her food on the conveyer belt and scanned the covers of the scandal sheets that flaunted their gossipy headlines. Robin almost didn't hear the grocery clerk address her.

"Back from your trip down south?" The checker flashed a welcome-home smile and started passing Robin's purchases efficiently across the scanner's eye.

It was such a welcome relief to have her friends recognize her. First Mr. Edwards, then Dub, now even Juanita at the grocery store. Something told Robin not to launch into a description of her present woes, so she smiled back and finished unloading her cart.

"I was real surprised when your roommate came in and told me she was getting married," Juanita commented as she passed the last item over the scanner. "What do you know about it?"

That explained why Cheryl hadn't come back to the apartment. She had finally convinced Hoke Smith that the time was right! "Not much. I haven't talked to her since I got back. How come you know?"

Juanita recited the total, and then answered Robin's question. "She came in here for some boxes. Seemed pretty down for somebody who was gettin' back from her honeymoon."

"I don't think that had anything to do with Hoke. I hear she'd had some bad news." Robin handed over the two twenties. "I'll have to call her and catch up. She'll be really shocked to hear from me." Robin grinned, thinking about

Cheryl's surprise when she learned that Robin was still very much alive.

Juanita counted out the change. "Well, it was nice seein' you again. Come on back now, y'hear?" She turned to her next customer.

Robin hefted her two sacks of groceries, balancing one on her hip, and turned to the magic eye. She smiled as the door opened for her, and headed home.

T.J. got up and poured himself another cup of the witches' brew he called coffee. After years of midnight shifts on the Birmingham police force, he'd gotten used to the stuff. If it wasn't black and thick, it wasn't done. He took a gulp of the strong liquid.

The outline for his paper had almost written itself, and he'd already begun the paper proper. T.J. couldn't believe how well it was going, thanks to Robin's organizing skill. And he'd thought that she was going to be a problem. If he continued to make the kind of progress he'd made this afternoon, he'd be done in plenty of time to get it to the typist on Monday. He consulted his stack of four-by-six cards and resumed writing.

He had covered two yellow pages with dark black ink scrawls when the sound of Robin's key in the lock alerted T.J. to her return. He shoved his chair back and went to help her with the groceries. Even one floor up was a long way to carry grocery sacks on a sweltering day like this.

Robin had already deposited two sacks of groceries beside the door by the time T.J. reached it. He brushed past her to go for the rest.

"Where are you going?" Robin asked as he reached for the door she had just closed.

"To get the rest of the bags from your car."

"What rest? What car?" Robin chuckled. "Forty dollars doesn't go very far these days."

T.J. looked at the two bags. "You mean that's forty dollars' worth of groceries?"

"No. Actually, it came to $37.23. You have some change coming." Robin reached into her pocket and came up with two damp and crumpled bills. Then she went back for the coins. "I had intended to pay you back for at least half of this," she added with a frown, "but when I stuck my cash card into the automatic teller machine, it ate it." Robin sighed loudly. "Now I'm going to have to make a trip all the way to Demopolis to straighten it out."

T.J. accepted the wadded bills and change from Robin and shoved it into his pocket. "I hate to say this," he said gently, "but that's probably tied in with the rest of the dead-Robin-Digby mess."

Robin looked up, obviously surprised. "You mean, the bank found out that I was supposed to be dead and canceled my account?"

He had just noticed the way her hair hung damply around her face, which was glowing with heat and perspiration. The pale blue dress had molded itself to her curves. He tried to stop himself from staring. "They've probably put a hold on your funds until your estate is probated."

Frowning, Robin inserted dryly, "That shouldn't be difficult, considering I don't have an estate to settle."

T.J. smiled, but his thoughts returned to the dress clinging to Robin's slender frame. "Why didn't you turn on the air-conditioning in your car?" T.J. asked, a heartbeat before Robin's comment about a car registered. He was really having a hell of a time keeping his concentration, with her looking like that. "Did you just tell me you don't have one?"

"Guilty as charged," Robin replied as she reached for one of the bags. "We need to get this stuff into the kitchen before the ice cream goes from milkshake to soup."

"You walked all the way to the store and back?" T.J.

picked up the other bag and followed Robin into the kitchen. "Why didn't you tell me you didn't have a car?"

"It's only two blocks. I'm used to the heat. And two sacks of groceries is hardly a stretch after a summer excavating in the jungles of Mexico." Robin rummaged through her bag until she located the ice cream and put it in the freezer. Then she went back for the rest.

"Well, I still wouldn't have suggested you go if I'd known you were carless," T.J. muttered defensively. "You could've gotten heatstroke. Look at you, you're soaking wet."

"I'll survive. Even when I had my car, I walked most everywhere I could. How do you think I lost the first ten pounds? Gas and upkeep were getting too high, so when I got the chance to go to Mexico, I sold the car to pay for the airfare. I figured I could use Cheryl's when I needed one.

"Oh, and I found out why Cheryl turned the apartment over to you. She got married." Robin pushed a damp tendril away from her eye. "I guess she finally convinced Hoke to marry her before he made his first million." She turned around and began to unpack the sacks of food.

T.J. was more interested in watching Robin bend and stretch as she put away the groceries than the explanation. He marveled at the efficiency with which she moved. By the time he realized that he should be helping, she'd finished putting everything away.

"I'm starved," Robin announced once the groceries had all been stacked away. "You cooked breakfast, I'll do supper. That was part of our deal, anyway. I can't believe it's already five o'clock, and we never got around to lunch."

"Do you always think about food? It seems like all you've done since you walked into my apartment is say you're hungry."

"*My* apartment," Robin reminded him.

"Okay," T.J. conceded. "Ours."

"Ours. No, I don't always think about eating, but my metabolism is a little out of whack just now. Two days ago I was in Cacaxtla. I spent a day and a half traveling. Now I'm catching up." Robin opened the freezer and surveyed the meager contents. True, there was more there than when she'd looked this morning, but pickings were still fairly slim. She selected a package of boneless chicken breasts she had just bought and set them out before they had a chance to freeze. She turned around to T.J.

"How's the paper coming?" Robin eyed the stack of note cards and the yellow legal pad that T.J. had been scribbling on.

"Pretty well. You really helped square me away. Hold off cooking for about an hour. I'd like to get a little more done before I quit for the night."

Robin raised an eyebrow. "For the night? I thought you had a deadline."

"I do," T.J. admitted. "But after last night and my headache this afternoon, I don't want to overdo it." He ran a hand through his hair. "You convinced me that I had all weekend. I think I'll take my time."

Robin fingered her damp dress. "I think I'll shower and change before dinner. Then I'll get started on freshening up my wardrobe. Do you have an iron?"

T.J. told her where the iron was stashed, and Robin went to get it. "Let me know when you're ready for me," she called over her shoulder. Then she turned and left him alone at the table.

It would have been distracting staying in the kitchen where T.J. was working, anyway. At first Robin had thought she could handle sharing this apartment with him and keep it simple. But as he had begun to reveal each of his many layers to her, she had become more and more attracted to him. In spite of her better judgment, Robin was already considering getting involved with another man.

And it worried her. She was just starting the second year of her new-woman five-year plan, and getting involved with T. J. Swift had not been a part of the schedule. At all.

Robin's change out of her damp dress was definitely for the better, T.J. noticed. She had slipped into a T-shirt and shorts, and was more than pleasing to the eye. Robin's outfit was a distraction that he didn't need, but really appreciated.

For a woman on the short side, Robin had incredibly good legs, T.J. marveled as he watched her put the final touches on the meal. It smelled almost good enough to distract his attention from those legs, provocatively displayed in a short pair of cutoff jeans. T.J. briefly considered suggesting some ground rules for dress and decorum around his—their—apartment. Then he looked again.

"Dinner's about ready. You'll need to clear your stuff out of the way," Robin announced as she began a systematic search through the cabinets above the kitchen counter. She made a tiny frustrated sound.

T.J. began to police up his materials, grateful for the excuse not to look at her. It was fortunate that he'd already finished what he planned to do for the day. Once he saw the latest in Robin's grad-student chic, he'd been too far gone to work. Where did she get those clothes? Only she would put on shorts so minuscule as to be nearly nonexistent, then top them with a Save The Earth recycling T-shirt, knotted at the waist and pulled snug enough across her chest to reveal more than it covered. That dress-code idea was beginning to grow on him.

He twisted a rubber band around the stack of index cards and closed his books, then swung out of the chair. "I'll just put these in the living room." T.J. would normally have simply shoved the school paraphernalia to one side, clearing out an area just big enough for his plate. It didn't take large reserves of intuition for him to know that that was a thing of the past. With the stack of papers and books under his arm, he prepared to leave.

Another exasperated sound from Robin's direction stopped him.

"What's wrong, hotshot?"

Robin whirled to face him and stood with her hands on her trim hips. "Don't you have any serving bowls? A platter? Something I can serve dinner on?"

T.J. swallowed and tried to look apologetic. He doubted he succeeded. What did he have to apologize for? "What you see is what you get. I usually just set the pot on the table." If he bothered to do that. There had been many a day when he ate canned stew or chili directly from the pan, holding it over the sink. He'd never been embarrassed about it before.

"Go on, then." Robin made a shooing motion with her hands. "Wash up. I'll think of something."

Yes, having a roommate of the definitely female persuasion was going to take a lot of adjustment. T.J. chuckled as he dutifully washed up.

There wasn't much Robin could do for this meal but put the pans on the dinette table. T.J. didn't even have enough plates for her to use one as a serving platter. She did manage to locate a plastic microwave dinner plate to place the breaded chicken breasts on. The gravy had to go in a cereal bowl. And Robin had the entire, slightly used contents of her hope chest stashed in the basement doing nothing.

She had wanted to make iced tea, but couldn't find a container large enough to mix it in. She settled on water. How that man had survived this long using jelly jars and two plates, she couldn't imagine.

Shrugging, Robin put the rest of T.J.'s meager supply of dishes on the table and waited for him to return. She busied herself tidying the area where she had worked.

He had come in so quietly that Robin didn't hear him

over the sound of running water at first. When she finished rinsing the frying pan, she turned off the tap.

"This looks like the best meal that's been cooked in this place for a long time," T.J. remarked as he pulled out a chair for Robin.

Robin was surprised. She hadn't quite expected that. But why not? He had actually been quite polite and mannerly in the face of her initial bad behavior. Robin dried her hands and hurried over to take her seat.

"Fried chicken, black-eyed peas, rice and gravy. Even coleslaw." T.J. picked up the container of store-bought slaw.

Robin had never been embarrassed about taking kitchen shortcuts before, but suddenly it bothered her. "I apologize for the store-bought slaw. I wasn't sure whether you'd like it, and I didn't want to take the time to make a fresh batch. I've been starved for real down-home cookin', after a diet of camp food with a distinct Mexican flavor." Robin speared a piece of chicken and put it on her plate.

"So I guess tacos are out for a while," T.J. commented as he helped himself.

"A long while. Anything else, I'll go for. Do you like Chinese?" Without further comment, Robin brought a fork-ful of rice and gravy to her mouth.

"I have indulged in takeout from Chang's from time to time."

Robin grinned. "That's one of Cheryl's and my favorite places. We'll have to get some when my money situation is straightened out."

T.J. acknowledged the comment, but went on eating.

Toward the end of the meal, T.J. made a comment as he refilled his jelly glass with water. "Don't you like tea with dinner?"

"Love it," Robin answered, still chewing on a piece of chicken.

"Why didn't you make any? I saw you unpack tea bags."

"I couldn't find anything to brew it in."

T.J. laughed. "I usually use the coffee carafe."

Robin made a wry face. There was no telling what iced tea brewed in a coffeemaker might taste like. She thought she'd pass. "Do you think we could bring up some of my things from downstairs? I think we could both benefit from my kitchen stuff. I don't mind an occasional challenge, but this is ridiculous." She waved toward the mismatched dinnerware.

"Probably could," T.J. answered, running his hand through his hair, and grinned. "I never claimed to be a kitchen person."

"It's a wonder you survived." But he had survived, Robin couldn't help noticing appreciatively. That teal polo shirt stretched too tightly across T.J.'s broad chest to suggest he'd been doing without. She was willing to bet T.J. had women running after him with home-cooked meals all the time.

"I don't know when I've enjoyed a meal so much. The least I could do is to help with the dishes," T.J. said after they had all but licked the pans clean. "After all, I did my share of eating."

"You're on. I never turn down kitchen help. I'll wash—you dry."

"Okay." T.J. glanced out the window across from the kitchen table. The hot, hazy afternoon had gone from milky white to dark gray. "We'd better get a move on. It looks like we may be in for a storm."

Robin glanced at the darkening sky. "Good. It might help cool things off."

"I suppose it would," T.J. agreed morosely. "As long as we don't lose the lights." He wasn't a nervous man, but he still didn't relish the idea of being caught down in the basement if the power went.

T.J. probably would have left the dishes, but Robin didn't seem the type to put things off. There was a dishwasher, but with the few dishes he had, it hadn't seemed worth the effort to fire it up. Maybe with Robin's stuff they'd put it to use.

"I'm done," Robin announced as she pulled the plug in the sink. "You finish drying, and I'll go get the key from Mr. Edwards."

"Sure. I'll be down right behind you." T.J. looked out at the darkening sky again and shuddered. He'd never been afraid of storms before, but since Saudi, everything had been different. It wasn't the storm that made him uneasy, but the possibility of all that thunderous noise. Noise that brought back entirely too many memories he thought were best forgotten.

T.J. stowed the last plate and turned off the light. He took one last uneasy look at the sky and went down the stairs after Robin.

She was already in the storage room, poking around among the cardboard boxes. She'd apparently selected one, because it sat against the doorjamb. T.J. shoved it outside the door as he came in. "Look what Mr. Edwards gave me on the way downstairs."

Robin looked up, and a startled look came over her as he handed her a folded piece of paper. "Leave the box where it was…" she called.

"It's a clipping about the body they found," he said after a quick glance. Then the alarm on Robin's face registered. "What's wrong?"

Robin's warning came too late. A sudden gust of wind from the high, barred window that Robin had opened in defense against the dank, stuffy air blew the heavy metal door closed with a resounding bang.

Dismay replaced Robin's look of alarm. "…or we'll be locked in," she finished weakly.

Chapter 8

"I can't believe you did that," Robin continued flatly.

T.J. looked around. "What?"

"Maybe nothing," she replied hopefully. "Please tell me you have the key in your pocket."

Still looking puzzled, T.J. gestured to indicate that he didn't. "Why? What's wrong?"

Robin sighed loudly. "Nothing much. Do you remember what Mr. Edwards told us about keeping the door propped open?" She was trying very hard to keep her voice level and calm.

Realization dawned on T.J.'s face. "We're locked in." He looked toward the door. There was no handle, just a keyhole. They were stuck in there until somebody could turn the key on the other side of the door and release them.

Another strong gust of wind blew in through the tiny open window and reminded Robin of the approaching storm. She pulled a box into the circle of light formed by the dim, bare bulb and sank heavily onto it. She puffed a strand of flyaway hair away from her face. "I guess we're stuck in here for the duration. Unless you have a file or some dynamite on you.'' She looked dolefully at the burglar bars on the window.

''Wait a minute! We're directly below Mr. Edwards's apartment. We could just bang on the ceiling until he hears us. Surely he'll come down to investigate.'' T.J. looked around and seized a golf club from a bag that leaned against the wall. He prepared to whack one of the bare support beams overhead.

''Save your energy. Mr. Edwards isn't home.''

''But I just got the clipping from him.'' T.J. stood holding the golf club uselessly.

''You just caught him on the way out. He goes to senior citizen night at the library on Thursdays. He won't be back for hours,'' Robin answered glumly.

Robin watched silently as T.J. put the club back and pushed another box into position beside Robin's. She knew that they were in no danger where they were. Even if there was a tornado—a definite possibility with these late-summer storms—she and T.J. were in the safest place they could be. But still, it was not comfortable to have T.J. stuck there with her.

Finally, T.J. made a suggestion. ''There's not much sense in just sitting here feeling sorry for ourselves. We could go ahead and sort through these boxes. Then we can make a fast getaway when the door's unlocked.''

That made sense to Robin. She hopped up off the box and tugged the cardboard flaps aside and peered inside. It was full of kitchen paraphernalia. Just the kind of stuff they had come down to get. ''This is a definite yes,'' she told T.J. and added, ''It would have helped a lot if Cheryl had bothered to label these boxes.''

They quickly developed a rhythm. Robin would check the contents of a box, then T.J. would set it aside. Soon there was a stack beside the door. As the stack of boxes grew, so did the ominous, rumbling thunder from the storm outside.

Wiping a trickle of sweat from her brow, Robin paused to listen. "The thunder is louder. The storm must be getting pretty close."

"And the rain isn't too far away, either. I can smell it in the air," T.J. commented. He, too, wiped at a rivulet of sweat. The steamy, hot air in the basement made his hair twitch in damp curls around his face, and his brow shone with perspiration.

"We're almost done," Robin remarked idly as she shoved another box toward T.J.'s growing pile.

"Then all we'll have left to do is wait." T.J. picked up the last cardboard box Robin had checked and positioned it beside the pile. "Is this it?" He looked around.

"I think so." All the boxes had been moved to the spot beside the door. Robin swept a pair of roller skates from the top of a dusty trunk close to the wall. "I guess we'll just wait." She patted the empty space beside her, inviting T.J. to sit.

He lowered his bulk to the spot next to Robin with easy grace. She hadn't fully realized how big he was before, but as they shared the perch on top of the trunk, she became acutely aware of his all-male presence. Robin instinctively scooted a little farther away from him.

T.J. seemed not to notice the way Robin had widened the space between them. "Oh!" He dug in his pockets. "Guess we have time to look at the article now." He handed her a torn sheet of newsprint and leaned back against the wall.

It was the article about the body that had been mistakenly identified as hers. Robin couldn't believe she'd forgotten all about it. Coed found dead, the caption read. Robin's blood turned to ice at the sinister sound of the title, but morbid curiosity made her read the short paragraph.

An Alberta man out walking his dog made a gruesome discovery yesterday: the decomposing body of a woman. Using fingerprints, police tentatively identified the body as an Alabama graduate student, but will not release a name until next of kin can be notified.

Robin shook off a shudder as she read the innocuous-sounding words. Though her name was not mentioned, just the idea that someone had thought the body was her was sobering. If it wasn't creepy enough being stuck down in the cellar, this put the icing on the cake.

A peal of thunder rumbled to a startling crescendo, and chills danced down Robin's spine. She tried to shake off the creepy feeling, but the dark cellar did nothing to ease her discomfort.

T.J. shrugged. "I guess we'll just have to be philosophical about this. We're locked in, there's probably a tornado watch. Surely, nothing else could go wrong."

In less than ten minutes, T.J. realized that he had spoken too soon. With a sudden gust of wind, the rain began. The thunder that previously had only rolled lazily across the sky turned violent. With a loud crash and a blinding flash of light, the storm announced its full fury.

T.J. pushed his way to the window and pulled it shut, getting soaked for his efforts. He picked his way back across the cramped room toward his seat on the trunk as the lights flickered.

Then the room went dark.

"Me and my big mouth," T.J. muttered as he groped his way across the room. He stumbled and uttered a curse as his shin struck an unidentified obstacle. He righted himself and waited for another burst of light. The next slashing streak illuminated the room enough for him to get his bearings. T.J. corrected his course and moved carefully to where Robin and the trunk waited.

As the darkness settled, a small, sure hand reached out to him. "Here." Robin's soothing voice beckoned. "Take my hand and let me guide you."

There was something calming and reassuring about Robin's hand in his. Without further mishap, T.J. reached the trunk and took his place beside her.

He knew it was irrational to fear the storm and the dark. He also knew it was neither wind nor night that he was afraid of, but the memories of another storm that he couldn't let go of. Not a natural storm that reminded mere mortals of the grandeur of nature, but a man-made storm. A storm so horrible that he had almost not lived through it.

He hated the noise, the light and the thunder. They reminded him of the sounds of war. Sounds that he would sooner forget. It was one thing to listen to all the noise in a warm and well-lit room. But trapped in a dark and closed basement? It was too much like a tomb.

"The electricity usually comes back on pretty quick around here." Robin's voice sounded so assured; T.J. was glad that she was trapped there with him. He didn't think he could endure it alone. He didn't want to.

He didn't want to go through it again at all. T.J. squeezed Robin's hand, which was still clutched tightly in his, as if he were trying to reassure her. But it was his own pounding heart he was trying to calm.

The storm only increased in intensity instead of abating. As it vented its full fury, it became apparent to Robin that the electricity would not return anytime soon. She wasn't too concerned about the storm or the confinement. Yet. It was merely inconvenient.

T.J., on the other hand, wasn't taking the situation so calmly. He paced the small room like a confined lion. With every rumble of thunder, his pace increased. With each spear of lightning, his muscles tensed until Robin wondered what would happen if they let go.

Robin reached out and touched T.J.'s hand. His fingers were cold, yet the last brilliant flash had illuminated his face enough for her to see sweat beaded on his brow. Hadn't he said something earlier about not liking storms? Or had she misread something between the lines?

She had to think of something to take his mind off the storm. Robin thought for a minute. Twenty questions! T.J. hadn't been very forthcoming about himself so far, and he still might not reveal anything. But Robin would have been willing to bet that he'd spend so much time trying to dodge her questions that he wouldn't have a chance to dwell on the storm.

"What's T.J. stand for?" That ought to get his attention. Robin grinned, though no one could see it in the dark.

The question seemed to catch T.J. by surprise. He hesitated, then said, "That's classified."

"I hardly think your real name is top secret. Maybe a little embarrassing. Dub Doubleday, famous football player and all-around great guy, goes by Dub because he's ashamed of his real first name. Lester." Robin wrinkled her nose. "Look at me. I'm admitting that I was once Mrs. Lester Dwayne Doubleday. If I can do it, so can you. It can't be any worse than that. Let me see if I can guess."

"What makes you think I'll tell you if you do?" T.J. replied slowly.

"If I come up with it, you have to tell. It's only fair. Agreed?"

"All right," T.J. agreed, albeit reluctantly.

"Okay. Let's see. Travis Jeremy."

"No."

"Timothy James?"

"Nuh-uh."

"Terrence Jeremiah?"

"Absolutely not."

"Am I getting close?" Robin asked playfully.

"Not even warm."

Robin decided she had better try another tactic. She had intended only to keep his mind off the storm, but the incorrect guesses had made her even more curious. Now she really wanted to know what his name was.

"That's not working," Robin muttered, more to herself than to T.J. "I'm going to concentrate on the *T* for now."

T.J. shrugged as another lightning bolt lit the room. "Whatever."

"Tobias."

He shook his head.

"Thaddeus?"

"Nope."

"Thurston."

"Yuk!"

"Troy? Tony? Theodore?"

T.J. chuckled. "No, no, no."

Robin laughed in response to T.J.'s warm chuckle. It was a relief to hear it. "How about Theophilus?"

Another bright flash of lightning revealed a wry grimace. "No way!"

"Tristan?"

"Where are you getting these names?"

"Well, it has to be something weird, if you don't want anybody to know." Or did it? Maybe it was something very simple. "I know," Robin announced, feeling smug.

"I doubt it."

"Thomas," Robin announced with finality.

T.J. said nothing.

"What? No denial? That's it!" Robin clapped her hands together excitedly.

"Yes," T.J. drawled slowly. "It's Thomas."

"Okay. It's so ordinary, it must be the middle name you're embarrassed about. Thomas what?" Robin paused for a moment. "I'll bet it's pretty ordinary, too." She thought for a minute. "I've got it. Thomas Jefferson!"

Another flash of lightning showed T.J. staring at her with incredulity written all over his face. "How did you do that?"

"Lucky guess?" Robin shrugged. "Why do you hide behind your initials? Thomas Jefferson Swift. What's wrong with that?"

"If you don't see it, I damn sure won't tell you."

It couldn't be the Jefferson, Robin reasoned. Thomas Swift?

No. Tommie? Tom? Of course! "I guess you've heard a lot of Tom Swifties in your day," she concluded, referring to the word games made popular by the children's books featuring the Tom Swift character.

"People were teasing me about my name before I even heard of the literary Tom Swift, much less knew what a Tom Swifty was," T.J. replied ruefully.

"Well, if it makes you feel better, this current crop of kids is clueless about both. And they will be until they make a video game about him."

"Too late to save me years of misery," T.J. said.

"Was it that bad?"

Another rumble of thunder crescendoed outside the cell-like room. Did she realize how much like heavy artillery that sounded? T.J. tried to shake the disturbing memory free.

"It was pretty bad to a ten-year-old kid. The adults were the worst. They always thought they were so clever, with their overdone adverbs. For a long time, I didn't even know what they were talking about." Abruptly T.J. got up and tried, again, to pace.

The going was difficult. It was hard to move around in the dark, cluttered room. Things kept jumping out in front of him. Or so it seemed.

He cursed mildly as he hit his shin on yet another obstacle. A memory from the past came to him. "'Ouch, I've hurt my foot,' he replied lamely," T.J. deadpanned.

He was rewarded with a low chuckle from Robin. "I guess it wasn't so painful that you blocked it all out entirely."

T.J. joined in with Robin's laughter. "No, it doesn't seem so bad now."

"'Well, come sit down before you destroy something,' she replied brokenly," Robin said, and stifled a giggle.

T.J. waited until the next lightning bolt flared and fixed Robin's position. As the light faded away, he groped his way back to the trunk.

As he reached his destination, T.J.'s foot caught on something. The roller skates. He pitched headfirst into Robin's lap.

"'Help, I'm being squashed,' she cried flatly." Robin giggled as T.J. righted himself.

Groaning, T.J. found his spot on the trunk. "Promise me you'll stop with those."

Another flash revealed a wicked expression on Robin's face.

"And promise you will never, never call me by the *T* name."

"I tomise," Robin said slowly, then dissolved into a fit of giggles.

At first T.J. wasn't certain he'd heard her correctly. But when another flash illuminated Robin's grin, he knew his ears had been working. Why, that witch! He had a sudden urge to kiss that smirk off her face. T.J. lowered his head.

The light was blinding, and simultaneous with an explosion of thunder. The tingly feeling that Robin felt had nothing to do with T.J.'s face coming toward hers. That bolt had hit almost on top of them. There was another detonation immediately behind the first, and again the air was charged with unleashed electricity.

T.J. clutched Robin tightly, holding her so close she could scarcely breathe. As she struggled to escape from his constricting grasp, Robin could feel T.J.'s heart pounding erratically as she was pressed against his chest.

This guy is afraid, Robin realized with certainty. And it has nothing to do with the thunder. Or does it?

She remembered what Mr. Edwards had told her about T.J. having served in Saudi and being wounded in Iraq. Was he having a flashback? What did they call it? Delayed stress. Somebody had told her once that thunder sometimes sounded like cannon fire. No wonder he was a wreck.

Robin sat quietly, imprisoned in T.J.'s viselike hold, until the intensity of the storm decreased. As the storm's fury finally spent itself, T.J.'s rapidly palpitating heart slowed to normal. Finally, the storm passed.

The storm was over, but they were still trapped. They still couldn't go anywhere. T.J. relaxed his grip on her. Now he sat, merely resting his head on Robin's shoulder. After a long period of silence, T.J.'s head drooped. His relaxed breathing told her that he was asleep.

Somewhere toward morning, the electrical power came back on, the sudden light waking Robin out of a fitful sleep. She would have turned it off, but T.J.'s head, heavy on her shoulder, wouldn't permit her to get up. She shifted her position to shield her eyes and tried to get comfortable. Squeezing her lids shut against the sixty-watt intrusion, she tried to catch a couple of hours of sleep before the long, confined night would come to an end.

The first thing T.J. noticed when he woke that morning was Robin's head nestled in the crook of his arm. He rubbed his eyes with his free hand and tried to figure out what she was doing there. As his vision cleared, so did the fog that had blurred his thinking. Embarrassment washed over him as he remembered the storm and his craven behavior. He sighed as he realized he was going to have to explain what had happened. For a once strong man, that weakness was a hard thing to have to bring into the light of day. T.J. shifted his position, trying to stretch his cramped muscles without disturbing Robin.

Muted sounds from outside indicated that it was still early morning and rescue would be long in coming. T.J. tried to look at his watch to get a fix on the time, but Robin's arm was twined around his, blocking his view. The sun was up, and the light was on. At least those were two things in their favor. People would soon be stirring. It wouldn't be long before they were free.

With nothing else to do but wait, T.J. settled back and tried to relax. It wasn't a new experience, resting with a woman in his arms. Just a long-forgotten one. A memory that T.J. had tried to suppress. Why were those long-dormant feelings reemerging now?

Robin stirred slightly in his arms. T.J. held his breath, loath to wake her. She snuggled closer to him, nuzzling her face against his chest, and a surge of warmth filled him. His first instinct was to push her away, to try to gently wake her up. As much as he tried to ignore the feeling, Robin did feel good in his arms. T.J. would have been content to stay that way all morning, but they both had other things to do.

The morning light finally did its job.

"What time is it?" Robin yawned sleepily and shifted out of T.J.'s arms.

"Early." T.J. flexed the arm that had been curled around Robin's sleepy form and twisted it around so that he could see his watch. "Not quite seven."

"I guess people will be out and about soon." Robin stretched languorously and pushed herself upright. "I don't hear anybody moving around upstairs. Do you think we should try to pound with the golf club and wake Mr. E.?"

"Let's see if we can attract someone's attention on the street first. I'd hate to wake the old guy up. He probably didn't sleep much, either," T.J. replied, remembering that he hadn't heard anybody come in after the lights went. Mr. Edwards might not have made it home yet.

"I guess we could try the window. Somebody might walk by." Robin picked her way carefully across the room.

T.J. pushed up and followed Robin. She climbed up on a milk crate and struggled with the window latch that had jammed when T.J. so hastily closed it the night before. T.J. reached behind her and jerked it free. The cool morning air brought in the sounds of traffic and an awakening day.

Robin stayed on her perch and craned her neck to see through the small, high window. "Well, I'll be." She laughed. "Guess who I see coming up the walk."

Not wanting to guess or wait for an answer, T.J. stepped closer to Robin's slender form and peered out. Mr. Edwards was heading toward them, whistling, and he looked as if he had slept in his clothes.

Robin glanced at T.J. and grinned. Then they both shouted Mr. Edwards's name.

Chapter 9

T.J. placed the last of the boxes on the pile that had formed in the middle of the living room. He had allowed Robin to carry up a couple of boxes and then had suggested that she get ready for her appointment at campus legal aid to meet with a lawyer. It wasn't that he didn't need her help. He needed to think.

Robin hadn't said anything about what had happened last night in the basement, but it had been obvious from her impromptu guessing game that she sensed that something was wrong. Even before he'd turned into a spineless wimp in her arms.

T.J. snorted in disgust.

He had never before felt like a weak man. Didn't feel like one now. But that storm! It had brought back all the terror of that night in Iraq. What was he supposed to tell her? How did he explain?

Saying nothing would have been T.J.'s first choice. But he had already learned that Robin Digby would not let it lie for long. She had an inquisitive mind and an innate curiosity that teased at something like a cat playing with a mouse. She wouldn't let it go until she was done with it.

And she wouldn't be done with it until she had all the answers. Answers that he would rather not give.

T.J. thought awhile longer and came to the only conclusion he could reach. It would be easier on them both if he just went ahead and got it over with.

It had occurred to Robin as she was ironing the dress she planned to wear that it might be a good idea to take something with her to her appointment at legal aid that would identify her as Robin L. Digby. Something other than the IDs that showed her puffed up like an unhappy balloon. That was why she was pawing frantically through a box of books, looking for her Auburn yearbook. If she remembered correctly, her senior picture looked very much the way she did today.

"What are you doing?" T.J. asked from somewhere behind her.

Robin hadn't heard him approach, and would have jumped ten feet at the unexpected sound of his voice if she hadn't finally found the yearbook. "Stop doing that!" she gasped as she tugged her annual out of the bookish jumble.

"Doing what?" T.J. did look cute when he was puzzled.

"Sneaking up behind me. You're always doing it. Try making some noise once in a while. Clear your throat, cough. Something." Robin clambered to her feet and flipped through the book.

"I'll try to remember to whistle 'Dixie' next time, but it is my house, too," T.J. reminded her. "You still didn't say what you were doing."

"Aha! Found it!" Robin looked up at T.J. who was still wearing the same clothes as the day before. He looked tired and badly in need of a shave. Robin felt guilty as she stood in front of him freshly showered and dressed. Doubly guilty when she recalled how their basement escapade had deprived him of a good night's sleep. She held the opened book out for him to see.

"This!"

T.J. glanced at the opened page politely, without really looking at it. "Very nice. But why are you wasting your time with it now? Don't you have to go?"

"I have plenty of time. I thought this might help prove who I am. This picture looks more like I do today, definitely better than those horrible ID pictures." Robin held the book for him again. "See."

He took the book from Robin's hands and looked again at the page. "You're right. That does look more like you. Why the big change between then and now?"

"It's a long story that I don't have time to go into now. Suffice it to say that it had a lot to do with Dub and how I felt about myself at the time."

There was enough time to tell the story, Robin just didn't want to go into it right then. It was still painful remembering how Dub had whittled away at her self-esteem until there was nothing to rely on but food to make her feel loved. Once she realized what Dub was doing to her, she had stopped allowing him to manipulate her and had made her own little declaration of independence. As the time passed and the hurt healed, the pounds had melted away.

T.J. looked at his watch and back to Robin. "Speaking of long stories…I have one I need to tell you." He paused and took a deep breath. "I need to explain about what happened last night."

Icy fingers traced patterns down Robin's bare arms. Gooseflesh formed, in spite of the August heat, as she realized what he was about to say. She wanted so much to know, but she was also afraid. She didn't want him to have to expose his vulnerability to her so soon, if he didn't really want to. How did she tell him it didn't matter, without it sounding as if she didn't care?

She stuck an emery board into the yearbook to mark the

place and laid it carefully down on the sofa next to her purse, then turned her attention to T.J. "I think I have a good idea," Robin said softly. "Mr. Edwards told me that you had been wounded in Iraq. I just assumed that it was some sort of delayed stress."

He looked relieved. Maybe T.J. wouldn't need to tell her anything after all. But Robin sensed there was more to the story than post-traumatic stress syndrome. "You don't have to tell me anything you don't feel comfortable with."

Robin picked up her purse and book and turned to go.

A strong hand caught hers and pulled her gently but firmly back when she would have gone past.

"Wait!" The needy look on T.J.'s face stopped her.

Curiosity made her stay.

Still holding his outstretched hand, Robin let him draw her back to the sofa beside him. "Okay. Tell me."

T.J. drew a long, shuddering breath and steeled his resolve to get the story out. It had helped to talk to the military psychiatrist, but once he got to Tuscaloosa he had tired of the bureaucratic shuffle at the local veteran's clinic. There was a group, but it had been too impersonal, so after a few sessions he had quit. And in Tuscaloosa there wasn't a large military community where he might have found someone to share his pain. There had been no support system to help him deal with his own terrors. At first it had been all right. But when the spring and summer storm season came upon him, with its battlelike pyrotechnics, the old nightmares had returned.

Robin really looked as if she already knew and understood. T.J. guessed that most people had heard of post-traumatic stress by now, but his situation was more complicated than that. He had more demons than just those dished up by war.

T.J. closed his eyes and tried to formulate his thoughts. Where did he begin? His personal hell had started years before. A year before Desert Storm. He'd start there. He took a deep breath.

It was easier not looking at her. T.J. fixed his eyes on a spot on the floor, a few inches from her sandaled feet. "You remember the picture of Ginger and Rusty?"

"Yes," she answered huskily.

"I killed them."

Robin jerked her hand from T.J.'s and raised it to her mouth to smother a gasp.

"Oh, I didn't do it with a gun, or a knife, or poison, or anything like that. But I was responsible."

T.J. recaptured Robin's hand. He needed the physical contact. He could feel her pulse in her wrist, racing and erratic. "I'd spent three straight weeks on graveyard shifts without a night off. I'd just come in after pulling a double shift on top of all of that. I dragged in at 8:00 a.m., about two steps short of dead.

"Ginger was just getting ready to go off to work. Rusty had missed the bus, and she was going to drop him off at school on the way." T.J. stopped, remembering the way she had looked that day when he came in. She had been flushed and glowing, the way she always was in the morning, and flustered because she was running late.

"She asked me to take a look at her car. 'The brakes were acting squishy,' she said." T.J. took a long, deep breath. "I chewed her out for not taking care of her car and told her I was too tired to look at it."

Robin squeezed his hand. "It's okay. You don't have to finish. I think I know."

He continued anyway. He had to. It was senseless to stop now. "It was the last time I saw her, and I chewed her out. You should have seen her face. Hurt and confused..."

"Please, T.J. You don't have to."

"But she forced a smile and kissed me anyway. I turned my head away. It was the last time we were together, and I turned away." His voice cracked and became a sob.

He swallowed and took a deep breath. "It had just started to rain, and the roads were slick," he continued flatly. "Somebody skidded out in front of her, and she couldn't stop. She swerved to miss the car, but I guess she didn't anticipate the semi coming from the other direction, and she couldn't stop." He swallowed again, forcing his heart out of his throat. "They were both killed instantly. The seat belts didn't do a damn thing.

"For a year, I just went through the motions. I just operated on automatic pilot. I was alive, but dead inside. When my reserve unit got called up to the Gulf, I was actually relieved. Hell, I was already dead. I figured the Iraqis would finish me off."

Gentle, warm fingers reached out and caressed his face. Robin's voice breathed a question: "You wanted the Iraqis to finish what you believed had already started?"

"Yes. God help me, yes." T.J. laughed bitterly. "Couldn't even do that right." He fingered the scar, then dropped his hand to his lap. He shook his head slowly.

"I was dead. Clinically dead. They said I had no pulse, no heartbeat. Lying on a stretcher in a casualty aid station, I died. I saw it all. They had covered my face with a towel and moved on to somebody else.

"Do you know what it feels like to hover over your own dead body?"

Robin shook her head. Her eyes were wide with feeling.

"I was happy. I thought I'd get to join Ginger and Rusty." He laughed again, less bitterly this time. "Next thing I know, people are all clustered around me, and I'm waking up from surgery."

Instinctively, Robin knew not to interrupt his thinking with words. The Lord only knew how weird she had felt when she was fully conscious and told she was dead. She shuddered at what T.J. had gone through. She wanted to gather him up in her arms and soothe his knitted brow, but he wasn't finished yet. She could feel it. He still hadn't explained why the storm had bothered him so. She squeezed his hand and smiled sympathetically.

T.J. looked away from her and stared out the window, as if trying to see far beyond his limited field of vision. He opened his mouth as if to speak. Then closed it. Finally, he sighed.

"It was friendly fire that hit me. Friendly fire. The good guys got me. Our side. Somehow even that seemed right. They knew who needed taking out." He shook his head slowly. "But I didn't die.

"I have a vague recollection of seeing Ginger. Talking to her. I tried to tell the doc about it. Ginger told me to go back. I didn't want to. But she made me." T.J.'s voice shook and cracked.

"The psychiatrist said it was just the drugs. Swelling of the brain making hallucinations. I think not."

"Maybe you were sent back because you weren't finished yet. You had something else to do," Robin suggested gently. She couldn't bear watching his torment.

T.J. shook his head, a disgusted look on his face. "No," he said. "I haven't been punished enough."

A sudden flash of insight made it all perfectly clear to Robin. "And every time you start to feel a little bit good about yourself, every time things start to run a little more smoothly, a thunderstorm comes along, with all its war sounds, to remind you why you're still here."

"Something like that."

It was funny. All the shrinks, the doctors, everybody had tried to talk him out of that idea, but Robin didn't. She understood. Robin had heard his long, sad story, and she hadn't tried to talk him out of it.

And she understood. And what was more, so did he. Or at least he was beginning to find some glimmer of insight. Something that would make the burden of guilt easier to bear.

Robin interrupted T.J.'s churning thoughts. "I can't presume to say that I know how you feel about all this, but I appreciate you telling me. I can see there have been times in the past couple of days when I've said things unknowingly that might have seemed insensitive.''

T.J. released Robin's hand. He hadn't realized that he was clinging to it like a lifeline throughout his cathartic monologue. He didn't seem to need it now. It was almost as if the lifeline were still there, invisible but strong. Her blue eyes looked squarely at him, unblinking and grave. T.J. wanted to look away, but he met her gaze.

"Thank you," he finally said.

"For what? All I did was listen."

"For listening," T.J. confirmed. And for not judging, though he didn't say that out loud. For caring. And not turning away. "You seemed to understand."

"We all have our own personal demons to fight," Robin replied—enigmatically, it seemed to T.J. "Mine's just a little more tangible," she said, half to herself. Robin glanced at her watch. "Are you going to be all right?"

Was she trying to get rid of him? T.J. had thought she was being so understanding. Why was she looking at her watch? "Oh, no." He uttered his realization aloud. "I forgot about your appointment."

Robin laughed a soft, tinkling laugh. "So did I. But I still have time to make it if I hurry. Do you mind if I dash off?"

"No." And he didn't, T.J. realized. He needed time to sort out his thoughts. To think. He looked down at his rumpled shirt. "I think a shower and clean clothes would do more for me right now than a session with a thousand psychiatrists."

"I've always sworn by the restorative abilities of soap and hot water. Why, just the other day it raised me from the dead." Robin's eyes widened as she realized what she had just said. She raised her hands to her mouth, as if to stuff the ill-thought words back inside. Her eyes seemed to say, *I'm so sorry.*

"It's okay, Robin. I know what you mean." T.J. laughed.

Actually laughed. Robin's unintentional comment seemed to point out the absurdity of his preoccupation of the past few years.

"It's about time I tried living again." He winked. "I'm off to the shower. Next time you see me, I'll be reborn."

The cool, almost autumnlike morning was a welcome respite from the oppressive Alabama summer heat. The sidewalk was strewn with debris from the storm the night before, and the sky was a brilliant azure blue, scrubbed clean by the rain. It had stripped the heat and the dust from the air as effectively as a woman with a mop.

Robin stepped over the litter of leaves and fallen branches and wondered if the storm could be more than a reminder to T.J. of his past problems. Could it be a symbol of a new beginning? T.J. had looked better by the time they had finished talking, she thought as she walked toward the law center, on the far side of the campus. Wouldn't it be wonderful if the storm marked a new beginning for T.J.? Just as an internal storm had sparked her own decision to no longer allow Dub to be the focus of her life, perhaps this storm of nature would help to cleanse him. Maybe that storm had been his catharsis.

Maybe the storm had done more than remind T.J. of his personal demons; it had served to cleanse his mind, as well as the hot, humid air. Perhaps, by telling her about his anguish and guilt over the death of his family, he could now get past it. Just as the rain-fresh morning signaled a new day, perhaps T.J.'s confession signaled a second chance.

Yesterday, Robin's only concern had been herself. She had worried about how to unravel the tangled web that Dub had spun around her. Now all that seemed unimportant. Her problems were technicalities. The proverbial red tape. A few well-placed snips with sharp legal scissors, and her life would be in order again.

T.J.'s problems weren't that simple.

Chapter 10

Rafe Bennett listened impassively as Robin unwound her tangled tale. He didn't blink, blanch, or bother to question what she said. Now he sat staring at her over his glasses, as if trying to read the truth in her face. Robin squirmed under his intense scrutiny.

Finally, he stopped his assessment and said, "Your story does sound a little far-fetched, but as they say, truth is often stranger than fiction. You were correct in coming to me before going to the district attorney.

"It would be best to establish your identity before going to see him. Lacking fingerprints on file, it will be difficult, but doable."

"What will I need to do to establish my identity?" Robin asked, feeling hopeful and discouraged at the same time. She had expected Bennett to take care of everything from here, but it seemed that the burden of proof about who Robin really was would fall directly on her own shoulders.

"Fingerprints would have simplified matters greatly, but there are other options. We'll have to establish your identity through witnesses. You need to give me a list of people who've known you since childhood. Since birth would be better.''

Robin's spirits brightened. ''Oh, that's simple. My parents, Cheryl Rodgers, half the people in Demopolis.''

It was Bennett's turn to look perplexed. ''Excuse my confusion. I had assumed your parents were dead, from what you told me. Why wouldn't they have come to claim the murdered woman's body and known it wasn't you?''

''My parents have been on an extended cruise in the Pacific. I doubt that anyone has been able to reach them. I was the one they left their itinerary and powers of attorney with. My brother Mack is overseas, working on an oil well in Kuwait. He calls once in a blue moon, but he doesn't really keep in touch much. After I went off to Mexico so suddenly, I'm not sure anyone else would have known how to find them.''

''You don't think they've heard of what happened, then,'' Bennett stated.

''Surely not. If they had, they would've been back here on the next plane. They wouldn't still be gallivanting around the Far East.'' Robin frowned. ''I'm hoping that they haven't heard anything, and that I can waylay them before they ever hear the news from anyone else.''

''When are they due back? Can you get in touch with them?''

''The first of next month. I have their itinerary somewhere in all my boxes. My roommate, Cheryl Rodgers, packed all my stuff away when she thought I had been killed, and put it all in storage for my folks, I guess—I haven't spoken to her since I got back. I'm still unpacking and sorting through everything.''

Bennett nodded. ''This is what I want you to do,'' he told her. ''Contact as many people as you can who will be willing to sign an affidavit testifying that you are who you say you are. And try to get them in to see me as soon as

possible. Today, if you can. And get in touch with your
parents. They will be the best witnesses you have.''

"What about Dub?''

"I don't think your ex-husband would be a credible witness to your identity, thanks to the previous incorrect identification he made. Since it would be to his advantage to
have you proven to be alive, it could be assumed that he
would lie to get off the hook. And it would be counterpro-
ductive to go to the D.A. with what you know until you
have something to prove who you are. But I will start the
wheels turning. I can check to see what they have on Doubleday and how they misidentified the body.''

Robin picked up her purse and started to reach for the
yearbook.

"Leave that here.'' Rafe Bennett's command startled
Robin.

"Why?'' It wasn't like Robin to question someone who
ought to know, but his demand didn't make sense.

"I may need it. I'll see that it's returned.''

"Okay,'' Robin agreed reluctantly. "I'll try to track
Cheryl down as soon as I get home. Now that she's gotten
married, I'm not sure how to reach her.'' Robin headed for
the door, but turned back. "I know that Dub is not completely blameless in all this. He brought it on himself by
claiming on that insurance policy when he had no right to,
but I know he didn't kill that woman. Is there any way we
can get him out of jail?''

Bennett laughed. "For the injured party, you seem awfully solicitous of Lester Doubleday.''

"I was so angry at him for what he did to me during our
marriage that I didn't see why he was doing it. That he was
hurting, too. I've had some time to think, and my eyes have
been opened very wide recently. I don't want to see him
suffer any more than necessary, and I think being jailed has
definitely gotten his attention. There are moments when I'm

still angry with him, but even pond scum has rights, I guess.''

"Well put. If we can get the murder charge dropped by proving you are alive and that somebody else died, we can probably get him released, since the motive would no longer stand. Since the victim was shot in the face, the killer had to know who he'd killed. I can't see how anyone could connect it with your ex-husband, since you're not the real victim.

"If they decide to charge him with insurance fraud, the bail should be low enough that he can post it and stay out of jail until trial, if there is one."

"Thank you, Mr. Bennett. You know, Dub may have been a weak man, but he wasn't intentionally cruel. I can't see any way that anyone could think Dub would have reason to kill that woman, whoever she was."

Robin adjusted her purse on her shoulder and turned for the door. "I'll let you know as soon as I have my witnesses."

It had taken a long shower and several cups of strong coffee to do it, but T.J. felt surprisingly good. Thanks to a couple of aspirin that Robin had thought to pick up when she got groceries, the aches and lethargy from the night spent perched on the hard trunk in the stuffy basement were gone. And the dark cloud that had hung over him for so long had thinned. It was still there, but there were breaks in it, and hopeful rays of sun peeked through. He knew he still had stuff to deal with, but he was beginning to think he could deal with it.

T.J. had even managed to complete a couple more pages of his rough draft by the time he heard Robin's key in the lock. He put down his pen and hoisted his body from the chair.

After living alone for so long, it was nice hearing someone else's key in the door. T.J. remembered with pleasure how he would wait after a long night shift and a day at home sleeping alone in the big, wide bed. How it had felt to hear Ginger's key in the lock, and see Rusty bounding in before the door was completely open...

T.J. smiled.

"What's funny?" Robin asked as she came in.

"I was thinking about Ginger and Rusty."

A smile brightened Robin's face. "And from the look on your face, the memory doesn't hurt."

It struck T.J. with the force of a hammer. No. It didn't hurt! For the first time since that awful day, he had been able to remember without pain. "Remarkable, isn't it?" he said, more to himself than to Robin.

She laughed merrily. "Sometimes healing is a gradual process, but I think yours happened all at once."

Realization dawned on T.J. "I think it did," he said softly. "At about eight o'clock this morning. Thank you."

Robin looked puzzled. "Why thank me? I didn't do anything. It was the storm that started it."

"Yes, the storm contributed to it, but you were the one who listened. You didn't try to talk me out of my feelings." He looked at her, really seeing her for the first time. "People kept trying to convince me I shouldn't feel that way. They didn't allow me to deal with how I felt, they kept trying to talk me out of it. You didn't. You accepted my feelings without question.

"And once I'd told you, and heard myself say what I had been holding inside for all that time, it sounded pretty stupid. And it sure didn't seem so important.

"I know I still have more working out to do about this thing, but now it seems possible. You know, before..." He paused a moment, groping for the right words. "Before, I didn't have hope." He took her hand and squeezed it. "Now I do."

"I'm glad I could help," Robin said softly, gently removing her fingers from his hand.

Oh, you helped, T.J. told Robin silently. Maybe now I can begin to live again. Maybe now I have a second chance at life. T.J. smiled and asked Robin about her day.

After the addition of some of Robin's things, the apartment had begun to look more like a home and less like a sterile box. Robin brushed a strand of hair away from her face, then unfolded the colorful afghan her grandmother had crocheted when she married Dub and draped it across the back of the sofa. Though it was not needed now, in the summer heat, the woolen throw added color to the drab beige of the apartment.

Robin stood back to survey her handiwork. Yes, the living room almost looked the way it had when she left it in June. A few more touches, and it would look like hers.

She was eager to get into the kitchen and unpack there, but T.J. had set up camp at the table, with his books and research. The kitchen would have to wait till later.

Wait. Robin was not in the mood to wait. She had reached her parents' ship in two quick phone calls, only to find that they had gone ashore to some island in the Philippines. Now she was waiting for them to call back. All she had done this afternoon was wait for everything. For T.J. to get done in the kitchen. For a phone call. For Cheryl to come and corroborate her existence. For her life to get back on track.

She was rummaging through another box of knickknacks when the doorbell rang.

"I'll get it," she called to T.J. out of habit more than necessity. He wasn't going to come out of the kitchen for anything short of an earthquake.

Robin pushed the box aside and straightened her clothes. Nervously, she went to the door.

"Don't ever do that to me again!" Cheryl Rodgers Smith demanded as she pushed through the door and enfolded

Robin in a bear hug. Then she pushed Robin away and looked her over carefully.

"Well, do I pass?" Robin's eyes were moist with tears.

"Yes, you pass. Yes, yes, yes. I'm so glad you're standing here in front of me in the flesh. And so much less flesh than the last time I saw you." Tears moistened Cheryl's eyes, too.

Robin pirouetted and then made a slight curtsy. "See what eight weeks of hard work in the tropical sun will do? Now what did you mean, don't ever do that again?"

"I'm so angry at you for putting me through this. Don't ever do it again," Cheryl's voice wobbled, then broke, as tears spilled from her eyes.

"But you knew I was going to Mexico. Why did you think it was me?"

"It happened so soon after you left. I only drove you to the airport, I didn't see you get on the plane. As much as I wanted to believe you were in Mexico, I couldn't be sure. You hear about all those sickos out there, trolling for victims. For all I knew, you could have been kidnapped before you got to the plane." More tears flowed, and Cheryl's voice broke with a sob. "The police said it was you. After all, who would think they'd make such an enormous mistake?" Her voice cracked. "I hadn't heard whether you arrived or not, and I didn't get so much as a postcard. And they said they had your fingerprints...."

"But I've never been fingerprinted," Robin protested. "And the site was so isolated, it was next to impossible to get mail in or out. It seemed like so much trouble, I didn't bother to try." Robin sighed. "Now I wish I had."

"I didn't know your fingerprints weren't on file. Or about the mail situation. I—" Cheryl's voice broke on another sob. "I grieved for you, Robbie. Hoke and I grieved together."

Seeing tears pouring from Cheryl's brown eyes prompted the tears that Robin had struggled so hard to hold back to fall freely. She buried her face in her friend's shoulder until they both had recovered sufficiently to talk. She forced a question. "Why are we doing this? This should be a happy occasion."

"I know." Cheryl sniffed and presented a weak smile. "I'm just so relieved."

"You know," Robin said as she wiped her eyes with the back of her hand. What had at first seemed like an irritation to her had been a real tragedy to her friend. Robin shuddered. It was all too weird. "Until you got here, this mostly seemed like an inconvenience. It didn't really occur to me that other people might have been affected by it."

Cheryl balled up her hand into a fist and punched Robin in the arm, just as she had done hundreds of times in the twenty-some years they'd been best friends. "Oh, Robbie, you don't know how much it hurt to have to say goodbye to you and think it was for good." Cheryl brushed a tear away. "I may never forgive Dub for putting us all through it."

"Hush, Cher. It really wasn't Dub's fault. At least not all of it. He couldn't help it that somebody else shared my name." Robin smiled crookedly. "But he deserves what he's getting for cashing in on that policy."

Robin made one last swipe at her tears. "I'm just glad word of this never made it to my folks. You know, I almost left a copy of their itinerary with you. I'm so glad I didn't. If you had located them and told them the news..." She blew a wayward strand of hair from her eyes. "I guess I can be thankful that Dub didn't follow through. He told the authorities that he'd notify my family, but didn't because he didn't know where they were.

"Suppose somebody had told them..."

"It's okay, Robin. There's no way they could have found out. If they had, they surely would have been home by now." She chuckled ruefully. "Score one for Dub," Cheryl remarked wryly. "Have you spoken to your folks yet?"

"Not yet. How do I explain all this to them?" Robin chewed on her lip as she pondered what to say.

"I don't really think you'll have to say anything. Just talk to them about your trip, then kinda work it in."

"Oh, yeah," Robin replied sarcastically. "'Hi, Mom. I had a great time in Mexico, and in case you hear that I was murdered, disregard.'"

"That's the general idea." Cheryl fumbled in her purse for a tissue and blew her nose. "Anyway, once you're talking to them, it will be obvious that you're here. You can just sorta mention to them that a funny thing happened when you got back."

"Real funny," Robin drawled. "It was about as funny as catching the plague."

"Well, you know. You have to prepare them."

"I know. Rafe Bennett says there might be quite a lot of media coverage once word of this megamistake gets out."

"Yeah. And the person who really killed that woman will know he didn't get off scot-free," Cheryl suggested.

Robin shrugged. "Well, that's not my problem." But she shivered, as if somebody had just walked over her grave. Maybe it was her problem, after all.

It became impossible for T.J. to ignore the happy commotion coming from the next room. He hadn't intended to intrude on Robin's reunion with her roommate, but he'd made good progress that afternoon and he deserved a break. He got up and stretched. A few more hours and he'd be ready to put together the final draft. All that upheaval, and he was still pretty close to schedule.

He sauntered out of the kitchen and tried not to stare too obviously at the striking auburn-haired beauty who was chatting animatedly with Robin. He'd forgotten how beautiful she was, or perhaps, in her grief and distress the last time he saw her, it hadn't shown. He wasn't sure what to say about his intrusion into their happy talk. Robin saved him from the quandary.

"Oh, T.J. I'm sorry. I was so happy to see Cheryl that I forgot about you working in there."

An ironic look came to Cheryl's face. "How could you forget about that gorgeous hunk of a man?" she simpered in a fair imitation of Mae West.

"Shush, Cheryl. You're a married woman." Robin looked at her friend sternly. "You'll have to tell me all about that later."

"Humph," Cheryl snorted. "Hoke just came to his senses, that's all. When we thought we'd lost you, we did a lot of serious thinking about what was really important in our lives. Hoke finally figured out what he was missing and begged me to make an honest man of him. All I had to do was wait for him to come around. It only took eight years." She grinned. "I guess I can thank Dub for that, as much as the thought nauseates me."

T.J. laughed. "It's nice to see you again, Cheryl. And under much happier circumstances, I might add."

Cheryl stuck out her hand. "Same here."

In spite of the redhead's flirty ways, her handshake was strong and firm. T.J. couldn't help thinking that Hoke Smith had made the right decision in choosing Cheryl. Even if he had taken a few years to get around to it.

And Dub Doubleday was a fool, he added as he looked past Cheryl to Robin.

"I'm going to fix myself a soda. Can I get you ladies something?" It had seemed selfish to hole up in the kitchen with all the food and drink. He was only being polite.

"Sure. Then Cheryl and I have to run off to Rafe Bennett's office before he goes home for the weekend."

"We're going to take Mr. Edwards with us. Mr. Bennett thinks that with two people testifying that I am who Dub is supposed to have killed, they'll have to let him go,"

Robin explained. "Of course, we'll have to have Dr. Armitrage verify that I was in Cacaxtla the whole time, too."

"Though I'm not sure he deserves it," Cheryl added. "Dub, I mean. Not Dr. Armitrage."

Robin made a face at Cheryl's comment. T.J. had a tendency to agree with Cheryl, but Robin seemed to think Dub deserved the benefit of some doubt.

"I'm afraid you won't be making any friends in the district attorney's office, either," T.J. commented. "They're going to have to start from scratch on the investigation, and by now the trail's pretty cold," he added as he turned toward the kitchen.

"Well, they can take their frustrations out on the other guy. That's what we pay them for," Cheryl suggested.

T.J. laughed. "I'll have to admit, they did a pretty sloppy job of establishing the identity of that Jane Doe."

"Okay," Cheryl agreed. "What about the real murderer lurking about? You don't suppose our Robin could be in danger, do you?"

T.J. rubbed his jaw thoughtfully and shook his head. "I wouldn't think so. I can't see where this guy is out preying solely on Robin Digbys."

Yet a possibility struck T.J. that he didn't voice. Suppose this guy was a little unbalanced. It might gall him that his supposed victim was alive and well.

He wouldn't go after this Robin. Would he?

Cheryl had grabbed her by the elbow and almost shoved Robin out the door. "You didn't tell me you had set up housekeeping with that hunk. Spill the details!" she hissed, as soon as they were outside.

"There are no details, Cher," Robin answered patiently. "It's strictly a business proposition. You left me homeless when you gave up the apartment, not that I blame you. I'm sure Hoke will be a much better roommate than I was. Since both T.J. and I claimed to have rights here, and neither of us wanted to give them up, with a little encouragement from Mr. Edwards, we decided to share.''

"Yeah, right. Some business proposition. I saw the way he looked at you.''

"How did he look at me? We were barely speaking to each other until today. You're imagining things.''

"I was not imagining those vibes you two were throwing off. There was enough electricity to turn on a radio.''

Robin shook her head. "Cheryl Louise Rodgers Smith, I don't know where you get these ideas. He's just a nice guy who agreed to share this apartment with me. Platonically.''

"And I love Patrick Swayze for his mind.''

Robin started to protest, but something stopped her. She did like T.J., and she had even when they were barely speaking. And they seemed to have more than a platonic relationship going since he had opened up to her. She could almost pinpoint the exact moment when he'd become more than just a disturbing piece of furniture to avoid in her apartment.

She had begun to feel something for T.J. She wasn't certain what. But it was definitely more than friendship.

It had been so long since T.J. had taken an interest in anyone but himself that the intensity of his feelings for Robin Digby surprised him. At first he dismissed them as interest, the normal process of getting to know someone else.

At first it had been much like getting to know a new college roommate or an army tentmate, but after the night in the storage room, T.J. had begun to see Robin less as an intrusion and more as a caring human being.

Robin was a reality. A real, living person. T.J. remembered the kiss he'd almost stolen the night before. That had been before the thunder and lightning had reduced him to a spineless caricature of a man. He'd probably blown his one and only chance with Robin, he thought. Now she saw him as the sorry specimen he really was. He'd destroyed the first love of his life through his own negligence. Did he deserve another chance at love? He hadn't thought so before, but now? Maybe.

T.J. crossed to the window and looked down to where Robin and her friend were getting into Cheryl's car. The afternoon sun brought out the blond highlights in Robin's hair. It was impossible to reconcile this beautiful, laughing person with the sad woman who had peered at him from her driver's license. He felt an unfamiliar tightening in his groin.

He must have stared so intently down upon Robin's head that she felt his eyes upon her. She looked up and waved. Then she ducked into the car.

Hope filled his damaged heart. He raised his hand in a half salute, then dropped it again. The tiny bit of hope that had welled so quickly just as quickly drained away. Her friendly wave had only been a polite gesture. It probably meant nothing.

Chapter 11

Robin drummed her fingers restlessly against the gray Formica tabletop. She should have heard from her parents by now, and it worried her that her message might have alarmed them unnecessarily. Oh, how she hated the waiting.

After they returned from Rafe Bennett's office, Cheryl had sprung for take-out pizza. Robin had made a salad, and T.J. had brewed tea in the coffee carafe that had actually been drinkable. But now Cheryl had gone home to her husband, the cleanup was done, T.J. was still working on his paper, and Robin had nothing to do. Except wait. And fret.

T.J. put down his pencil with slow, deliberate care. Robin could see that she was annoying him, and that he wanted very much to be patient with her. But even a saint has a breaking point.

"Don't you have something you can do?" he finally said, without trying to hide the irritation in his voice.

Robin sighed, loud and long. "I wish I did. And it's driving me bananas that my parents haven't called."

"For cripes' sake. They're halfway around the world.

For all you know, it's the middle of the night there. Do you want somebody to drag them out of their beds to the phone just to talk to you?''

"Of course not," Robin snapped back. "I just need to hear from them." She started to pace.

"Robin," T.J. said through clenched teeth. "Go read a book."

"I'd love to read one, but I don't have anything to read."

"Well then, go work on your notes from your summer research project."

"I can't concentrate on anything like that right now," Robin complained. "I'm too keyed up."

"Well, you're going to have me all wound up, too, if you don't stop pacing."

Robin stopped for a moment and looked at T.J., then resumed her back-and-forth march.

"Will you please do that somewhere else?" Though it had technically been worded as a request, Robin knew it was a command.

"All right. I think I'll go for a walk. It's still light out. Anyway, my folks probably won't call till tomorrow." The last words were more for herself than for T.J.'s benefit.

She stalked out of the kitchen. After stopping to grab her purse, she hurried out. And she felt not the least bit guilty when the door slammed noisily behind her.

T.J. didn't fail to notice the slamming door. He regretted making Robin angry, and he was even more sorry he had run her off. But, damn it, the research paper was just as important to him as straightening out her mess was for her.

Yet the quiet in the house didn't ring true. Instead of giving him the peace he needed to get his work done, the silence echoed with unspoken recriminations. As much as Robin bothered him when she was there, her absence bothered him more. And it really hadn't been that unpleasant.

T.J. got up, poured a glass of iced tea and sat back down.

He stared at the paper in front of him, but it seemed as if every scrap of knowledge he had once had had deserted him.

He took a sip of his tea and absently set the glass down on top of the clean draft he had carefully lettered for the typist to read. T.J. stared into space for a few minutes until he figured he could think.

When he looked back at his paper, he uttered a curse. The condensation from the cold glass had dripped down and made an inky puddle on what he'd written, blurring the water-based ink.

T.J. snatched the glass off the table and uttered a string of curses that would have made a Teamster blush. He wiped at the pool of murky water, but that only made it worse. Crushing the ruined sheet of paper angrily in his fist, he threw it across the kitchen.

Draining the glass as he went, T.J. stalked across the room to the sink, dumped out the melted ice cubes and jammed the glass into the dishwasher. Now he was going to have to copy at least one page over. If not more.

He cursed himself again, silently this time. Maybe having to do those pages over would reestablish the momentum he had lost.

And maybe pigs would fly.

The instant Robin reached the street, she regretted flouncing out on T.J. as she had. Not that it wasn't probably best that she be out of the house and out of his hair. But that they'd parted under less-than-cordial circumstances mattered to her.

She knew that her restless fidgeting had been interrupting his concentration. And though T.J. might be finished with the hardest part of his paper, too many distractions could cause him to make a careless mistake that could cost him his grade. But she had things to worry about, as well.

As much as Robin wanted to go back and apologize, she

thought it best to stay out of his way until he finished with his evening's work. She had probably already thrown his schedule way off; maybe by staying out of the way she could give him time to get back on track.

She stood at the bottom of the steps in front of her building and tapped her foot while she wondered what to do next. Across the way, a woman sat in a lawn chair, enjoying the last heat of the sun's rays while reading a paperback novel.

The woman reading gave her an idea. She'd go to the drugstore and pick up a couple of mysteries. Then Robin remembered the woeful condition of her finances. She had exactly two dollars and change. There was no way she could pay for a new book with that.

Then the thought struck her. There were several used bookstores within walking distance, and books were considerably cheaper at any of them. Robin consulted her watch. The evening was still early enough that she could make it to the Book Rack before it closed. She stepped out onto the sidewalk and headed south.

Robin didn't spend much time in the bookstore. She didn't need to. She spotted two dog-eared mysteries by one of her favorite authors on her first pass through the section. Then, as she carried her selections to the checkout counter, Robin remembered a credit slip from a visit the previous spring.

Tucking the two books under her chin, Robin rummaged through her purse until she located her wallet and sorted through a collection of various expired coupons and grocery receipts until she found the certificate. She could buy the books without having to spend the last of her cash.

Feeling inordinately pleased with herself, Robin left the store humming a cheerful tune. She had two books tucked into her pocketbook, and she still had two dollars in her wallet. She stopped along the way and purchased an ice-

cream cone and savored its cool creaminess as she sauntered along the street.

There was still some decent light left, she reasoned as
she enjoyed the pleasant evening. So she didn't head
straight home, but strolled aimlessly through the cooling
city, in the general direction of the apartment.

Without consciously doing it, Robin found herself wan-
dering in the direction of Palm Ridge, the cemetery where
Dub had buried the dead woman. Curiosity overruled her
common sense, and Robin altered her course to head there.
More specifically, to the site of the grave of the other
woman called Robin.

As she reached the cemetery, the shadows, long from the
dying sun, seemed to reach and grab at her, and Robin
almost changed her mind about the sundown visit to the
graveyard. Then she noticed movement a few avenues
away.

Shading her eyes with her hand against the setting sun,
Robin strained to see who was there. Partially blinded by
the glare, all Robin could make out was a kneeling figure.
And that person was kneeling in front of a new grave.

The short hairs on the back of her neck rose, and her
skin cooled suddenly as gooseflesh provided unwelcome
air-conditioning in the close evening air. Certainly, there
must have been more than one interment in this cemetery
in recent weeks, but the possibilities were too much to ignore.

Robin hurried forward. Perhaps if she could talk to the
man—she was almost certain it was a man she had seen
silhouetted against the setting sun—she would finally discover a missing piece to the puzzle she'd been unwillingly
made a part of.

If only it weren't so far away. Eager to catch up with
the man, Robin shortcut across the plots and, in her haste,
caught her toe on a low-lying marker, stumbled and fell.

Robin righted herself quickly, but her unguarded yelp of pain must have been enough to warn the man.

By the time she had regained her feet and wiped the dirt and grass from her hands, Robin could see that he had gone.

The evening light was nearly gone, and Robin debated whether to turn back or go on. But the opportunity was too good to pass up, and she was already there, she rationalized. Robin hurried on.

If the marker bore someone else's name, then Robin would know she had gotten all worked up over nothing. And if the name on the stone was hers...

Well, she'd cross that bridge when she came to it.

By the time Robin reached the grave, the sun had just slipped below the horizon. It was nearly too dark to see, much less read. But in the murky light that remained, she could make out the legend. Robin Leigh Digby. The birth-date was hers, and the date of death was just one day after she'd left for Mexico.

No wonder Cheryl and Dub and everyone else had believed she'd died. Robin shuddered, goose bumps raising her flesh in spite of the balmy summer evening.

She couldn't tear her eyes away.

How many people could say they'd looked at their own graves and lived to tell about it? Robin shivered again. As far as she was concerned, one too many.

As she turned to leave, Robin noticed something else. There was a fresh bouquet of flowers still wrapped in florist's plastic lying on the grave, next to a cement vase containing a wilted spray. She must have interrupted the man before he could replace them.

Robin reached for the flowers, to arrange them in the waiting container, then thought better of it. They could be a clue.

It was too dark to see, much less read, but she was hoping that she might be able to tell something from the wrapping. Robin picked up the bouquet and hurried home.

* * *

After several tries, T.J. finally managed to copy the blurred sheet. Once that was done, it was relatively easy to finish the rest. That should have been the end of it. He should have been relieved.

T.J. supposed it should be a relief to have the paper finally written, but worry about Robin had supplanted any elation he might have felt. It was almost nine o'clock, and she had been gone for nearly two hours.

He glanced out the kitchen window into the thick summer darkness. Heat haze and the lights of the city had obscured the stars. There was nothing out there to see but the alley behind the building, but looking seemed like something to do.

How could one irritating, fascinating, maddening woman have gotten to him so quickly? And after all this time of caring about no one and feeling nothing.

"Come on, Robin," he muttered to himself. He chuckled. First she had driven him crazy while she was there; now it was driving him to distraction that she was not.

"You're some piece of work, Swift," he murmured as he straightened out his stack of note cards and lined up his pencils with mathematical precision. She even had him talking to himself. "First you can't wait to get rid of her, and now you want her back."

"Who do you want back?" a cool voice asked from somewhere behind him.

T.J. whirled around, feeling guilty, sheepish and embarrassed all at once. Robin was watching him from the doorway, and on her face was an expression he couldn't quite have described. "I didn't hear you come in," he told her.

Robin propped one hand on her hip while she leaned against the doorjamb. "I shouldn't think so. You were slamming those books around as if you were trying to knock the life out of them."

He could feel heat color his face. You'd think by the time a man reached the age of thirty-two, he'd be over that adolescent phenomenon. Maybe his tan would hide it, but that kind of luck would be too much to expect. "I guess I was taking out my frustrations on them."

Narrowing her eyes, Robin looked at him as if she were trying to compute the answer to a complex math problem in her head. "Who are you really mad at? Me?"

His heart skipped a beat. Had she taken up mind reading, too? "I'm not mad at you," he answered, more carefully than he should have. So much for staying cool.

"You are, too. I can tell by the tone of your voice that you are."

"I am not."

Robin rolled her eyes. "You're mad, T.J. Spill it. What's your beef?"

T.J. arranged his stack of books so that they all lined up with the edge of the table. Anything to keep from answering. Then he started on the pencils, as he groped frantically for an answer. "I'm angry because you were gone so long. And that you didn't call." He drew one long breath. "And I'm angry because I'm angry."

Robin eyed him carefully for a moment, then smiled a Mona Lisa smile. "Why, T.J. I didn't know you cared." The smile widened to a crooked grin.

Grins were infectious, and T.J. found himself returning hers. Funny, he thought. Funny that she could put her finger on it so quickly, when it had taken him so long to come to the same conclusion. He didn't know what to say, so he said nothing.

Wondering what to do about the impasse, and wondering who would be the first to break the silence, T.J. tried not to look at Robin. But, just like trying not to look when someone else said not to, it was impossible. Ignoring her didn't work. She wouldn't go away, and he didn't really want her to. His eyes were drawn to her.

"You blinked first," Robin finally said, and laughed. He liked the sound of her laugh. It had been so long since T.J.

had experienced pleasant feminine laughter so close at hand. She turned to leave the kitchen, but apparently thought better of it.

"Don't you want to know where I've been?"

T.J. blinked. Again. "It isn't any of my business where you've been."

"Well, as of this minute, I'm making it your business," she told him, and held up a bunch of flowers.

"If you're expecting me to come up with a vase, you're looking at the wrong person. You'd know better than I do where you'd have one. You just unpacked all that stuff from the storeroom."

"I am not looking for a vase," Robin replied, carefully enunciating the words for him, as if he were dim-witted.

"Then why are you showing them to me?" They were nice enough flowers, T.J. supposed, not that he was an expert on those kinds of things. Flowers had always been Ginger's territory. They were a little wilted, but they'd probably perk up with a little attention from someone who knew what he or she was doing. "Don't you think you should put them in water or something?"

"Yeah, I guess I should." Robin stepped into the room and brushed past him. She reached under the sink and came up with a mason jar. "But before I take them from the wrapper, there's something you should know about these flowers." Robin watched him, as if he should make the next move.

T.J. wondered if maybe he should. Was there some significance he'd missed about that inexpensive-looking bunch of posies? "Okay, I'll bite. Where'd you get them?"

"I found them on my grave."

That finally got T.J.'s attention. Robin had been wondering if she was going to have to hit him on the head with it before he caught on. He opened his mouth, as if to say something, then stopped.

T.J. watched Robin for a moment before saying anything. "What possible reason would you have for going there?"

Robin shrugged. It wasn't as if she had planned to go to the cemetery. "It just happened. I got done at the bookstore, and it was still early. Oh, I got two mysteries cheap."

"Robin!" T.J.'s tone told her to get to the point.

Unwrapping the plastic from the flowers, Robin explained. "As I said, I got finished at the bookstore and it was still early. I didn't want to interrupt you again, so I figured I'd kill some time before going back. So I went for a walk. It was still light, not too hot, and I needed to burn up some excess energy."

T.J. shot her another get-to-the-point look, and Robin got the message.

"Without really thinking about it, I found myself in the vicinity of the cemetery."

"So you just thought you'd drop in."

"Yeah. I was curious. It isn't a crime."

"No, but you could have been involved in a crime," T.J. pointed out.

Robin didn't get the connection. "Don't be ridiculous. I wasn't doing anything illegal."

"Not you, Robin," T.J. clarified. "But you could have been a victim. Do you know how many women are molested because they are alone in deserted places at that time of day?"

He did care, Robin realized. It also occurred to her that he was entirely right about the possibility of danger. Especially since she had seen that man there.

She must have taken too long to respond, because T.J. interrupted her thinking. "It isn't exactly legal to remove flowers from graves."

"I hadn't thought of it that way. I was more interested in how they got there. It was too dark to really see them, and I thought I might find some kind of clue," Robin said as she ran water into the jar.

"And was there a clue?"

"Probably not." She touched the plastic wrapping from the flowers as the jar filled. "This is a kind of bouquet you can pick up at any grocery store."

"You probably destroyed any fingerprints there might have been."

"We're not exactly set up for fingerprinting here, T.J.," Robin reminded him.

"But we could have shown it to the police."

"Why? They think they have the mystery solved. They don't even know about me yet."

"Dub probably sent them, anyway," T.J. suggested.

"Dub's still in jail. Remember?"

"Maybe he had somebody bring them over for him."

"T.J., Dub now knows that it wasn't me he buried. Why would he be putting flowers out for a dead woman he doesn't know? Besides, I saw who put them there." She turned off the tap.

T.J. hadn't appeared too interested in the discussion up to this point, but that last statement made him straighten.

"Who was it?"

"It was nearly dark—I could barely see. But I don't think it was anybody I know." Robin brushed the excess water off the vase and placed the wilted bouquet into it. "But I am pretty sure it was a man."

"If it wasn't somebody you know," T.J. announced exultantly, "then it must be..."

Chapter 12

"Somebody who knows the dead woman," Robin finished.

"Bingo!" T.J. grabbed Robin and spun her into his arms.

"Whoa, boy. I'm gonna drop this if you don't let go of me," Robin protested.

T.J. let go. But only long enough for her to put down the flowers. He grabbed her arm. "Don't you see the significance of it?"

"Of course I do, T.J. That person knows who is really in that grave," Robin answered, shaking free.

T.J. rubbed his chin thoughtfully, then ran his fingers through his hair. He stopped when his fingers touched the raised ridge of scar tissue. "And he may just know who did it."

Robin blanched, the high color of excitement leaving her cheeks. "He might even have done it," she said carefully, her eyes wide.

T.J. took Robin's elbow and steered her out of the kitchen. "Let's go sit down," he told her as they reached the sofa. "There's got to be a logical explanation for that man being there."

"Why? I thought my idea was pretty reasonable." She made herself comfortable on the cushions.

"It think it's pretty far-fetched," T.J. told her as he positioned himself on the other end of the couch. "How likely do you think it would be for a man who killed somebody to come back and lay flowers on the grave."

Robin shrugged. "He was revisiting the scene of the crime."

"It wasn't the scene."

"Oh, yeah." She tried again. "Maybe he was sorry. He felt guilty."

"I don't know. He'd be running the risk of getting caught."

"Yeah, but for all he knows, he got away with it. Dub is still in jail. My reappearance from the dead hasn't been made public yet."

"Could be." But T.J. couldn't dismiss another thought that had come to him. "Would it be possible that Dub arranged for somebody else to put those flowers there before he knew you were alive? Then, since he was in jail when he found it wasn't you he buried, he wasn't able to cancel it."

"Possible, I suppose," Robin said. "But not likely. Dub never brought me flowers when I was married to him. It would be way out of character for him to do it when he thought I was dead." She fiddled with the fringe on her grandmother's afghan. "He might have paid for the funeral for old times' sake, but flowers…"

"Well, it's a thought. It wouldn't hurt to ask him."

The jail hadn't gotten any more cheerful since the last time Robin visited Dub there. It had been nine-thirty at night when they came up with the idea of talking to Dub, and they couldn't just waltz in then and demand to see him.

Robin and T.J. had been forced to wait all night to see if it had been Dub who ordered the flowers. Now Robin paced in the grimy visitors' room, waiting for Dub to be brought down from his cell.

The door on the other side of the grim room grated open, and the guard ushered Dub in. Robin's ex-husband looked expectantly toward the cubicle where she waited, but his face fell when he saw her.

"What's the matter, Dub? I thought you'd be happy to see me," Robin said as she slid into the seat across from him.

He had the grace to apologize. "I'm sorry, Robbie. I was expectin' somebody else. My lawyer."

"Sorry to disappoint you. Maybe he'll be here soon. For now, you'll just have to make do with me."

"Did you come to try to get me out of here?"

"I'm working on it. But until the powers that be are satisfied that I am your true and only late ex-wife, they're not going to let you go," Robin told him, feeling not at all apologetic. It would still take her weeks of paperwork before she could undo Dub's handiwork.

"Robin's lawyer has spoken with the district attorney. He still needs more documentation," T.J. volunteered.

Apparently Dub hadn't noticed T.J. until then. He looked startled, but recovered and asked, "Who's this guy?"

"This is my roommate, T. J. Swift. He was kind enough to drive me over here, since I can't even afford busfare, thanks to my unfortunate demise."

T.J. nodded to Dub, who gave him an appraising look in return. Robin was sure that Dub had misinterpreted the *roommate* label, and it gave her no small measure of satisfaction to watch him squirm.

"I see" was all that Dub said.

He didn't see, but Robin didn't care to correct him. She smiled inwardly. "I came here to ask you something about the funeral arrangements."

Obviously puzzled, Dub asked, "Why should they matter to you?"

"It doesn't matter. Just tell me what kind of floral arrangements you made."

"Floral arrangements?"

"You know, Dub. Flowers—for the grave."

"I didn't…"

"You didn't arrange for flowers?"

"No. Why?"

"That's all I wanted to know. See ya." Robin picked up her purse and turned to leave, ignoring Dub's incredulous stare.

She signaled for the guard and waited impatiently for him to let them out. When the door opened, T.J. followed.

"You were pretty rough on him back there, Robin," T.J. told her as the door closed.

Robin shrugged as she hurried down the drab jailhouse hallway. "No harder than he was on me during our fiasco of a marriage."

"Maybe so, but the man is in jail. And it wasn't his fault that the police identified the body as you."

"I know, but Dub brings out the worst in me. He may be in jail now, but when he gets out, he can pretty much go back to his life as if nothing had happened. I don't know how long it's going to take me to straighten out the mess mine is in."

They stopped and waited at a bank of elevators. Finally, one came to a stop and the doors opened. A man stepped out.

Robin stepped inside, but T.J. stopped and stared after the man. The elevator doors didn't wait for him.

Punching the hold button, Robin urged him in. "Hey, the elevator's going down without you."

T.J. looked at Robin and stepped quickly inside. As the doors closed behind him, T.J. was still looking down the hall after the man. "Did you see that guy?"

"Yeah." Robin shrugged. "So?"

"That was Miles Yarborough."

"The high-priced criminal attorney?"

"Yeah. He must be slumming." T.J. looked thoughtful. "I wonder who he's here to see?"

With the question about the flowers answered, two more had arrived to replace them. Who was the man who had left the bouquet? And what was his connection to the dead woman? T.J. would have been considerably happier if Dub had arranged for the floral tribute. He should have been putting the final touches on his draft, but his mind kept hanging on the flower conundrum.

Robin was pacing again. But this time he couldn't blame her for his lack of concentration. He was stuck on the mystery man and the flowers. At least Robin hadn't gotten the deeper significance of Dub's answer. That the other man could be a threat to her. She was upset because she still hadn't heard from her parents, and it had been over twenty-four hours since she placed her first call.

"Do you think they forgot to give them my message?" Robin asked, sounding plaintive.

T.J. looked up. He knew what she meant, and he wasn't getting much done on his paper, anyway. He'd spent the past couple of hours wondering about the flower man. "Do you want to try to call another time?"

She looked apologetic. "Do you mind? I know your phone bill is going to be a bear, but the radioman on the ship could have misplaced the message. Or copied down the number wrong. My folks might be trying to call my old number."

"Go ahead."

Robin grabbed the phone and checked the slip of paper she had left lying under it. She jabbed in a long series of numbers. Again she reached the radioman in the ship's communication center. Again he took the message. He assured her that he would pass it on to her parents as soon as they got back. He'd neglected to mention to her that they'd gone on an extended onshore excursion when she called before. No wonder they hadn't called back.

Robin placed the receiver back on the cradle. "I guess all I can do now is wait. And wait. And wait."

T.J. put down his pen. "Look, Robin. You're driving us both crazy. Let's go rent a movie."

Robin perked up instantly. "Okay. Have you seen *Four Weddings and a Funeral*?"

"Hasn't everybody?"

Her face fell. "I haven't."

"Well, it was a good one. I'll watch it again."

"Yay." Robin grabbed her purse and headed for the door.

"Just how is it you managed to miss one of the biggest movies of 1994?"

"It wasn't Dub's kind of movie," Robin explained. She didn't think T.J. needed any further explanation.

The headline proclaiming Lester "Dub" Doubleday innocent had supplanted national events on the front page of the *Tuscaloosa News*. There was a color photograph of Dub standing in front of the courthouse with his attorney. Miles Yarborough. Robin should have known.

Robin's eyes first widened with shock, then narrowed with anger, as she read the story that accompanied the tabloidlike headline. Dub had called a press conference to announce that his arrest had been a mistake because the apparent victim was still very much alive. There was a brief mention of Robin's return and her part in freeing Dub. The rest of the story portrayed Dub as the injured party, focusing on the way the local police had botched the identification of the body.

"What has your forehead so bunched up with wrin-

kles?'' T.J. asked as he came out of the kitchen munching
an apple.

Robin folded the first section of the thick Sunday paper
to frame the offensive story and waved it in T.J.'s direction.
''Look at this,'' she sputtered. ''That...that lowlife has
twisted the story around so much that he looks holier than
Mother Teresa. Next thing you know, he'll be suing for
wrongful arrest.''

''I doubt that he'd have a leg to stand on,'' T.J. said
calmly as he came up behind Robin and took the wadded
newspaper from her hand. A shiver raced up Robin's arm
as T.J.'s fingers briefly touched hers.

Shrugging off the tingly feeling, Robin wheeled to face
T.J. ''Have you read that?'' She indicated the offending
sheaf of paper. ''He barely mentioned my part in getting
him out. And didn't bother to discuss the insurance issue
at all.''

''I'm sure he has a team of publicists trying to turn the
tide of public sympathy in his direction.'' T.J. paused to
skim the contents of the article.

''He can barely afford a public defender, much less a
publicity agent. And now he's going to pay a high roller
like Miles Yarborough.'' Robin snorted. ''The nerve of
him, taking advantage of this to come out smelling like a
rose. He probably thinks the publicity will get him some
big moneymaking deal.''

T.J. waved his hand to calm Robin, which just inflamed
her all the more. She seethed as she watched T.J. read the
article again, more carefully this time. But her ire began to
subside as she noticed the way the muscles in T.J.'s lean
jaw twitched as he chewed on his apple. The muscles of
his chest played hide-and-seek beneath the tightly stretched
fabric of his rust-colored T-shirt as he moved his arm to
turn to the next page. The color of the shirt was a near-
perfect match for the chestnut highlights in his hair. How

could she be noticing this, when Dub Doubleday was still taking her life and using it to suit his selfish needs?

Robin chastised herself for allowing herself to be distracted from her righteous indignation. She was at the beginning of a well-thought-out five-year plan, she reminded herself. A plan that certainly did not include Dub, or T.J., or men in general. Being distracted by an attractive, sensitive man did not fit into her plans at all.

She had almost persuaded herself to revise her plan when T.J. spoke. It took a few moments for his voice to penetrate the point-counterpoint that was going on in Robin's mind. "I'm sorry. I was woolgathering." Robin was grateful that her tan hid the flush that crept up her face.

"So I see," T.J. drawled. He smacked the folded newspaper section against his hand. "This story doesn't really have any lies in it," he suggested gently.

"No. It's just so full of omissions you could use it to strain soup," Robin responded wryly. "I know that he has to make himself look like a good ol' boy, so that when he gets called on the insurance bit, he'll get off. But, darn it, he's got my life all tied up in knots along with his."

T.J. placed a gentle finger on Robin's lips. She knew his gesture was an attempt to soothe her. It did anything but. Her breath caught in her throat, and she had to make a conscious effort to keep her breathing rhythmic and slow. T.J.'s strong fingers did indeed make Robin forget all about Dub Doubleday and his imperfections, but they did nothing to keep Robin and her five-year plan on track.

It was going to be a lot harder to live with her than he'd planned, thought T.J. as he sat trying to proof the last few pages of his paper. She was a distracting presence in the room, though she'd done nothing overt to attract his attention. In fact, the clothes she was wearing were nondescript, and her tanned face was scrubbed clean of makeup. Yet, something about her kept pulling his eyes away from the yellow legal pad.

Robin was flopped in a patch of sun on the faded carpet in the middle of the living room floor, reading a paperback mystery novel. Though there was nothing seductive about the pose, every shifting movement she made when she turned a page or pushed her thick, tawny hair from her eyes called his attention to the lithe, firm body that lay hidden beneath the faded jeans and T-shirt she wore. His imagination filled in any details he couldn't see. Even the dress code he'd once considered instituting wouldn't help him now. Not even if she wore a nun's habit.

"I hate that," Robin announced abruptly. She sat up and placed a marker in her book. She crossed her legs and stretched.

T.J. almost dropped the legal pad. He hadn't really been looking at it for several minutes, anyway. "What did you say?"

Robin chuckled. "I'm sorry, I didn't mean to disturb you. Just when I thought I'd figured this mystery out, the author threw in a red herring."

"Just like real detective work," T.J. commented. "All the evidence says one thing, witnesses say something else, and neither of them tell the complete story."

"Sounds a lot like archaeology. It takes more patience than skill. Do you know how many days I spent digging and ended up with nothing but dirt?"

"I'm sure not nearly as many as I have wading through piles of evidence that led exactly nowhere." T.J. put the legal pad down. "You know, it sounds like you and I have a lot more in common than I thought."

"At least as far as our jobs are concerned," Robin conceded. "We both do a lot of detective work. Brains, brawn and patience required. And not necessarily in that order. Indiana Jones–type adventures are only for the movies."

"What made you interested in archaeology? It doesn't

seem like something the average American girl would turn to." T.J. tried to picture Robin knee-deep in a trench sifting through tons of sand to come up with a couple of pieces of broken pottery.

"My grandfather discovered what appeared to be an ancient Indian campsite one winter when he was clearing an unused section of his land for a cornfield. When he began plowing, he found an unusually large number of arrowheads and primitive implements just below the surface. He was smart enough to recognize it for what it was, and abandoned his plan to cultivate there. After that, he spent all his spare time excavating the site. My brother and I used to spend summers helping him dig. Mack just thought he was being used as forced labor, but I got swept up in the mystery and history of the thing."

Surprisingly, after Robin's explanation, T.J. could picture Robin as a grubby teenager, sifting through the red Alabama dirt. "I bet you read *National Geographic* from cover to cover." T.J. winked. "And not for the photos of naked women, either."

"Guilty as charged. In fact, I have every back issue from the time I was twelve. They're at my parents' house."

"Speaking of your parents, have you heard from them yet?"

"No." Robin frowned. "And I'm a little concerned. I wonder if they even got my message."

"Maybe not. You can't be sure if it was delivered, or if your parents bothered to check for any messages at all. I'd try to reach them again."

"I'd considered that." Robin checked her watch. "I wonder what time it is in the Pacific."

"Very early, I'd wager. Or very late."

Robin sighed. "I'll probably just get somebody in the communication center, anyway. I guess it couldn't hurt to leave another message." She scrambled to her feet and reached for the phone.

Just as it rang.

The sudden shrill sound startled Robin so that she drew
her hand back from the instrument with a swiftness that
was more reflexive than voluntary. The instrument shrilled
again as Robin tried to gather her scattered thoughts. How
could the mere sound of an ordinary phone ringing, one
she'd heard regularly for the past year, cause such an unlikely reaction? Her heart raced out of control.

T.J.'s calm voice from the other side of the room nudged
Robin back to action. "Do you want me to get that?"

Robin drew a long breath. "No, I'm here." She reached
for the receiver as the bell rang a fourth time.

"Hello." Robin's salutation was more question than
greeting, her anxious voice a croak.

There was nothing on the line except a distant-sounding
musical tone.

"Hello? Is anyone there?"

There was a clicking sound, then more of the strange
notes.

This is all I need now. Not some kid playing with the
phone, thought Robin as her curiosity turned to irritation.
"If you don't say something, I'm going to hang up."

There were more tones and then, finally, a tinny, distant
voice. "Robbie, don't hang up."

"Mom?" The voice was so weak and faraway that Robin
could barely make it out. She covered her other ear with
her hand. "We have a really bad connection. You'll have
to speak up—I can't hear you."

"Robbie, we got your message." The voice was stronger
now, and clear enough to hear. "We're on the way home.
What's wrong?"

"Oh, Mom. You and Daddy don't have to cut your vacation short. It's not that important. Go ahead and enjoy
the rest of your trip."

"We were getting tired of living out of suitcases. We're

in Los Angeles, and we'll be in Birmingham tonight,'' responded Robin's mother's faraway voice.

It was so good to hear her that Robin almost forgot why she had left the message in the first place. "Okay, Mom. I'll pick you up."

"It's not necessary. We left our car at Aunt Esther's in Hoover. We'll just go by and get it. You don't need to come get us."

"I don't mind. I need to talk to you about something important." Robin couldn't help wondering if her elderly aunt Esther had heard about her demise. Her eccentric aunt only read the *New York Times* and listened to public radio. Robin doubted that her aunt would learn about her through either of those sources.

"Mom, before you hang up... There's been a really weird mix-up here. No matter what you hear, I'm very much alive. The reports of my death are all a mistake. Do you understand?"

It was evident from her mother's shocked silence that she'd heard and not completely understood what Robin told her. "Mom, don't worry. Everything is okay. I'll meet you at the airport and explain everything. Tell me your flight number."

The worried tone in her mother's faraway voice did nothing to reassure Robin as the woman gave Robin the information. Both her parents had been recovering from heart problems before their trip. Would this strange and unexpected news upset them too much? Robin listened to her parents' goodbyes, then reluctantly hung up.

"Do you want me to drive you to the airport?" T.J.'s gentle, caring voice came from somewhere behind Robin.

Slowly she turned around. It was then that she realized that she had promised to meet her parents at an airport over fifty miles away. And that she had sold her car!

Heat burned Robin's cheeks as she answered. "Would you mind? I forgot that I don't have a car anymore."

T.J. chuckled. "I think I figured that out before you realized it. No, I don't mind." He patted the legal pad that lay on the sofa next to him. "I've finished the paper. We could stop somewhere for dinner. I haven't been out to eat in months, unless you count takeout from Chang's."

"Thank you. That'll be nice," Robin replied so promptly that T.J. almost didn't realize that he had, for all practical purposes, asked her for a date. It had seemed like the most natural thing in the world.

And she had accepted.

The last time he asked a woman—a girl, really—for a first date had been over ten years ago. That girl had been Ginger, he recalled fondly. It had taken him weeks to gather the courage he needed to ask her out. The fact that Ginger accepted readily had surprised him so much that he had almost forgotten to follow through with the details.

But she had accepted the invitation, and they had connected as if they were meant for each other. It had been the last time he was required to put his ego on the line for a woman. Until now. And he had done it so easily.

Maybe Robin didn't see this as a date, the way he did. Was he wrong in thinking of it that way? After ten years of being out of circulation, he wasn't certain they even did things the same way they had when he was a twenty-one-year-old college senior.

"Where do you propose to take me on this date?" Robin asked, looking strangely at T.J.

"There's a new steak house on the approach to Highway 59. I seem to recall you mentioning that you were hungry for American food." T.J. surprised himself with his prompt answer. This date business was getting easier by the minute. Maybe it was a skill, like riding a bicycle. You never really forgot. Or, like wine, it got better with age.

"Oh, I know that place," Robin responded brightly. "I haven't been there, but several people have told me about it. I'd love to try it."

So that was it. In the past few days, he'd acquired a roommate, finished a paper that had been plaguing him for weeks, and asked a woman out for a date.

T.J. wondered if lightning was waiting to strike him. Or at least remind him of his past failures. Things were just going too well.

Chapter 13

Whatever had possessed Robin to refer to her outing with T.J. as a date, she didn't know, but she had. And now she had to figure out what to do about it. He had been just as adamant about keeping their friendship platonic as she had. Maybe more. But that had been before they spent the night trapped in the basement together. That had been before everything changed.

Robin stood, half-dressed, in front of her closet, debating what to wear. She didn't have many choices. Since her weight loss, there were very few things that fit right. Oh, there were plenty of things to wear, but few that would make an impression. But did she really want to make one? Robin sighed.

That was just it. She did want to make an impression. Not because T.J. was an attractive man, but because for the past few years, Dub had so worn her down that she hadn't felt desirable. Not to Dub, not to herself, not to anyone. There was something about the way T.J. looked at her from beneath those feathery gold eyelashes that told Robin that he was interested. And Robin liked it. There was something about the glint in those amber eyes of his that seemed to say, *I want you.* Robin hadn't seen a look like that in a long time, and it felt good. Too good.

She reminded herself that she still had four more years to go on that five-year plan she had so carefully made out. Four more years to find out who she really was and to become her own person. Robin found herself wondering if she could have a man in her life and complete the plan, too. The sensible side of her brain told her no, but the romantic side said yes.

Robin wanted so much to believe the romantic side. Sure, she'd made a terrible mistake in letting Dub take from her until she had nothing left. She'd let him do it, and she'd learned. Had she found enough strength and confidence to be able to give and not be used up? Dub had almost extinguished the light that once shone from within her. Was she strong enough to withstand another assault on her emotions so soon?

The clock on the dresser showed that it was nearly five o'clock. Robin had no more time to stand in front of her closet and debate. She grabbed the hot-pink halter dress she had kept for years in hopes of wearing it again and pulled it over her head. She hadn't been able to squeeze into it in ages, but now it fit like a glove. With a few quick touches to her hair and a last glance at her makeup, Robin took a deep breath and pushed open the bedroom door.

T.J. let out a long, low whistle as Robin entered the living room. He hoped that she hadn't heard him, but he was certainly glad she had chosen to wear that pink thing. Dress code be damned. He liked seeing a woman look like a woman, and though Robin's jeans and T-shirts had done nothing to disguise her gender, this dress was a definite improvement.

He still had difficulty reconciling the vibrant young

woman here with the frumpy woman in the terrible photo IDs she'd shown him, but he knew in his head that they were the same. T.J. would have had no trouble sharing the apartment with the plain woman in the pictures, but he almost enjoyed the challenge of trying to stay sane with this one around.

Robin smoothed the flowing skirt of the dress. The fabric clung to her breasts like a second skin, teasing T.J. with its ability to touch her when he could not. Should not.

"I know I've said this before, but you do clean up good," T.J. drawled appreciatively.

"Thanks. I haven't seen my folks in months. I wanted to show off the new me. Or the old me."

T.J. tried to conceal the vague disappointment he felt at Robin's words. Why couldn't she be dressing for him? He knew that they'd agreed to be friends and only friends. But that had been before he got to know her. He'd had no desire to get close to the irritating woman who accused him of apartment-stealing in the middle of the night. The only thing he'd wanted to do then was to get rid of her.

Swallowing hard to clear his throat of the disappointed lump that had lodged there, T.J. said, "It's a little over two hours until your parents' flight comes in. We have to hurry if we're going to eat."

Robin laughed that tinkly little laugh he'd grown to love. "We can't have that. I'm starved."

"Is that all you think about? Food? You've done nothing but eat since I met you." T.J. had made the comment before, but Robin seemed not to take offense.

"I think of plenty of things, but it's been a long time since lunch. Besides, you always manage to put away twice as much as me."

"Touché," T.J. answered testily. "I'll let you get away with that for now."

"Oh, thank you so much," Robin murmured slowly. "I do so like a man who overlooks a woman's shortcomings."

Shortcomings? As far as T.J. could tell, Robin had very few. He thought he was going to enjoy the evening, even if it didn't lead to anything else. Even if it wasn't a real date.

Robin didn't question whatever it was that created her high spirits. It was enough that she felt loose and free and happy. Her parents were coming home, and she had T.J. sitting across from her. She felt that the solution to her problems was close at hand. Her mom and dad could help clear up the question of her identity, and T.J. could...

Robin cut off another piece of the petit filet in front of her. "You know, I haven't eaten steak in ages." She popped the morsel into her mouth and savored the flavor.

"Well, I know it can't be because you're a vegetarian," T.J. commented as he sawed off a huge chunk of his T-bone. "You've cooked meat since you've been back from Mexico."

Swallowing the bite of meat, Robin gestured with her finger to signal that there was an answer coming. "Umm, that was good. I started watching the amount of red meat I ate when my parents both developed heart conditions. Dad had a bypass, and Mom's cholesterol was way up there. Steaks and roasts were among the first to go." A wicked smile crept across her face. "It really irritated Dub that I'd reduced his meat choices to chicken and fish and minuscule portions of ground beef."

"He had been used to eating at a training table," T.J. commented.

"Yeah, but he hadn't trained in years. He had started to get paunchy. He kept dreaming of making a comeback, but he didn't do anything about it. He ate like a pro jock, but he didn't work out like one."

T.J. arched his eyebrows in acknowledgment, but didn't comment. He speared another chunk of meat.

Robin brandished her fork. "Then he had the nerve to

blame his failure to get another football contract on what I was feeding him.''

"Or what you weren't," T.J. added dryly as he picked up his mug of non-alcoholic beer.

"He could have used some of that, too," Robin commented, indicating the pseudobeer.

T.J. laughed. "It doesn't have the same kick as the real thing, but the taste is still there."

Grimacing, Robin said, "I always thought the kick was what you drank it for. I've tasted the stuff. It's vile."

T.J. pointed to Robin's diet cola. "To each his own. I've never understood the rationale behind decaffeinated diet soda. You might as well have water."

"With bubbles." Robin smiled and held up her glass to toast. "And flavoring."

"What're we toasting?" T.J. asked as he brought his mug up to meet Robin's glass.

"Certainly not Dub." Robin looked across the table at T.J.'s wholesome good looks. *Certainly not Dub.* "We'll toast my parents."

"To your parents." T.J. touched Robin's glass.

Along with the gentle pressure and clink of the glasses, Robin felt a tingle. Her fingers had only met T.J.'s for a brief second, but something had passed between them. This time she couldn't blame it on bad carpet.

What made the light suddenly shine in Robin's clear blue eyes? T.J. wondered as he sipped at his drink. She had been effervescent enough to start with, but now she glowed.

An awkward silence built between them, and T.J. was at a loss as to how to fill it. He sawed off another chunk of meat and set to chewing it methodically. Then he glanced at his watch and poked his fork into his baked potato.

Robin hadn't worn a watch. "Is it getting close to time to go?"

T.J. swallowed quickly, nearly choking on his food. He

took a swig of his beer. So much for grace under pressure, he thought ruefully. He swallowed again. "We still have time."

"Good. I'm enjoying myself."

"That's good." T.J. wished he could have shrunk into his seat. What a stupid answer! Why was he so tongue-tied?

He'd never had problems talking. It was something red-haired little boys seemed to develop early, in self-defense. His hair might have darkened significantly with age, but he still knew how it felt to have to prove that there was something lurking in the brain that lay hidden beneath the once carroty thatch. He hadn't been class clown, but he'd managed to be articulate enough for two teenage boys.

"I sure hope I didn't worry my folks this morning, when I told them about the late great Robin L. Digby," Robin remarked pensively.

"I don't think you worried them," T.J. replied. "But I'll bet you have them damned curious."

"*They're* curious? The police wouldn't tell me anything. I'm dying to know about that other woman." Robin made a sheepish face. "Okay, that was a poor choice of words, but you know what I mean."

"Yeah, I know. Dub's part in the mess notwithstanding, I do have a vested interest in this myself."

The arriving flight was just being announced as Robin and T.J. approached the gate. Robin stood on tiptoe, straining to get a first glimpse of her parents.

Laughing, T.J. nudged Robin. "Look, the plane is just now taxiing up to the boarding ramp. You have a few minutes before they'll be out."

Robin smiled sheepishly. "I'm just anxious about my parents coming. All the time I was in Mexico, I worried about them, so I guess I won't be convinced they're all right until I see them looking hale and hearty."

T.J. sobered. "You don't think they came home early because of their health, do you?"

"It had crossed my mind." Robin craned her neck toward the gate. A flight attendant pushed open the pleated partition and locked it into place. "It won't be long now."

"Tell me what they look like. I'll probably see them first, since I'm at least a head taller than you." T.J. glanced in the direction of the gate. So far, it was vacant.

"You don't have to gloat about your superior height," Robin retorted lightly. "I could just look between everybody's legs." She laughed, then described her parents.

As the first of the passengers began to come through, Robin felt T.J. squeeze her hand. She looked up into his warm amber eyes and smiled. Her heart lurched as he returned a grin. It's so nice having T.J. here with me, Robin thought as she scanned the approaching crowd.

Robin glanced around and noticed several people holding flowers. A young man presented a pretty young woman with one red rosebud, and was rewarded with a kiss. Should she have gotten something for her parents?

T.J. seemed to be reading her mind. "I don't think your parents expect anything but you."

"I suppose," Robin replied, her voice tight with emotion. "I just want them to hurry and get off. What if something's happened to them and they didn't make the flight? Or one of them's sick?"

The concerned look in Robin's eyes touched T.J. more than her words could. He wanted so much to hold her, to squeeze her to him and reassure her. But T.J. knew it was too soon in their relationship for that. If it was a relationship. Instead, he turned back to scan the thinning group of stragglers coming through the gate.

One last couple emerged, laden with bags, gifts and camera. T.J. smiled. He noticed Robin's face brighten as she, too, spotted the couple.

"I think I can see why they were so late getting off the

plane," said T.J. as he followed Robin toward them. They were tanned, fit, and far from the sickly invalids Robin had suggested.

"Mom, Dad, you look so healthy!" Robin exclaimed as she stepped into a double embrace.

"You act as though we were on our deathbeds," the older version of Robin said as she stepped back and appraised her daughter. "I can see I'm not the only one who's had a change for the better from a summer away."

Robin pirouetted. "What do you think?"

Mr. Digby grinned, the expression making him look inexplicably boyish. "You look just like you did when you were twenty-two. I thought that dress was too skimpy then, too."

"Are you still scandalized?" Robin teased.

The old man's expression grew stern and his voice gruff. "Naw, you're a grown woman now, and I can appreciate a well-turned figure as well as the next old geezer."

"You're hardly a geezer," Robin replied, as her mother gave her husband a sharp poke with her elbow.

"Aw, Lurleen. I can still look," Digby protested.

"Stop bickering, children," Robin demanded. Her expression softened. "Now, tell me about your trip."

Lurleen looked at T.J. He had been holding back, reluctant to interrupt the reunion.

"Why don't you introduce me to this nice young man you've been hiding," Lurleen said pointedly, as she extended her hand toward T.J. "Then I want to know all about this murder mystery. Our travelogue can wait."

"I'm sorry. Folks, this is T. J. Swift." Robin paused. "He's my roommate. Strictly platonic," she added.

T.J. watched as a montage of emotions showed on the Digbys' faces. Lurleen arched an eyebrow, but said nothing. T.J. felt that he needed to explain. "I've taken over Cheryl Rodgers's room. There is nothing untoward going on between me and your daughter.'' Though he was beginning to wish that there was.

Robin's father broke into a wide grin. ''Call me Digger. Just about ever'body does.'' He fished a card out of his pocket and handed it to T.J.

''I'm just about the best well digger in all of Demopolis,'' Digger explained proudly.

T.J. laughed, feeling a little uncomfortable. Why did he feel like a sixteen-year-old being given the once-over by his date's parents?

Lurleen Digby cut in. ''Don't worry. He won't pressure you into having a well dug.''

''Good.'' T.J. laughed, feeling more at ease. Robin's parents were proving to be nice people. ''I don't have anyplace to put a well.''

Robin interrupted, rescuing him. ''Hey. Don't you have some baggage to claim? Or is it all hanging off you?'' Robin gestured toward the clutter surrounding and draped over her parents.

Digger grabbed a carry-on bag. ''Here, T.J. You help with this stuff. Let Robin catch her mother up about things while we go get the bags.''

T.J. hefted a hang-up bag and hoisted another carryall as Lurleen Digby pulled her daughter aside. ''Where did you find this handsome, sexy man?''

''Mom, it's a long story,'' Robin replied as she herded her mother toward baggage claim.

Lurleen arched an eyebrow. ''Well, I've got good ears and plenty of time. You will explain why he's your roommate and not your boyfriend.''

T.J. wondered about that himself as he followed Digger away.

Two days of traveling were beginning to show on the faces of Digger and Lurleen Digby. Once the initial excitement of greeting had passed and the family had caught up on events, it became apparent that the couple were running on reserve energy. Possibly on willpower only.

"Mom, Dad, you really look worn out. You're not planning to drive home tonight, are you?" As relieved as Robin had been initially, some of her old concerns about her parents' health had returned as she watched how quickly their strength waned as they walked out to the street in front of the terminal.

Lurleen Digby reassured her daughter as Digger stifled a yawn.

"Don't worry, hon. We'll stay at Aunt Esther's tonight, and head back in the morning. She'll want to hear all about our trip before she'll even let us go to bed."

"Maybe you should stay in a hotel."

Digger dismissed the suggestion and yawned again. "Lurleen, don't we have a birth certificate from the hospital that has Robbie's footprint on it?" He turned to T.J. "Reckon she could use that?"

"If you do have that," T.J. answered, "it would be very helpful. Footprints don't change any more than fingerprints. That may be the quickest way to prove her identity."

"Well, I'll see if I can find it. Tomorrow. After we've had a good night's sleep."

"Do you want me to come home and dig for it?" Robin volunteered, a second before she remembered that getting to Demopolis would be a problem without a car. She grimaced.

"It's okay, Robin. I can drive you over after I've gone to the typist," T.J. said, after correctly interpreting the face. "I have some free time until the semester starts."

Robin shot him a grateful look. "Thanks, T.J. I do have to straighten out the mess at the bank."

"What's wrong at the bank?" Digger asked. "Have they messed up a deposit or something? Maybe I can make a call to Cart Jameson, and get it straightened out."

Dealing with a small-town bank did have its advantages,

but even Robin didn't think her father would be able to untangle this snarl. She smiled sadly. "I wish you could, Daddy. And I wish it was as simple as a misplaced deposit." Robin's dim smile faded even more. "They got wind of my untimely demise, and have frozen my account until my estate is settled."

Lurleen looked astonished. "I didn't think they read the obituaries to find out if any of their customers had died anymore, in this computer age."

"They don't. I called the bank, and they told me that much. But they wouldn't talk to me over the phone. I have to come in and prove I'm really me," Robin told her mother.

"But we've been doing business with that bank for near forty years," Digger complained.

"I pointed that out to them. They weren't impressed. Apparently the bank's under new management. I talked to several different people, and I'd never heard of any of them before Friday."

Digger stifled a yawn. "Well, we'll just see about that when we get home." He yawned again, this time without bothering to conceal it.

Lurleen stretched and covered her mouth politely, then looked at her husband fondly. "Let's go, old man. We can't do anything about that tonight. And Aunt Esther is probably wondering where we are."

"Are you sure we can't drive you there?" T.J. asked as Digger summoned a cab.

"Not on a bet. Aunt Esther's is just a couple of miles from here," Digger explained as a taxi pulled over. "I never could see the attraction myself, but Lurleen here just loves to ride in them things." Digger started handing baggage to the cabbie. "Besides, old Esther'd never let you get away without talking your ear off."

"Believe us. We're saving you from Aunt Esther," Lurleen said with a tired grin. "She's a little peculiar, and I don't think you're quite ready for her just yet.'' She pulled Robin aside as her husband and T.J. supervised the loading of the luggage. ''He's trying to be subtle, in his own tactless way.''

''Subtle? Why?''

Lurleen's tone was conspiratorial. ''He wants to give you two some more time alone.''

Robin had to laugh. ''Mom, we live together in the same apartment. We're together all the time. Besides, we agreed not to get involved.''

Lurleen glanced over at the handsome, well-muscled man hefting baggage into the cab's roomy trunk. ''Do you really want to stick to that agreement?''

''No comment,'' said Robin, feeling her face grow hot.

''I like your parents,'' T.J. said as he guided his car into the traffic on Highway 59. Robin hadn't said much since her parents left, and T.J. wondered if she was still worried about them.

''They looked good, but I think I'll call Aunt Esther when we get home, to see if they arrived all right.'' Robin leaned wearily back against the upholstered seat. She looked vacantly out toward the dark countryside.

''Tired?'' T.J. asked as he carefully steered the car around a lumbering produce truck.

''Yeah. I don't think I'm caught up yet from my own trip.'' Robin raised a hand to conceal a yawn. ''Imagine how beat they must be.''

''They should sleep well tonight at your aunt Edna's.''

''Esther's,'' Robin corrected. ''Once she lets them get to sleep. She can talk on and on.'' She paused a moment. ''At least their homecoming wasn't as upsetting as mine was.''

''Finding out that you've been declared dead can be a real shock,'' T.J. commiserated. *He should know.*

''Tell me about it.'' Robin looked as though she were trying to stifle another yawn. She didn't succeed. ''I have to talk to the D.A. tomorrow. I wonder what he wants,'' she added pensively.

''He's still got to sort out all the details concerning the misidentified murder victim. He may also want to make certain you're not an impostor trying to get your old buddy Dub off.''

Robin sat up straight. ''I hardly think I'd be doing that. I ought to be pressing charges. I'm still furious at him for putting me through all this.''

''Make sure Lightfoot knows all that. A little righteous indignation should go a long way in convincing our illustrious district attorney that you're not a party to Dub's alleged scheme.'' T.J. glanced at the woman sitting beside him. Robin looked worried, tired and beautiful all at the same time. ''For now, don't worry about it.''

''That may be easier said than done.'' Robin settled back into the corner created by the edge of the seat and the door.

''You'll be fine.'' T.J. was right. It soon became evident from the soft, gentle breathing coming from the huddled pink form that Robin had succumbed to sleep's dark comfort.

T.J. drove contentedly on through the night. The gentle motion of the car and the engine's hum seemed to lull Robin into deeper sleep. He did nothing to disturb her.

As the darkened countryside outside the car gave way to the brighter lights of Tuscaloosa, the straight, smooth highway was replaced by stop-and-go city streets. Robin began to stir.

''Wake up, Sleeping Beauty. We're almost home.''

Robin blinked and sat up. She looked around sleepily. ''I must have fallen asleep.''

''With a resounding crash.'' T.J. smiled. He hadn't minded that she had winked out on him. In fact, it had been pleasantly comfortable driving along with her beside him.

Rubbing her eyes, Robin looked at the road ahead. ''We're almost there.''

"Just a minute or so," T.J. said as he turned the car onto Reed Street.

"There it is. And look! There's a parking space right in front."

"I'll take it." T.J. steered the car into the slot. He switched off the lights, pulled the key from the ignition and released his seat belt.

Robin fumbled with her seat belt and muttered an out-of-character curse. "I can't get this thing undone."

"Hold it. That blasted buckle gets hung up sometimes. I've been meaning to get it fixed." T.J. leaned over and deftly released the latch.

"Thanks," Robin said, in a breathless sort of whisper.

Funny, but T.J. felt short of breath, too. He caught the gentle scent of Robin's musky perfume. It drew him closer to her, and he brushed his mouth lightly against her slightly parted lips. The brief contact brought him to his senses.

He jerked away, embarrassed by his unplanned action and stunned by his body's response. He drew in a ragged sigh and wondered what to say. If he should say anything.

They had made an agreement to share the apartment platonically. As friends. He had no business complicating things with even something as trivial as a kiss. A kiss that was anything but insignificant, he realized.

T.J. turned back to look at Robin, his breath rapid and rasping. She had been as startled as he, if the way she touched her trembling fingers to her lips was any indication.

He knew he would have to say something. To make it right. "I was out of line. I shouldn't have done that." He knew full well that he didn't mean it. Not one hundred percent, anyway. He was damned glad he'd kissed her, but he wasn't happy that his impulsiveness might just have jeopardized their living arrangements.

"It's okay." Robin snatched her fingers away from her mouth and licked her just-kissed lips nervously.

Her unconscious action nearly sent T.J. over the edge,

destroying every one of his good intentions. To keep from surrendering to his body's sudden demands, T.J. shoved open the door and stepped hastily out of the car.

Robin followed him up the steps like a faltering shadow as a man hurried past them, head down. He brushed close enough to knock Robin off balance. Then the man hurried down the street.

T.J. had never seen him before, but something about the man's careless haste sent signals to the policeman in him. He didn't want to alarm Robin, but he smelled trouble.

And trouble he found, as he inserted the key into the lock. There, on the woodwork and around the striker plate, were fresh gouge marks that hadn't been there when he locked the door earlier in the evening. The man he saw leaving hadn't been carrying anything as obvious as a crowbar, but he could have used a knife. Hell, if the man had used a crowbar, he probably would have gotten in, and he and Robin would have walked into more trouble than they already had.

As if they didn't have enough.

The latch clicked and the door swung inward, giving T.J. another opportunity to see the damage the intruder had inflicted. He ran a finger over the splintered wood. Given just a little more persistence, the guy could have succeeded. He wondered if the break-in had anything to do with the dead woman.

"What are you looking at?"

T.J. looked up guiltily. The last thing he wanted to do was worry Robin. And if he showed her this, he surely would. "Thinking of an excuse," he answered, too quickly, as he stepped inside and used his body to block Robin's view of the damaged door frame.

"An excuse for what?" Robin followed him in.

Keeping between Robin and the scarred frame, T.J. closed the door carefully behind him. "To do this," he whispered huskily, only then realizing that it wasn't a lie conveniently fabricated for the moment. "To finish what I started earlier." He placed his hands on her shoulders—bare, thanks to the sexy pink dress—and drew her toward him.

"You want to kiss me? Again?" Robin's voice was breathless, eager.

"Yes," he said, his voice a rasp. His lips found hers, and he felt the hungry way they yielded to him. He couldn't settle for another chaste kiss like the one that had happened earlier tonight in the car. An image of the two of them naked, their arms and legs entwined, hit him like a nuclear explosion. His groin tightened.

He realized then that that first kiss had only been a preliminary. Now, he wanted more.

Robin supposed abstractly that she should protest this violation of the pledge of celibacy, but even as the thought flitted through her, she knew she wouldn't. It had been far too long since she felt wanted. T.J.'s lips pressed against hers with an urgency something deep within her strained to answer. Robin didn't stop to analyze this sudden need for him; she just fed the hunger that gnawed at her heart.

Without consciously doing it, Robin let her arms find their way around T.J.'s neck. She raked her fingers through the short, unruly thatch as T.J.'s hands traveled down from her shoulders to the sensitive skin at the base of her bare back. Shivers of delight raced through her as he stroked, kneaded, and caressed.

Raw desire exploded within her, and she found herself pressing against his solid, heated form. She felt his hard ridge of pulsing want against her, and need replaced desire. Her breasts became heavy, and her nipples contracted into hard, sensitive buds. She arched against him and felt a warm, sweet ache swelling within her.

T.J. groaned as he tried to pull away.

"No, don't stop," Robin whimpered, removing her mouth from his only long enough to form the words.

He wrenched himself away, leaving Robin bereft and needy. "If you don't let me stop this now, I don't know if I can," he rasped.

Desire filled her, making her limbs languid and heavy. "I don't want you to stop," Robin whispered, with what little intelligent thought she had left.

"Are you sure?" T.J.'s voice was thick with desire, and though his words might have been trying to send her away, his exploring hands continued to urge her on.

Robin could no longer think or talk, but she managed to nod.

Whatever happened now would be up to T.J.

Chapter 14

He almost missed that tiny nod of assent, so simple but so eloquent. "You're sure."

Robin smiled then. "Yes," she whispered.

T.J. waited no longer, but scooped her up into his arms and carried her into his room and laid her gently on the bed. He sank down beside her, feeling a brief twinge of awkwardness. It had been too many years since he'd undressed in front of a woman who wasn't his wife. Had the game rules changed since he was sidelined?

Apparently so.

As he hesitated, Robin scooted into a sitting position and reached behind her for the fastenings of her halter top. The strips of fabric that tied it together at the back of her neck loosened, but remained in place. Then she reached for the buckle on his belt and quickly released it. The sudden movement caused one strap of her halter top to fall free, revealing the rounded bare breast beneath.

That was all the urging T.J. needed. While Robin worked at his zipper, he pulled his shirt over his head without both-

ering to unbutton it. At the same moment he emerged from
his shirt, Robin released her hold on his belt.

T.J. pushed himself to his feet and kicked off his shoes
and socks, stepped out of his pants and turned back to
Robin. She had slipped out of her sandals and was struggling with the closure at the lower back of her dress, the
one barrier that remained between them. T.J. lowered himself to the bed and gently brushed her hands away and
deftly sent the zipper whispering down its track.

Without a word, Robin wriggled free of the dress and
the tiny shred of silk that remained. Her white breasts, knotted with desire, contrasted with the tan of her arms, looking
surreal in the room, lit only by the dim light sneaking in
from the short hall. She placed a cool hand on his chest
and slid it slowly down his torso until she reached the wide
elastic band of his briefs, which were straining to contain
his urgent need. She hooked one finger under the band and
tugged. T.J. did the rest, sliding them down his legs with
hands too clumsy with need.

As he kicked away the piece of cotton, Robin touched
his shoulder and pulled him around to her. She kissed him
once, then drew him down to cover her.

As she arched against him, pressing her mound against
his swollen need, T.J. could do nothing to hold back. He
entered her then, swiftly, strong and hard. And, with only
a few desperate thrusts, emptied himself into her.

He knew he should have taken more time, given her a
chance to come to completion. But before he could apologize for losing control so quickly, Robin arched against
him. She writhed and moaned with her own release, and
T.J. collapsed on top of her.

"Thank you," she whispered from beneath him. "It's
been a long time since I last felt wanted and desired. Thank
you," she murmured again.

T.J. arched back his head, closed his eyes and answered.

"No. Thank you." How could he explain that Robin had made him finally want to live again?

There was no way words could describe the immense weight that had been lifted from him, so T.J. said nothing. He rolled off her and pulled her close into his arms. He held her next to his beating heart until her soft, even breathing told him she had gone to sleep.

Sometime during the night, Robin had wakened in the unfamiliar room and the unfamiliar place in T.J.'s arms. Panic filled her as she realized the implications of what she had done. Not just that she had slept with a man she barely knew; that was bad enough. But also that she had probably ruined any chance she and T.J. were going to have to live together simply as roommates. This was bound to complicate things. What if T.J. took it as an invitation to continue in the same way?

She had to get some distance between them. She needed time alone to think. She slipped carefully out of T.J.'s arms, quietly, so as not to wake him, and crept back to her own room.

Morning finally came, earlier than usual, because sleep, once she'd returned to her own bed, had been slow in coming. Robin's restlessness had everything to do with what had happened the night before, she knew. Still, she had wrestled with the memory until the first rays of the sun began to lighten the sky. And now, she was no closer to finding a way to undo what she—no, they—had done.

She was unaccustomed to rising so early, but saw no point in remaining in bed. Her appointment with Gardner Lightfoot, the district attorney, was at ten, so she still had hours to kill before it was time to go. After showering and dressing with care to impress Mr. Lightfoot, Robin headed for the kitchen.

T.J. had taken over the breakfast chores, as they had agreed, but Robin had decided to cook this morning, since she was already up. Maybe, if she could butter him up with breakfast, she could broach the subject of what had happened last night. And, of course, insist that there be no repeat of it.

But all she could think about was the night spent in his arms.

Though it was not much past seven, T.J. was already in the kitchen, hunched over his yellow legal pad, studying with deep concentration. Robin came to an abrupt halt outside the kitchen door. Damn! That brought an end to her plans to bribe him into seeing things her way.

It was too late to surprise him with breakfast now.

T.J. was dressed much the same as he had been the first time she'd seen him less than a week before. Had it really only been five days that she'd known him? The color was different, but he still wore formfitting nylon jogging shorts. And nothing else.

That first time, she'd been able to look at him with some kind of objectivity; this morning, she could not. Her pulse raced, and she was certain she could hear the blood rushing through the veins in her ears. It was impossible to look at T.J.'s practically nude and very masculine form and not remember how it felt being kissed by him or relive the night spent in his bed. Or not to want to experience more.

No, she told herself, there could be no more. Not if she didn't want to complicate her life again, just when she was trying to simplify it.

Five-year plan be darned! one renegade lobe of her mind shouted, while Robin's more rational side told her to take it easy. She didn't want to blow her well-planned future; both sides of her brain knew that. But her impulsive, emotional side seemed willing to postpone it a bit, if T.J. could be a part of her present.

Robin banished the tempting thought with a violent shake of her head. She would not allow another man to sway her from her dream. Careers and men didn't mix.

Robin had given up her dreams for a man once; she wouldn't do it again.

Opening her mouth to speak, Robin found her words stuck in her throat. She tried to clear the obstruction, and that sound alerted T.J. to her presence. He looked up from his papers and smiled. He had looked weary when Robin first saw him this morning, but the smile of greeting brightened his face and put light into his golden eyes. And it put an end to Robin's plans to untangle the mess she'd gotten herself into.

"Hi. I was just going over my paper one last time before I take it to the typist. I've already made coffee." T.J. gestured toward the machine on the counter.

"So I see. And smell." Robin returned T.J.'s welcoming smile. "Do you always get up this early?" she asked as she crossed to the coffeemaker. "I had planned to make breakfast to repay you for dinner last night."

"Sorry. I already ate." T.J. indicated an empty cereal bowl near his elbow. "If I'd known, I'd have stood in bed."

"That's an intriguing notion," Robin said as she doctored her coffee. An image of the two of them, naked together, flashed unbidden into her brain, and she felt heat coming to her face. She looked away.

T.J. looked puzzled, then caught the joke Robin had almost forgotten she'd made. "Stood in bed. Oh!"

"And they say blondes are slow on the uptake." Thank goodness T.J. hadn't made a reference to what had gone on in his bedroom. Robin breathed a relieved sigh and carried her coffee to the table and slid into the chair angled catty-corner to his. "Why did you really get up? You proofed that draft three times yesterday."

"I had trouble sleeping."

Robin raised a brow, but tried to keep her expression neutral. Had he been unable to sleep for the same reason as she?

* * *

T.J. wondered whether to worry her about the splintered door, then decided to go ahead. She'd gotten her night's sleep. *Or had she?* He'd been surprised and disappointed to wake and find her gone. At first, he'd thought that she'd taken the event much less seriously than he. Now he couldn't help noticing the faint shadowing around her eyes that she'd tried to conceal. She'd done a reasonably good job of it, but T.J.'s trained eyes had picked up on it right away.

He drew a deep breath. He'd rather talk about what had happened last night, but the attempted break-in was more pressing. "I didn't want to tell you this last night." He paused.

Robin's blue eyes widened. With alarm. "Oh?"

He wondered if she thought he was going to give her the brush-off. They'd have to talk about that later, but the door was more important for now. "Remember that man who ran past us as we were coming in?" T.J. watched as Robin nodded over the coffee mug poised at her mouth. "I think he was trying to break in here."

Robin put the mug down so fast and hard that the steaming brown liquid sloshed all over the table. She jumped up and grabbed a paper towel and began to mop at the puddle that was quickly advancing toward T.J.'s paper. "What makes you think that?" she asked breathlessly.

"There were pry marks on the door and the framework. I think he probably heard us pull in and took off." T.J. watched as Robin mopped the spill with deliberate, mechanical motions.

"But I didn't see any marks. And why would anybody want to break in here? We don't have anything," Robin protested.

"You didn't see anything because I distracted you from the door once I'd seen it. I don't know why anybody would want to break into a student apartment, but it happens all the time." I don't know why *yet,* but I intend to find out, he thought.

He had a feeling that it had something to do with the death of Robin Digby, but he didn't know why. Yes, he did. The article in the Sunday paper had alerted someone that Dub was no longer considered a murder suspect and that the woman buried under Robin's name wasn't who the police had thought she was. It had alerted him that the police would again be looking.

T.J. would bet anything that the stranger was doing his own investigation before the police got to it.

"Shouldn't we call the police or sheriff or someone?" Robin had stopped mopping the coffee and was now worrying the sodden paper towel.

T.J. hated the frightened look that clouded Robin's blue eyes. "I already did."

"When? This morning?"

"Yes. While you were in the shower, I called in and told them what I found and described the man."

"Why didn't you call me when they came? I saw him, too. Why didn't you tell me in the first place?" The alarm that had first shown in Robin's eyes had given way to anger.

"They haven't come yet. There's not really anything to look at. Nothing was taken, and as far as the police are concerned, this is nothing but a throwaway call."

"But can't they find fingerprints?" Robin's indignation switched to worry again.

"They'll be over to take a look, but I doubt they'll find anything." T.J. pushed himself out of the chair and stretched his cramped, tight muscles as he rose. "This is more of a formality, to put a report on record in case Mr. Edwards wants to file a claim against his insurance company."

"Will they need to speak to me?" asked Robin in a tiny voice.

"Maybe. Just to confirm my description. But I am a trained observer. I doubt that you noticed much." Especially since he'd done such a good job of diverting her attention.

Robin shook her head. "I really didn't see him. I just got the impression of a man passing me. All I can say is I'm pretty sure he was a man." Her elbow propped on the table, she rested her head heavily against the heel of her hand. "Some witness I am. I couldn't say whether he was fat, thin, or short or tall."

T.J. placed his hand on Robin's shoulder. "It's okay. You weren't expecting to have to describe the man. You might have if you'd thought you were being threatened."

The kind gesture, though meant to reassure Robin, did not have a similar effect on T.J. He drew his hand back, as if it were burned. The brief physical contact had only heightened his own sensual awareness of her. He wanted to hold her, to reassure her.

He wanted to kiss her senseless and lose himself again in her yielding body, as he'd done last night.

But he left hastily and took a shower.

A cold shower.

Wiping the excess ink from her fingers with a rough paper towel, Robin stepped into the district attorney's private office where Gardner Lightfoot and her own attorney, Rafe Bennett, waited. At first Robin had been offended at the suggestion that she submit to the fingerprinting procedure, but since she had nothing to hide, she'd gone ahead with it. If Gardner Lightfoot thought he'd disprove Dub's claim of innocence by showing that Robin was somebody else, Robin would gladly prove him wrong.

Robin glanced around Gardner Lightfoot's imposing office and found the seat the district attorney indicated. "How long will it be before you get the results?" she asked as she wadded up the paper towel and looked for somewhere to toss it.

Lightfoot picked up a leather trash can from behind his desk and held it for Robin. She tossed the paper in and prepared to answer whatever questions he might throw at her.

"I couldn't say for sure, ah…Miss Digby. Perhaps as soon as the end of the day."

It galled Robin that Lightfoot had paused as he spoke her name. As if he weren't sure it really was hers. But she'd show him. Robin glanced toward Rafe Bennett.

"You realize, Robin, that all this fingerprint check will do is prove who you are not," Bennett pointed out.

"I know. It'll show that I'm not somebody else pretending to be me. But it won't prove that I'm who I say I am, since I've never been printed before." Robin smiled wryly. It was probably one of the few times anyone could regret having a clean arrest record.

Gardner Lightfoot looked at her appraisingly. "What reason can you give me to believe that you were not in cahoots with Dub Doubleday?"

She had to give it to him. Gardner Lightfoot didn't believe in beating around the bush. Robin paused and tried to compose an answer to the man's question. She knew it was the man's job to leave no question unasked, no stone unturned, but still she couldn't help being offended. She drew a deep breath and swallowed.

"I don't have all day, Miss Digby."

"I'm sorry. I was trying to phrase my answer so that I don't come across as vindictive, while at the same time making it crystal-clear that I do not have and don't want to have anything more to do with Dub Doubleday. Never would be too soon." Robin glanced at Rafe Bennett, then looked at the older man. Though he seemed kindly enough, the austere furnishings conveyed what his avuncular face did not. He was a no-nonsense man who meant business.

"You don't have to be polite for me, Miss Digby. I just want to hear the truth."

"The truth is, Mr. Lightfoot, that until last Thursday I hadn't seen my ex-husband in over a year and would have been happy not to ever set eyes on him again." Robin twisted the skinny leather strap on her purse.

"How is it that Mr. Doubleday had an insurance policy on you?"

It was a fair question, but the implication that Robin was somehow involved in Dub's stupidity irritated her. "Dub was still under contract with the Dolphins when we married, so he put me on their group policy. The policy was paid ahead for several years beyond the end of his initial contract—Dub's former business manager had seen to that. When we separated, I told him to remove my name." Robin looked down and examined her stubby nails. "Dub was nothing but a good ol' boy. He was a good athlete, but had it not been for that, he'd never have gone to college, gotten a degree—even if it was in phys ed. He never had any real ambition. If not for football, he would probably have been content to go to work in his Dad's air-conditioning business. No thinking required." Robin sighed.

"But, he'd gotten a taste of the good life," Lightfoot concluded. "And who could blame him for wanting to hang on to it?"

"Yes," Robin agreed. And she had to grudgingly admit that she'd been swayed briefly by it, too. She'd just faced reality sooner than Dub.

She sighed again. "His philosophy was not to do anything today that could be put off until tomorrow. Foolishly, I thought that if he realized there would be a refund coming, he'd cancel the insurance policy. I should have known better."

It still angered Robin to know that Dub had squandered all the money that she had earned teaching junior high social studies, and later, when their resources thinned, what she had made selling cosmetics door-to-door in her spare time. She had let Dub handle the family finances to give him something to do while he waited to rebuild his career or start something new. Robin had thought that he was managing well.

But the money that he always seemed to have in his pocket had come from their joint savings account, instead of the shrewd investments he'd claimed. Now she had nothing to show for years of working two jobs.

"So you were making a life together." The man's statement was almost a question. Lightfoot watched Robin through the triangle he had formed with his hands.

"Well, I was. I'm not so sure about Dub anymore," Robin responded bitterly.

"Explain."

"Dub never faced reality. He kept saying he wanted to get back to football, get a job, something. But there was always some reason why he couldn't or wouldn't actually do anything." Robin's voice caught as she remembered the pain of the realization that he wasn't ever going to take on his financial responsibilities, and that he'd been playing her for a fool.

"Do you think he was deliberately stringing you along?"

"Not at first. We became engaged when he graduated from Auburn and signed his first big contract with the Dolphins. I still had a year of school left, so we agreed that I would finish, and we'd be married after I graduated. Then he hurt his knee in that motorcycle accident between his first and second seasons. The next year looked doubtful, but we married anyway. He managed to limp through that second year, but his contract wasn't renewed."

"Then what?"

"He dragged us home to Demopolis, blaming everyone but himself. By that time, he'd had a little taste of the good life, and he wanted to keep it. He kept talking about a comeback, but he lacked the gumption to do anything about it.

"His injuries would probably have healed with time and proper training, but he wouldn't try. He just sat and waited."

Lightfoot frowned. "I'm beginning to get the idea of the man your ex-husband is. I'm surprised you took it."

"Well, you know how it is, Mr. Lightfoot. We southern women are trained to stick by our men through thick or thin. I thought if I gave him enough time, he'd come around." But no more. Robin was tired of making allowances for Dub's lack of initiative.

"What about the insurance policy? Why didn't you cancel it?" the district attorney asked. Robin was certain he was trying to catch her in a lie.

"Dub told me he would take care of it. Knowing Dub, I should have done it myself, but I tried to leave the man some shred of dignity. That was a big mistake. It might have been too much work for him to cancel it, but when the opportunity presented itself to cash in big on that policy, Dub just couldn't resist the temptation."

Rafe Bennett interjected, "That last statement is purely conjecture on my client's part."

Lightfoot nodded. "Do you think Dub had anything to do with the actual murder?"

"No. I can't see how he could." Robin tried to convince herself that Dub couldn't have gone looking for another Robin Digby to substitute for her. One whose fingerprints were on file.

"You never heard of another Robin L. Digby?" The attorney consulted a file that lay open in front of him. "A relative, maybe?"

"No. I thought I was the one and only!"

Lightfoot frowned as he scanned the file. Then he looked back at Robin and studied her very carefully.

The scrutiny made Robin want to squirm, but she forced herself to remain still and quiet.

"Remarkable physical resemblance," Lightfoot muttered. "What's your social security number?"

Robin told him.

"Birth date?"

"July 17."

"What year?"

She told him.

"Amazing. Same year. No wonder everyone took it for granted that you were she." The man looked up at Robin and smiled broadly. "What is your middle name?"

Puzzled, Robin answered. "Leigh."

"Hers was Lee also. Spelled *L-E-E*."

"Mine's *L-E-I-G-H*."

"Wait! There's more. Her social security number has one digit different from yours. Where you have an eight, she had a three. Your birthday was the seventeenth, hers was the eleventh. Both of those discrepancies were probably dismissed as copy errors or typos. Nobody bothered to check further, once your ex-husband turned up to claim the body." An expression that could almost have been described as admiration flitted across Lightfoot's face. Then he sobered.

Robin resisted the urge to remind Lightfoot that she and Dub were no longer married, but thought better of it. She waited to see what he would do next.

"I'm really going to have to git after somebody for not checkin' closer. We're going to have a deuce of a time gettin' to the bottom of this now. And I have a good mind to go after Mr. Doubleday for obstruction of justice."

Robin understood Lightfoot's disgust. She felt the same thing, and for much the same reasons. She had thought that Dub had finally stopped complicating her life when she walked out on him, almost two years ago. Though it was probably unintentional, Dub was still doing it. "Will you keep me apprised of the investigation?'' Robin finally asked.

''I'll try. Technically, you're not entitled to information on an ongoing investigation. But I understand your desire to know.'' Lightfoot closed the file.

''Thank you.'' Robin got to her feet. ''I never met that other woman, but I feel as though our lives are connected.''

''They are, Ms. Digby. They are.''

The notion wasn't comforting at all.

T.J. pedaled his bike joyfully. He had taken up bicycling after the head injury forced him to give up jogging. At first he'd rejected the notion that a hunk of spokes and metal could replace the rush he got from running, but it had. It felt great to be free of the pressure of the research paper and to feel the force of the hot wind against his skin as he sped through the streets of Tuscaloosa. He had delivered his draft to the typist and had consequently completed three hours of credit before the new semester began. And he had the rest of the week to do nothing before classes started on Monday.

Since he had decided to add the law concentration to his criminal justice course load, he'd been too busy to think. Most of the time, the pressure had been welcome; it had helped him to forget. Now remembering was becoming easier. Oh, he'd never forget Ginger and Rusty, but the ache that came when he thought about them had lessened. It wasn't his fault that they had been killed.

Bad things happen to good people all the time. He could deal with it. He had to. Maybe, with time, the pain would disappear entirely.

He downshifted to accommodate the gentle slope of the narrow street, and another thought came to him. With the independent study research paper out of the way, maybe he would have time for a life this term.

Right now he had nothing to worry about for the next

few days. Almost nothing, he reminded himself as he careened around the corner to his block and jumped the curb. He skidded to a halt in front of the apartment steps and almost dislodged the take-out bag strapped to the tiny cargo platform in back.

Robin, looking remarkably chipper, was coming up the walk from the opposite direction. He waited for her.

"You wouldn't believe what I found out about the other Robin," she called as she hurried toward him.

T.J. was eager to hear what she had to say. Eager to see her, he realized. But a little voice reminded him that they had an important matter to discuss. "Yeah, what?"

"It's stranger than fiction. You wouldn't believe how much we have in common. How our lives are intertwined."

T.J. handed Robin the aromatic paper bag.

"What's this?" Robin asked as she took the bag and T.J. hefted his bike up the steps. Then she sniffed. "Umm. Chinese. What's the occasion?"

"I know it's still early for lunch, but what the hell? I figured we needed to celebrate me getting my paper in. And I thought you might be tied up at the district attorney's office too long to take time for lunch before we go to your folks' house."

"I could have rustled up something, but this is great. I haven't had Chinese food in ages. Thanks."

"No problem," T.J. responded as he watched Robin peer into the bag. She might think that she had it all sorted out, but there was something about the way she'd said "intertwined" that nagged at him. Something told him that the next few days were going to be anything but restful.

"Do you suppose Robin Digby was married?" Robin wondered aloud as she related the details of her visit with Gardner Lightfoot to T.J. over lunch.

"Could have been. Why?" T.J. looked thoughtful as he dipped an egg roll into mustard sauce.

"Well, *L-E-I-G-H* is usually the feminine spelling of Lee. When it's spelled *L-E-E* it's frequently a surname or the masculine form. Suppose she was originally Robin Lee, who married somebody named Digby." Robin reached for the phone book. "That could be a clue."

"What're you doing?" T.J. said with his mouth still full. He jerked his head around to watch.

"I'm looking for Digbys in the phone book."

"That's a good idea, but I'd expect that the detectives have already tried that."

"I'm sure they did, but they stopped looking once they saw my name," Robin muttered. She remembered the way they had ignored the correct information about the victim and identified her. She flipped through the alphabetical white pages listings, ruing the day she had spent the extra money to have her name listed in the book, when the phone was already listed in Cheryl's name. "Darn. I'm the only one listed."

"You could try the listings for Lee," T.J. suggested. Then he quickly countered the idea. "No, that wouldn't work. If her files were on record as Digby, she would have to have been married for a fair amount of time."

"Oh. I would never have thought of that." Robin started to put the phone book down, but changed her mind. "It can't hurt to look. If nothing else, one of those Lees might be related to her. Let's see what we can find." She flipped through the pages to the *L* listings.

"Any luck?" T.J. leaned over her shoulder, making her heart flutter.

"Ah, here they are." Robin's enthusiasm dimmed a little as she realized the number of Lees on the page.

"Damn," T.J. muttered. "There are two columns of them."

"And that's not all," Robin added, with a sigh. She turned to the next page. "There's almost another full column of Lees, and—'' she groaned ''—there's a bunch of *L-E-I-G-H* Leighs here too.''

T.J. took the phone book out of her hand. "Look, Robin. There's no way you can narrow down this list to a manageable size, and you can't call every one of these people. There must be a hundred names here."

"More like three hundred," Robin told him, then laughed at T.J.'s surprised look. "I once got very bored when I was a teenager and restricted to my room. I counted the numbers of lines in a column in the Demopolis phone book. Allowing for the occasional space and large-print entry, there are approximately one hundred names in each column. And considering how much smaller Demopolis is, there may be more here."

"Speaking of Demopolis, don't we need to get going? If we don't get on the road now, the bank will be closed for lunch, and we'll have to wait until half the afternoon is gone before you get your banking business done." T.J. set the phone book down by the phone with unmistakable finality. "Your folks are expecting us. We can't keep them waiting."

"You're probably right. And I do need to get my checking account up and working again. We'll talk about this when we get back from my folks'.

"For now it's more important that I get financially solvent than I find out about the other Robin. But I'm not going to give up on it." She turned around and looked for her purse. "The police may eventually find out who killed her, and maybe even why. But I want to know about her. Her life. She didn't know anything about me, but considering what her death did to my life, I need to know everything about her."

Robin shuddered as she followed T.J. out the door. All of this was very unsettling. Creepy. And she didn't think she would get another good night's sleep until she had the entire affair settled.

And somehow she knew it wasn't going to be easy.

Chapter 15

The trip to Demopolis had been successful, and Robin waved triumphantly to her parents as she slid into the car beside T.J. Still clutching the hospital birth certificate with her newborn footprint on back that Lurleen had kept filed in the old family Bible, Robin leaned back and sighed. "I wish the rest of this could be so easy to straighten out."

"How did your father get the bank mess cleared up so fast?" T.J. asked as he backed out toward the road.

"Never underestimate the power of the good-ol'-boy network. You just have to know the right people." She chuckled. "You should have seen old Carter dressing Camryn Jameson down."

"Why shouldn't the bank president be able to chew out an employee?"

"He should, especially since she's his Harvard-educated daughter." Robin chuckled again. "At the time, he was wearing bib overalls and smelled like fish bait."

T.J. looked puzzled. "On a business day?"

"It's a long story. But Mr. Jameson came out of retirement just long enough to remind his thoroughly modern daughter what customer satisfaction means. And he told her what she could do with her modern management methods. And I told her what she could do with my checking account," Robin continued, tapping her bulging purse. "I withdrew the entire contents. What little there was." Then she sobered. "Now if only we could convince Mr. Lightfoot as quickly."

T.J. paced restlessly outside the judge's chambers as he waited while Robin obliged Lightfoot with a footprint. He smiled as he thought about her reaction to the minor indignity. She had marched off cheerfully enough, but stepping onto an ink pad and doing what it would take to prove she was who her parents said she was wasn't anybody's idea of a good time.

He hoped it would be enough to keep her mind off investigating the other Robin Digby. He had tried to convince her to stay out of it during the long car ride to Demopolis and back, but so far, Robin hadn't been swayed. He was afraid she was going to continue with her investigation. And if she did, he would have to go along with her. If for no other reason than to keep her out of trouble.

Robin's jubilation over settling the bank matter should have been enough for one day, but it hadn't been. Once she finished chortling over her victory, her attention had gone straight back to the murder mystery; she was already plotting her attack plan on the three-hundred-name list of Lees. T.J. had only one other hope that he could steer her thoughts another way. The district attorney.

The heavy wooden door creaked open, and Robin appeared. She hopped on one foot, carrying a shoe, as she tried not to track black ink on the floor. Her grin surprised him.

"All done?" T.J. asked, already knowing by her expression that she was.

"Yep. They'll believe I'm me once they get corroborating records from my hometown hospital." Robin balanced herself on one foot and glanced at her watch. "And I still have plenty of time to go home and clean the rest of this gunk off my foot and make a dent in the Lee list. That little wipe they gave me was hardly enough to swab one toe, and all the towel did was smear it."

T.J. sagged. He hadn't really expected Robin to forget about it. But he had hoped. He shoved himself to his feet. "Are you free to go?"

Robin nodded and took his arm to stabilize herself on one foot.

Shaking his head, T.J. steered them toward the exit. Robin's one-footed progress was too slow to suit him, so T.J. did the only thing he could. He swept her into his arms and carried her out to the car.

"Are you sure this isn't just a ploy to play touchy-feely with me?" Robin joked as his arms closed around her.

That hadn't been his intent, but he couldn't say it didn't feel damned good. After the last time, he wasn't so sure he should be doing this, but they were a long way away from his bedroom. And by the time they got home, Robin's foot would be dry and she could go in under her own steam. "No," he muttered as he shouldered open the swinging glass door. Liar, he told himself.

Coward! Now would be a good time to talk about what they were going to do about their broken vow of celibacy. But with Robin in his arms, there was no way he could think of anything but her. And celibacy had nothing to do with it.

And he'd thought he'd have a restful few days off before the fall term began.

"I think," Robin said, with more confidence than she really felt, "that I'll just call the Lees with men's names. And initials. That ought to narrow it down some."

"And what do you plan to say when you disturb all these people? You're not going to ask them about the body, are you?"

Robin shook her head patiently. Did he think she was a complete idiot? "No. I'll just ask if Robin is there, and whoever answers will probably tell me it's a wrong number." She slapped her hands together, as if dusting them off. "I'll apologize, and that will be the end of it. We can mark that name off the list."

T.J. let out a deep breath. "That could work. But it's gonna take the rest of the day."

Robin shrugged. "I have plenty of time. And so do you, I might add. Or do you have something better to do?"

"No," T.J. agreed grudgingly. "But I could certainly find something else to do that would be more fun, if I thought about it hard enough."

"Maybe we'll get lucky and hit the right Lee on the first try. Then you can play." Robin reached for a yellow high-lighting pen from amid T.J.'s study paraphernalia and collected the phone book. Then she settled down on the floor by the phone. "Here goes." She picked up the receiver.

"I still don't know what you're going to do if you do find somebody who knows Robin."

"Stop hovering over me! If you don't want to do this, go outside." She made a shooing motion with her hand, then dialed.

T.J. started to say something, but Robin waved him off. "Hush. It's ringing.

"Hi. Is Robin home?" She listened a moment, then murmured an apology and depressed the disconnect button. "One down," she told T.J. and drew a yellow line through A. C. Lee's name.

She watched T.J. out of the corner of her eye as she dialed the next number. She knew he disapproved of what she was doing; the way he had his arms crossed over his chest showed that as well as his discouraging words had. But this was something she had to do.

The phone rang ten times before Robin gave up and put down the receiver. "I guess nobody's home." She picked another number.

"Cross that one off the list," T.J. ordered from his position on the sofa.

Robin sighed and looked up at T.J. "I didn't get an answer, so I'll have to call them again later. That might be the very one."

T.J. made a face, but he didn't say anything. Robin dialed again.

It was well past dinnertime by the time Robin had reached the lower level of the first column, and it was obvious to T.J. that she was discouraged, tired, and not a little hoarse. But he wasn't about to say, "I told you so." Not in a million years.

So far, all she'd gotten were wrong numbers and endless strings of unanswered rings. She'd give up soon. T.J. was sure of it. Surely she was as hungry as he. If glancing constantly at the clock wasn't hint enough, his grumbling stomach confirmed his impatience. If she wouldn't quit because she was hungry, she'd have to stop anyway before long. Her voice wasn't going to hold out much longer.

Robin dialed yet another number, listened to it ring and cleared her throat. "Hi, is Robin there?" Her eyes widened, and she beckoned to him frantically to come and listen.

T.J. launched himself up off the couch and hurried across to where Robin still sat cross-legged on the floor. He lowered himself down beside her and bent his head toward the earpiece. He could barely hear what sounded like an elderly person.

"No, ma'am," Robin murmured. "I'll call back later." She placed the receiver carefully on the hook. Then she clenched her fists and shook them in a gesture of excitement. "I think I just hit pay dirt!"

His stomach grumbled, and T.J. wondered what was more important at that moment. Food, or learning what Robin had just discovered. Reluctantly he settled on the latter. "How do you know?"

"When I asked for Robin, she said she was out of town and she didn't know when she'd be back. Called her Robbie." She looked hopefully up at T.J. "You know, she didn't sound upset or anything, but the connection was bad. I could barely hear. Do you think she really believes that Robin is out of town?"

T.J. stroked his chin, fingering the nick, healing now, that Robin had caused just the other day. "It could be. Some people aren't very conscientious about checking in with their loved ones when they're away." He looked pointedly at Robin.

She grasped the unspoken suggestion. "Look, T.J. I was out of the country, at an isolated dig, in a remote area. I didn't have a phone by my bed or a mailbox on the corner." She pushed herself to her feet, grimacing as muscles cramped from sitting on the floor protested. "Oh, I remembered something else. She wanted to know if I was calling about the ad about the shotgun. I probably should have pursued that." She stood, shaking the kinks out of her legs, and looked thoughtfully off into the distance. "Wasn't the dead woman killed with a shotgun?"

"I hardly think that someone would be advertising in the paper about a shotgun if it had been used in a crime."

"But maybe there was a gun that had gone missing about the time of the death. We have to find out."

"We?" T.J. asked, knowing full well what she meant. He blew out an exasperated breath. "If you'd just sent a couple of postcards to your friends after Robin's body turned up, you would not be in this mess." *We* would not be in the mess, was what he really meant. And they would never have met, he realized suddenly. And just as suddenly he realized that he would have missed out on her. If nothing else, Robin had been the one to start him living again. And even if their "fling" went nowhere, it would still be an important milestone for him.

"Yeah, and every Monday-morning quarterback knows how to win the game. I don't want to talk about this now. I'm starved. Now that I have money, how about I treat you to fast food on the way to Robin's house?"

T.J. was so interested in the food part of Robin's statement that he almost didn't hear the rest. When it registered, he groaned. He should have known that she wouldn't leave it alone.

Robin and T.J. sat inside the brightly lit hamburger place, finishing their dinner of burgers and fries. The place was oddly deserted for this time of night, but then, most of the college kids were away on summer break and wouldn't return till next week. The emptiness of the place afforded them the privacy they needed to speculate on the information they had found out that day.

"You know, I think that shotgun is the key to all this," Robin told T.J. between bites of cheeseburger. She stopped to think as she chewed.

"More than just being the murder weapon?" T.J. popped his last bite of hamburger into his mouth and crumpled the paper wrapping.

"Well, yeah." Robin dipped her fry into a puddle of ketchup. "The ad in the paper."

"Robin, you don't even know what the ad was about. They could have been advertising to buy a gun." He took the french fry Robin had just doctored and put it in his mouth.

"Hey. I wanted that." Robin prepared another one and ate it before T.J. could get to it. She picked up another fry and brandished it at T.J. as she would a pointer. "Too bad we don't know what's in the ad."

"I know one way to find that out," T.J. told her as she popped the naked fry into her mouth. He jerked his head toward the plate-glass window. "There's a newspaper stand out there. We'll see if the ad's in today's paper." He snagged some of the loose change off Robin's tray and hoisted himself out of the booth.

"Good idea," Robin said, her mouth full. "That way I can finish my fries without your help." She watched as he headed for the door, then bent to take a sip of her soda. She had to admit that T.J. was one fine specimen of a man. Even with the scar. Too bad they'd made that stupid agreement about keeping it platonic. Even though they'd already strayed from their good intentions once, she knew it should never happen again.

But she couldn't help thinking about it. That platonic thing was one bright idea she wished she hadn't had.

"Here it is," T.J. announced. He folded the paper into a compact rectangle and pushed it toward Robin. Then he tapped his finger on the spot.

Robin took the paper from him and turned it around to face her. She scanned the terse description, a frown marring the smooth lines of her forehead. "That doesn't look very sinister, does it?"

"Did you expect it to?"

"Not really. But this is odd." She tapped the ad with the tip of one of her remaining fries. "She doesn't want to sell a gun, she wants to buy one she sold by mistake. I wonder what that's all about?"

"Who knows? Maybe Mrs. Lee had a garage sale and sold a gun. One that Mr. Lee didn't want to part with." T.J. drained his soda glass. "You know how women are. They get this wild idea about cleaning closets and having a garage sale, and everything goes."

Robin whacked him with the paper. "Your male chauvinism is showing. Maybe Mr. Lee sold Mrs. Lee's gun."

She had a point there, but T.J. wasn't about to admit it. He was sick of all that politically correct garbage. What he was talking about had nothing to do with male bias or anything else. It was human nature, pure and simple. But he knew better than to tell Robin that. "I guess the only way to find out is to go see them." He pushed himself up out of the booth again. "I'll call and ask about the gun."

"But we don't have one to show her," Robin pointed out logically.

"I know, but we can say we thought she was selling." He shrugged. "Anyway, it'll get us into the house. You got any better ideas?"

"No," Robin answered in a small voice. Though T.J. enjoyed hearing her concede defeat, the triumph he felt was just a little bit hollow. He wondered why as he made his way to the pay phone in the corner.

Mrs. Lee's house was old, as Robin had expected, but it appeared to be well-cared for. It was in a long-established part of Tuscaloosa, where the streets were wide and shaded by trees that were as old as, if not older than, the houses they sheltered. She studied the Victorian-style house, with its porches and gingerbread trim. "It's a cute little house," Robin commented, half out loud, as T.J. angled the car into the curb. "You wouldn't think that anybody who lived here would be involved in anything so awful."

"We don't know that they've done anything, Robin," T.J. reminded her. "All we know for sure is that somebody in the house wants a particular type of gun that they sold by mistake." He shut off the lights, pulled the key out of the ignition and pushed open the door. "This could be nothing but a giant wild-goose chase."

Robin scrambled out behind T.J. and followed his sure strides up the sidewalks. The edges were neatly trimmed, the lawn was cut, and flowers abounded in the tidy beds that edged the front porch. She had a very sneaky feeling that this visit would lead to nothing. But they had to try.

T.J. rang the illuminated bell button and lifted the big brass knocker for good measure.

A light in the front hall went on, illuminating a lovely set of stained-glass windows that flanked the door. In another minute the door flew open, and there stood a tiny old woman, silhouetted in the doorway. "You didn't need to beat the door down, young man. My eyesight may be gone, but I can still hear." She softened the querulous statement with a merry grin. "Why don't you all come in? It is still hot as day outside."

"Thank you," Robin murmured, and followed the sprightly old lady inside.

"You know, I fought getting this air put in for years, but now that I have it, I couldn't live a minute without it." She led them into a quaint old parlor, just like something you'd read about in a Victorian novel.

"This is such a lovely room, Mrs. Lee. It looks so comfortable." And it did, with its big overstuffed chairs. Even the white lace antimacassars did more to make the room look inviting than to warn her away.

"Oh." The lady laughed, a merry tinkling laugh. "It isn't Mrs. Lee. It's Miss." She shook her head. "I finally unpacked my old hope chest and used the goods I had put aside. It was plain I wasn't going to get asked, and I surely wasn't getting any younger."

"Well, Miz Lee, I'm sure you must have had dozens of suitors. And it was their loss that one didn't offer for your hand," T.J. told her gallantly as he sank into one of the huge old chairs.

Miss Lee laughed. "You do go on. But I must admit that I had my share of gentlemen callers. Mother told me I was being too choosy, and I reckon she was right, because they finally stopped coming around."

T.J. cleared his throat. "Now, Miz Lee, about the gun."

"Please call me Dora. I know, I'm old-fashioned, but I just can't abide being called Miz. It makes me think of all those women burning their unmentionables. I'm an old maid, and a fancy new name won't make it not so." She looked over her glasses at T.J. "You didn't bring it with you?"

Suddenly Robin felt guilty about imposing on this sweet old lady under false pretenses. She started to say something, but T.J. answered.

"I'm sorry. Did I misunderstand you? I thought I understood that you had a gun to sell." How T.J. could lie to that woman without so much as batting an eyelash, Robin didn't know. But she had to admire the skill with which he did it.

Dora seemed to shrink in size as she slumped in her chair. "Oh, I had so hoped that you had the shotgun I was looking for." She sighed a delicate, ladylike sigh behind her hand. "I had hoped that you would have it, and Robbie could stop being angry at me." She smiled sadly. "You see, I sold an old gun of his and he threw such a fit about it. I thought I'd best try to get it back."

"Robbie is angry with you because you sold his gun?" Robin leaned forward in the chair, waiting for the answer. *And how long has it been since you last saw her?* she wished she could ask.

"That boy, you'd think I'd sold a pot of gold out from under him. It was just a rusty old shotgun."

Miss Lee went on to explain what had happened, but Robin really didn't hear what she had to say. She was too fixated on the fact that she had called Robbie a boy. He couldn't have been the murder victim. They were back to square one. And had wasted a lot of time getting there.

Robin pushed herself up. "I'm sorry we took up your time, Miz L—I mean, Dora."

"Pooh," Dora responded. "I don't hardly see anybody

anymore. It's nice to be able to talk to such a nice young couple. You two be good to each other now. I'm so very happy that you don't have to end up old and crotchety and alone like me.'' She pushed herself agilely up from her seat and escorted them to the door.

T.J. offered Dora his hand, and she took it, and giggled when he raised it to his lips. ''Why, Miz Dora, it was a pleasure meeting you. If I had met you a few years sooner, we could really have had us a time together.''

Robin had a few comments to make about T.J.'s shameless flirting, but she'd have to hold it till they got to the car. She waited until he and Dora quit drooling over each other and then followed them out to the porch.

Another car, an ancient light blue Pinto, had pulled up to the house while they were inside, and a seedy-looking young man was making his way up the walk.

''Oh, it's my nephew, home early. Robbie, come meet these nice people.''

Robbie, it appeared, was in no mood to be sociable, for he brushed past them, muttering what could have passed for a greeting and trailing the sour smell of stale alcohol and something more pungent. Robin made an effort to ignore the young man's rudeness and turned to Dora Lee. She took the elderly woman's hand. ''Thank you so much for being so nice to us. I'm sorry we couldn't help you locate your gun.''

''Thank you,'' Dora replied in return. ''I enjoyed having you. Please drop by anytime. I love entertaining. Lord knows I don't get to much anymore.'' She inclined her head toward the door Robbie had disappeared behind. ''Robbie and I don't seem to enjoy the same kind of people.''

She let out a long-suffering sigh. ''But what can I do? He's my only brother's—may he rest in peace—youngest boy. And he does need some guidance from time to time. I do what I can.''

''Well, thank you again. We have to go,'' Robin mur-

mured, withdrawing her hand from Dora's birdlike grip.
She felt T.J.'s hand on the small of her back, firm and sure,
guiding her away from Miss Dora. Grateful, and regretful
at the same time that she'd left such an obviously lonely
old lady in Robbie's dubious company, she followed him
down the steps.

As soon as the door closed behind Miss Lee, Robin muttered under her breath. "Did you get a load of Robbie Lee?
He smelled like a brewery. And he looked like somebody
you'd find on a wanted poster."

"That wasn't all he smelled like," T.J. added tersely.
"Get in the car." He yanked open his door and all but
shoved Robin in behind the steering wheel.

"What was it?" Robin scrambled across the seat, already
pretty certain how T.J. would respond.

"He reeked of marijuana," he confirmed as he slid in
beside her. "But I have no way of telling whether he had
been smoking it, or just hanging around somebody else who
had." He slammed his door shut and jammed the key into
the ignition.

"I'll have to take your word for it, T.J." That was one
thing Robin knew nothing about, but she wondered how it
was that T.J. knew as he switched on the lights and pulled
out into the road. But he had been a cop. She supposed
they would have to know.

"Well, that was a waste of time," T.J. muttered as he
climbed the steps to the apartment. "I can see no way to
connect Robbie Lee with Robin Lee Digby, except by the
similarity of their names." He unlocked the front door.
"He may be a dirtbag, but I don't think he's our suspect."
He rolled his eyes as he turned the knob. Robin had really
done a number on him. She had him talking like some sort
of paperback-novel cop. And he didn't like it one bit.

"Don't you think we should report him to the authorities? Pot is still illegal in Alabama, you know." Robin followed him inside.

"The police force is not going to waste their time running in some two-bit druggie who hasn't otherwise done anything wrong. We didn't see him smoking the stuff. We didn't see any of the stuff on him. You're going to have to give him the benefit of the doubt." T.J. tried to convince himself that he was right in discouraging Robin from pursuing it, but the thought of that lovely, genteel old woman and that…slime didn't set well with him.

He looked up from his thoughts to see Robin flipping through the phone book. Not again. "Can't you give it a rest? At least until tomorrow?"

Robin didn't seem to hear him. "They could have an unlisted number," she mused. She closed her eyes for a moment, then opened them wide as a thought struck. "It doesn't have to be an unlisted number. It could be a new listing."

She held up the phone book and pointed to the date in the lower left corner. "See? It was published in December. There've been almost nine months for new Digbys to move into the area."

"Who? Don't you have enough listed numbers to contend with for now?" Why couldn't the woman just let it rest? T.J. resisted the urge to go and take the phone book out of her hands and put her to bed. His bed. The rogue thought flashed into his mind, but he dismissed it as quickly as it had come. He had no business thinking such thoughts. He had made a promise. A promise he had already proved he couldn't keep.

"Just let me check this one thing, and I'll give up for now." No longer needing the book, Robin reached for the phone.

"You don't think it's as simple as calling directory assistance?" T.J. groaned. "I'm sure the Tuscaloosa police have already done that.'' He ran his fingers through his hair and followed Robin to the phone.

''The police picked my name out of the phone book and stopped looking once Dub stepped into the picture. I think it's very unlikely that they looked any further.'' Robin ignored T.J. and dialed directory assistance.

''I bet you won't find anything.''

Robin covered the mouthpiece. ''Bet I will. It's ringing.'' She removed her hand and affected a girlish tone. ''Yes, ma'am. My name is Eloise Digby, and I'm just starting as a freshman at the university. I have an uncle who lives here in town, and my mom suggested I give him a call once I got settled in. But I've lost the number. Can you help me out?'' Robin made a face at the way she had aped the voice and mannerisms of a flighty young woman.

She listened as the operator spoke.

''Yes, ma'am. He's my uncle Buster.'' Robin smiled mischievously. ''Digby. No, I don't know his first name. I thought it was Buster.'' She forced a giggle.

Robin waited for an answer while T.J. watched her, a bemused expression on his face.

The operator must have given her a listing, because Robin told her, ''No, ma'am. I already tried that one. It's some cranky old lady. My uncle Buster just moved here a few months ago. Is there another place to look for new numbers?'' She grinned at T.J., who made a thumbs-up sign.

''Herman R. Digby on Martin Lane. Yes, ma'am. That sounds like it.'' Robin copied the number and the address. ''No wonder they call him Buster,'' she added. ''Thank you, ma'am.'' She hung up.

T.J. looked at Robin with renewed admiration and just a little concern. He was constantly amazed at how resourceful she could be, but he tried to temper his elation. Robin was an amateur playing detective, and things could always backfire. "Okay, so you got a listing for another Digby. Who says it's the one you're looking for?"

"It might not be, but I know how we can find out." Robin picked up the phone receiver she had just put down.

"What are you going to do?"

Chapter 16

"I'm going to call Mr. Digby and ask him a few pointed questions," Robin explained, as if it were the most logical conclusion in the world.

"Do you know what you're doing?" T.J. crossed the room to stand by Robin as she dialed.

"So far I do. When I don't, I'll play it by ear."

T.J. watched as Robin dialed. He knew he would have done much the same thing when he was a cop, but Robin wasn't a policeman. She could easily get in over her head.

"Hi. This is Cherry Mims. I'm an old friend of Robin's from school." Robin's voice sounded almost too bright and cheerful. "I'm just passing through town and thought I'd give my old friend a call. Is she home?"

Robin covered the mouthpiece. "He's not saying anything." She removed her hand. "I'm sorry to hear that. No, she can't call me back—I'm just passing through. I'm at the Dairy Den on the highway. I'm sorry I missed her." Robin hung up the phone.

"I think that's Robin's number."

"What makes you so sure?"

"When I asked to speak to her, the man who answered didn't say anything. You know, like he didn't know what to say. But I could almost hear the cogs turning in his head."

"Then he came up with an excuse for Robin not being there," T.J. concluded.

"Yeah. He said she was out of town, and he wasn't sure when she'd be back." Robin made a wry face. "Mine wasn't much of a marriage, but I can't see any husband just letting his wife run off to who knows where without knowing exactly when she'd be back."

T.J. remembered his own marriage. "I certainly would expect my wife to let me know her plans." It took him a moment to realize that he'd been able to remember Ginger without the pain and guilt that had so tormented him.

"So. He must be our guy."

"Maybe," T.J. agreed grudgingly.

"I sure would like to get a look at him."

"Robin, you're not Kinsey Millhone," T.J. said, remembering the paperback mystery Robin had been reading.

"I know," she replied. She brushed a wayward strand of blond hair from her face. "I'll be careful."

"I don't think this is a good idea," T.J. grumbled. But he could already tell that his warning would go unheeded. If Robin was that intent on visiting Herman Digby, he'd have to go with her.

"But you will wait until tomorrow," he told her firmly, fully expecting her to protest.

"Yes, Mr. Swift. I'll wait until the morning. I would like to be on my toes when I go to meet with a possible killer." She cleared her raspy throat. "And maybe my voice will have recovered by then."

He didn't like the way she had described this Digby person, but at least she was going to wait until tomorrow to do anything. Maybe, just maybe, he could talk her out of it by then. In the meantime, it'd been a long day. He stretched and yawned and headed for his bed.

The problem was that he'd be alone. After last night, he didn't think he'd be able to sleep alone. But he didn't know how Robin felt about it. He'd intended to talk to her about what happened, but he'd sabotaged his plans by bringing up the pry marks on the door.

Was Robin feeling the same alone in her room across the hall?

The next morning, Robin sat on the edge of the tub and blew a strand of oversprayed hair away from her forehead. She had scrubbed at the black smudge on the bottom of her foot until her skin tingled, but the ink, though lighter, still remained. But the good thing was that Lightfoot would soon have his answer. She had wanted to attack the stain with nail polish remover, as she had after the fingerprinting session, but she hadn't taken the time. Now it appeared that the stain would be there until it wore off. She shrugged and tugged on her stockings; the bottom of her foot wasn't going to show, anyway.

The white heels and nylons were not what Robin would have chosen to wear on a hot late-August afternoon, but were necessary for the image she was trying to project. She carefully lined her lips and filled them in with the rose-colored lipstick she had chosen out of her sample case. It wasn't her color, but it would do. Blotting her mouth with a tissue, Robin stepped back to survey the finished look.

"Not bad," she murmured as she fluffed a wayward strand of the teased and sprayed hair back into place. It made her look as if she were wearing a blond helmet, and she certainly didn't look anything like she usually looked. Maybe having to supplement her teacher's salary selling cosmetics had been worth it, after all. "Not bad. Not bad at all."

If nothing else, selling makeup had taught her what not

to do. She had used all the wrong colors and wrong techniques, and she looked her very worst. And that was good, for now.

Robin gathered her cosmetic case and the purse that matched her shoes and turned off the light over the shaving mirror. "Let's see what T.J. thinks about this getup," she said to her image in the mirror. Then she left the room.

T.J. was sitting on the sofa with a ragged city map stretched out on the coffee table in front of him. "I think I've found the street," he said, without looking up. "It's in the Alberta neighborhood."

"Good. Isn't that close to where the body was found?"

"Not too far," T.J. replied absently. He continued poring over the map, paying absolutely no attention to Robin.

Annoyed that T.J. hadn't bothered to pry his face away from the map, Robin cleared her throat. "How do I look?" It wasn't subtle, but at least it got his attention.

T.J. placed a long, tanned finger on the map to mark the spot and glanced up.

"Well?" Robin asked, without giving T.J. a chance to comment. "Do I look like your average door-to-door cosmetic lady?" She struck a pose and smiled like a television spokesmodel.

"Is that what you're supposed to be?"

Robin's smile dimmed. "Yes. What's wrong with it?"

T.J. laughed. "Nothing, now that I know the reason for the Halloween getup. The makeup doesn't do it for me."

"It is a disguise, T.J. I don't want him to be able to recognize me."

"Or point you out in a lineup later," T.J. added dryly.

"Very funny, Mr. Swift." Robin made a face at him. Then she wriggled her mouth from side to side, flexing her cheeks. "I had forgotten how confining all this stuff is in this weather. It's positively claustrophobic. Are you ready to go? I don't know how long I'll be able to stand all this pancake."

* * *

Alberta had recently found favor with the younger generation, and the attention showed. Interspersed among the aging, faded fifties-era houses with overgrown yards was a collection of newly refurbished homes with manicured lawns. Even the shabbier homes showed signs of renewed interest.

T.J. turned the car onto Digby's street, where the house in question sat between two extremes. The house on the left looked neglected and shabby; the one on the right was a shining finished product. Digby's stood somewhere in the middle.

The trim had been painted and flowers had been planted, but the plants stood drooping in the sun, and weeds were taking over the small patch of cleared ground. A ladder leaned against one wall, as if waiting for the painter to return. It looked as though someone had started the improvement project and not gotten around to finishing.

"I don't know how I let you get me into this," T.J. muttered through tightly set jaws as he cruised the neighborhood for the third time. "I think if we drive down this street one more time, the neighbors will get suspicious."

Robin patted his clenched jaw. "It's only been three times, and it doesn't look like many people are at home."

"I'm going to park around the corner," T.J. said as he steered the car around the block one last time. "I'm still not sure about this," he grumbled. What had he been thinking about when he agreed to go along with Robin's scheme to impersonate a cosmetics peddler to get a look at Digby?

Her safety, he reminded himself. Robin would have done it anyway. And at least this way he'd be nearby to help. Robin wasn't trained for this, and she could get into trouble.

T.J. eased up to the curb. He almost decided to drive on, but Robin pushed the handle and the door creaked open. Resignedly he let her go. Maybe Digby wouldn't be home, he hoped. But the blue car in the driveway told him otherwise.

"It's okay, T.J. I'll be fine. I did drama all the way through high school and college."

"This is not a school play, and it's not your acting ability I'm worried about," T.J. replied grimly as he watched Robin swing her slender, well-shaped legs out of the car. "It's Digby I'm thinking of. He doesn't have the same script as you. We don't know anything about him. He could be a raving lunatic. You don't have any experience with self-defense." He tried not to think about any other reasons.

"I wrestled my way out of the back seat of a car a few times," Robin told him flippantly. "Besides, he sounded absolutely normal over the phone."

"That doesn't prove anything. So did Ted Bundy."

"I'll be very careful. I'm not trying to make a citizen's arrest—I just want to get a look at the guy." Robin stood up and smoothed the lines of the mint-colored summer suit she wore.

"Don't take any chances."

"Wouldn't dream of it." Robin leaned back into the car and gave T.J. a light peck on the cheek. "For luck," she explained as he reached up to touch the spot.

The kiss had been unexpected and distracting, which was probably what Robin had intended. By the time T.J. had recovered from the suddenness of it, Robin was already at the corner.

Cool it, T.J. told himself as he watched Robin stroll confidently up the walk. Just pretend this is a routine surveillance. You've done it a hundred times.

It almost worked. Until Robin got to the first house and rang the bell.

T.J. uttered a curse and started to swing out of the car and go after her. He thought better of it as he reached for the door handle. Apparently nobody was home. Robin took something from her purse and wedged it into the gap be-

tween the screen and the door, then turned around and
traced her steps back up the walk. She continued on to the
next house, the one that sat next to Digby's. Then T.J.
realized what she was doing.

If Robin was going to carry off the appearance of being
a door-to-door saleslady, she was going to have to go door-
to-door. T.J. settled back in his seat as Robin repeated her
performance at the second house. He had to admire her
resourcefulness. He hadn't thought to do it, and he was the
one with professional training.

Robin headed for the next house. Except for the recent
neglect, it looked ordinary enough. The requisite minivan
sat in the shady carport, and a battered and ancient light
blue Honda sat at the curb. He'd bet the woman of the
house used the van.

The uneasiness that T.J. had almost succeeded in
squelching returned with the speed of an out-of-control
train when Robin knocked on Digby's front door.

She had promised that she wouldn't go inside. But there
she was, big as life, smiling at the man who answered and
following him in! T.J. gripped the steering wheel in anger
and frustration. How could he have agreed to this?

Without waiting to think, T.J. turned the key in the ignition and steered the car around the corner to Digby's
place. He maneuvered the car around to a position across
the street, facing the house. He knew it was premature to
go dashing to the rescue, but he needed to be close enough
to see or hear.

Robin was inside the house all of five minutes, but to
T.J. they seemed like the longest minutes of his life. His
breath caught when he saw her reappear on the step, apparently unharmed. He signaled for her to get in the car,
but Robin didn't respond.

She purposefully strode down the sidewalk and turned
away down the street. As she walked parallel to the car,

she signaled slightly with the hand that faced away from the house. The gesture said, "Let's play this out."

It made sense, and T.J. had no choice but to watch. He could hardly drag her into the car off the sidewalk. That was no way to keep her undercover. He watched helplessly as Robin walked up a toy-littered flagstone walk to the next house. If she followed the pattern, she would spend a brief moment at the door and move on.

T.J. glanced at Digby's house. He saw no one, but the slight movement of a curtain behind a closed window, where there ought to have been no breeze stirring, suggested that someone was watching.

Robin appeared to be deep in conversation with a young woman at the house next door by the time his gaze rested on her again. Was she simply chatting with an overfriendly and bored housewife, or was she still playing detective? He knew what the answer was.

The fluttering curtain at Digby's front window still bothered T.J. and reminded him that his parked position across the street was ill-advised. Reluctantly he started his engine and pulled away from the curb. To make a U-turn in the middle of the street would be too obvious. He'd have to circle the block to get close enough to pick Robin up.

Robin couldn't sell cosmetics she didn't have, but she quickly concocted a scheme where she was taking a survey. She asked a few questions and hit paydirt when she mentioned that she'd called on the lady next door who was apparently out of town.

"She and I used to go garage-sale shopping together," the young woman volunteered.

The garage-sale element was a link she felt she should explore, so Robin went on with her. "Oh, you haven't been out lately?"

"Well, Robin and I haven't. She's been out of town for a few weeks." She stopped to consider. "It could be longer. I didn't think to mark it on a calendar or anything. It was really odd, though,'' she went on to explain. "We had planned to go out that particular Saturday, but when I stopped to pick her up, her husband said that she'd been called out of town suddenly. Something about a sick relative in Arizona.''

"That's too bad. I guess it must be hard to get out with a little one to chase after.'' The story the woman repeated was close to the one Digby had given her the night before. Today he hadn't been so forthcoming. He'd acted as if she'd be back anytime.

"I'll say. Robin used to be a big help with Jason here. She said she was practicing for her own. She and Hank have been trying to have a baby.'' She smiled benevolently down at the toddler playing in the yard. "We were real lucky the last time we went shopping. My husband stayed home with Jase, and we were able to shop child-free.

"That was the day she bought the shotgun.''

Robin had been only half listening, but the mention of the gun got her attention. "Do you remember where you got it?'' Maybe that sounded too eager, but she couldn't think of any other way to work the question into the conversation.

"I'm not sure. Robin drove that day. But I do remember being in an older part of town—Victorian houses, I think. And there was such a sweet old lady there.''

It had to be Dora Lee. Now all Robin had to do was figure out how to escape and tell T.J. what she had discovered.

The woman was still talking to Robin when T.J. finished his circuit of the block. It was obvious that Robin was trying to get away, and it was also apparent that the woman was reluctant to release her. There was nothing sinister about the woman's attentions, however. The scattered litter of toys assured him of that.

He remembered how Ginger had yearned for adult company when Rusty was small and she was held hostage all day in a child's world. She'd complained that her mind was going to waste and insisted that she had to exercise hers or lose it. So, in spite of his objections, Ginger had gone back to work when Rusty was old enough to go to nursery school.

A pang of regret came and went as he thought about it. If Ginger hadn't gone back to work, she might be alive today. A ray of realization dawned. This was the first time that T.J. had been able to assign even the slightest part of the blame for her death on someone or something other than himself. After all, a complex collection of circumstances had led to her death, not just his negligence. T.J. drew in a deep breath and tightened his grip on the wheel.

Was this the beginning of healing? He had spent so much time consumed by his guilt over failing to keep his wife and child from harm that he felt empty without it. Yet it was not the same hollow emptiness he'd felt in the past when thinking about his family. Maybe *emptiness* was not the right word. But there was still a void.

Realizing that he was being derelict in his duty to watch out for Robin, T.J. banished the puzzling new emotions that were seeping into his awareness. His primary challenge now was to provide protection for this woman. To keep her safe. He had to succeed this time.

All he could see was a cluttered yard and a flagstone walk lined with shrubs.

The fat yellow tiger cat had planted her chubby body right in the middle of the cluttered flagstones, and Robin couldn't resist the urge to stop and pet her. She stooped down and rubbed her furry head. Rewarded with the deep rumble of the animal's idling engine, Robin lingered over that comforting sound a moment longer than necessary.

In typical catlike fashion, the striped animal allowed

Robin to stroke her until she'd had her fill of human attention, then got up and ambled off. Robin straightened and watched the cat's meandering progress across the lawn until she settled into a shady nook in a clump of shrubbery.

Chatty Kathy, as Robin had privately dubbed the housewife, had told her that the neighbors in the house Robin was approaching were seldom home. That made Robin's job easier. She could stroll up the walk, knock, then, for appearances' sake, leave a card as she had before. It would be conveniently blown away in the wind, and nobody would be the wiser for it. Robin didn't have a card to leave, but she would come up with something.

She'd hated lying about the survey to Kathy, but she had dutifully jotted down several comments about current issues on a steno pad from her purse. If the woman suspected Robin was an impostor, she hadn't shown it. She'd been too eager for adult conversation to question Robin's motives.

Robin rang the bell of the remaining house on the block and waited for no one to answer. She knew that T.J. was probably having a conniption by now, and she wanted to hurry. Not because she was alarmed or concerned about her safety, but because she was about to suffocate in the heavy makeup. And she wanted to tell T.J. what she had found.

As expected, no one was at home. So Robin scrounged for another old pizza coupon in her purse and propped it up on the knob. She turned and walked briskly down the walk.

T.J. had situated the car just around the corner, and Robin hurried toward it. She could tell by the way he drummed his fingers against the wheel that he was not amused by her unplanned improvisation. But she was too elated by what she had discovered to care.

She tugged open the car door and slid inside. "Guess what I found out!" she began. "Robin Digby bought a shotgun at a gar—'' Her excitement faded instantly as rough hands grabbed her wrist and yanked her across the seat.

T.J. felt two conflicting urges as Robin slid into his waiting grasp. The first was to kiss her. The second was to wring her pretty neck.

He settled on the former.

He pulled her in so roughly that Robin didn't close the door. T.J. didn't care. He snatched her angrily toward him and crushed her against his chest.

Robin struggled at first, but quickly settled, though she still breathed in ragged gasps and her heart pounded against his. T.J. regretted alarming her, but she had scared the hell out of him, and he would make her pay. As soon as her frightened heart began to beat more slowly against his own pounding chest, he eased back and looked into her blue eyes.

"Don't ever pull a stunt like that again," he demanded, his words raspy and hoarse.

Before Robin could utter a word in response or an excuse, he stopped her. Before she could open her mouth to protest, T.J. covered her lips with his.

The kiss had only been intended to be brief, but as their lips met, it became something else. The moment they touched, something happened. It was as if someone had opened a circuit between them and reignited the passion they had managed to ignore for the past thirty-six hours. T.J.'s blood surged with electric desire, and his senses were heightened. Once again, he felt more than merely alive. He felt the all-too-familiar tightening in his groin.

And then he remembered that they'd agreed that it could never happen again. Or had they? They'd agreed it could never happen at all when they'd agreed to share the apartment as friends only. They had talked all around what had really been bothering them yesterday. In fact, they hadn't talked about it at all.

Robin didn't struggle, but let him crush her with his bruising passion. She gave him nothing, but allowed him to take. As his anger diminished, she began to respond, parting her lips to receive his discovering tongue. Her tongue darted out to meet his, nearly sending him over the edge. What T.J. had intended to take, Robin offered freely.

T.J. groaned. This was not the place to be necking like a couple of teenagers with only a steering wheel between their eager bodies to keep them honest. He dragged his lips away from hers and ran his fingers through his hair. He turned toward the front of the car and stared through the windshield.

"Close the door," he found himself saying with surprising calm. As Robin stretched to comply, he felt that he had to make it right. He'd promised to keep their relationship platonic, for God's sake. "I didn't mean for this to happen."

Robin touched a gentle finger to T.J.'s still-yearning lips. "Don't," she whispered huskily. "I wanted it, too."

Chapter 17

Robin couldn't believe she'd admitted that to T.J. And she'd been the one who insisted they would have to keep their relationship platonic. After their megamistake of the other night, she just didn't know anymore. If their little apartment-sharing experiment was going to work, they were going to have to clear the air. But for now...

How could she be so inconsistent?

Robin directed a sidelong glance at the man driving the car. That was why. T.J. He was strong and kind, and moody and silent. And as needy as she was, in his own way. Even with his mouth set, grim and angry, he was too appealing to ignore.

They were some pair.

No, she told herself silently, punctuating her thought by balling her fist and slamming her thigh. She was not going to spoil her plans, not yet. She wasn't the first woman to be distracted by a set of well-developed muscles. Nor would she be the last. This would be the last time for her, though for now, she wouldn't spoil the moment.

No, no, no. The fist pounded again and again. What was the matter with her?

"Is something wrong?" T.J. asked without removing his eyes from the road.

Grateful that his gaze was not on her, Robin lied. "No. I just got a cramp. I haven't worn heels in a long time," she told him, relieved that he couldn't see the falsehood on her face.

"We're almost home. Maybe a hot bath would help."

"What?" What was he talking about? A hot bath in this ninety-plus-degree heat? Robin had already forgotten the lie. "Oh, for the cramp. With this heat, a cool shower would be more likely." A cold shower!

T.J. said nothing as he parked the car. His jaw was set and his expression was still grim. He must really be angry, Robin realized as she swung her legs out of the car. She followed him up the apartment steps, belatedly remembering to affect a limp.

As soon as T.J. unlocked the door, Robin hurried past him to the bathroom. She hoped he was going to think that she was hurrying to take the bath he'd suggested. What she really needed was to get out of those clinging, hot nylons and heavy makeup. And she needed time alone to sort out her feelings and think.

How could she let a kiss destroy her resolve and all her plans? It wasn't even the first time he'd kissed her, but those other kisses had almost been jokes, compared to this one. He'd meant it—though maybe not at first—and Robin had meant it right back. Even if she hadn't intended to in the beginning. She wasn't a dewy-eyed virgin; she could have resisted. She had a mouth to say no with.

Robin stripped out of the hot nylon that clung to her legs and tried to work out her confused thoughts.

Just say no. It sounded good. *Just say no.* It looked good on paper. Yes, the theory was good, but would it hold up in practice? It hadn't seemed to work so far.

Robin scrubbed at the heavy makeup, smearing it with her urgent ministrations. She looked about for cold cream to make the job easier, but realized that she had left it in the cosmetic case in the other room. Damn, she'd have to make do with soap.

She wasn't going to face T.J. again until her skin was clear of paint and her mind free of confusion.

The paint part would be easy.

Strengthening her resolve to resist T.J.'s magnetic pull was going to be dauntingly harder. She realized that she was as drawn to him as iron filings were to a magnet. And had been since the moment she saw him sprawled across his research paper.

But she didn't want to abandon her plans just yet. Not after only one year. Revise them a little. Maybe. Make a small amendment. Change. That was it. Robin needed to be more flexible. Change was good.

T.J. swore as he slammed the phone receiver down. Not that his angry reaction made any difference. The deputy on the other end had already hung up. He'd forgotten how closemouthed public servants could be when they wanted to.

"Remind me to tread very carefully around here," came a soft voice from behind him.

T.J. turned around. Robin had just emerged from her shower, and stood glowing just inside the living room. She had scrubbed herself free of all the concealing makeup and stood there wearing another one of those overlarge summer dresses, pale yellow this time. There had been nothing wrong with the carefully made-up lady Robin had impersonated earlier, but T.J. definitely liked this one better.

"I didn't hear you," he replied slowly.

"Obviously. You were making an awful lot of noise. Want to talk about it?"

"Not really." T.J. crossed the room and sank wearily to

the couch. "I just had a damned frustrating conversation with the sheriff's department."

"Why?"

"I was going to let them know what we found out today."

Robin dropped her shoes and stockings and sank down onto the seat beside him. "What did they say when you told them?"

"I never got that far. I got such a damned runaround that I never told them a thing. I thought Gardner Lightfoot told you he'd keep you apprised of developments." T.J. ran a hand through his hair. His fingers made contact with the ridge of scar tissue, and he stopped. He'd been trying to break that lousy habit for years. Maybe running into that scar every time he messed with it would finally do it.

"Mr. Lightfoot promised to tell me. Kind of under the table, off the record. I don't think that applied to you," Robin reminded him.

T.J. uttered a curse. "Whatever happened to professional courtesy? Police departments used to share information." He got up and started to pace.

He'd called the sheriff's department in the first place to distract himself from that ill-advised, badly timed, wonderful kiss. God, that woman made him weak in the knees.

"But, T.J., you're not a policeman anymore. You're just an ordinary citizen like me," Robin told him gently.

Not like her. She was anything but ordinary.

"Damn them all," T.J. ranted. Damn Dub Doubleday for making her feel the way she does about involvement. Damn Herman Digby. Damn the head wound that had taken him away from the work he loved.

He swore again and strode to the door, angrily jerking it open.

"Where are you going?"

"Out." He didn't care where. He just needed space to think. And he didn't care how long it took. After years of trying to avoid feeling anything at all, he was suddenly overwhelmed with emotions. He had to clear his head. He needed to breathe.

He had to get away before he did something rash.

Long shadows were already marching relentlessly down the street, and T.J. had still not returned. At first, Robin had not been concerned, but as afternoon turned into evening, and evening leaned toward dark, she began to worry.

She had gone ahead and prepared supper, assuming that T.J. would be back by the time it was ready. The meat loaf had dried and the potatoes gone mushy before she stopped waiting. She dished out a scant serving and stared at the unpalatable lumps. She might as well throw the whole mess out, for she couldn't think about eating.

After dumping the cold and inedible dinner into the yawning mouth of the trash can, Robin switched on the television and tried to watch. She'd made at least five trips to the large front window before she gave up on TV, too. With nothing else to do, Robin dragged a kitchen chair to the window and prepared to watch all night, if need be.

It wasn't a long watch. As the fading vestiges of twilight disappeared into the dark, T.J. appeared across the street at the end of the block.

He was walking slowly, and the relaxed swing of his arms and the way he carried his shoulders proved that he had come to grips with his frustration. Robin couldn't see his face, but she would have bet he was smiling.

T.J. seemed to be walking in slow motion, and Robin's heart raced toward him in fast forward. If he didn't hurry, she would explode. Now that he had reappeared, apparently safe and sound, Robin wanted nothing better than to vent her irritation at him for worrying her so. And his languid pace only fueled her anger.

When he stopped to chat with a neighbor at the corner,

Robin could wait no more. She rushed out of the apartment and charged across the street.

T.J. saw it before Robin did. A parked car suddenly set into motion.

The car pulled out into the street, its driving lights off. T.J. stepped forward to signal the driver that his lights weren't on when he realized with abject certainty what was going to happen.

The car's trajectory had it aimed at precisely the spot where his and Robin's paths would intersect.

The doused lights were intentional!

Robin still hadn't noticed the car, but had hastened her step as she saw T.J. hurry forward. If she didn't stop, she would be directly in the automobile's path.

"Wait! Don't cross the street!" T.J. shouted. But Robin kept coming.

She stopped and looked at T.J. blankly, cupping her hand at her mouth, and called back. "I can't hear you over that car coming."

The car slowed down, as if allowing Robin to cross in front of it, and Robin started forward. But she had evidently noticed that the car was running dark. She turned, as if to motion to the driver, just as he flashed on the high-beam lights and accelerated. Robin was trapped in the headlights' blinding glare.

Adrenaline surged before T.J. had a chance to think, and he charged into the street. Heedless of his own safety, he made a tackle that would have been the envy of any varsity linebacker. Grabbing the stunned woman tightly in his arms, T.J. rolled them both out of harm's way.

Robin's heart thudded erratically as T.J. held her against his own rapidly heaving chest. He had evidently knocked the wind out of her, for she lay beneath him, struggling for air. T.J. tried to calm his own racing heartbeat as he drew in deep, calming breaths.

In the moments it took for Robin to breathe, slow realization came to T.J. *Somebody had figured out that they were on to him.* Just as they had found him, he had found them. He hadn't even had to work at it as hard as they had. All he'd had to do was to look in the phone book. He remembered the man who had tried to break in. Hell, he had probably already been there at least once.

The only question was, which one of the two suspects was it?

It was time to call in outside help.

Robin had caught her breath and found her voice. "What did you do that for?" she spluttered, pounding her fist against him. "And get off me."

He started to roll away, but something stopped him. He had almost lost someone who had in a few short days come to be very important to him. He didn't want to let go. Not now. Not ever.

"Let me up," Robin muttered, still struggling to roll free. "What do you think you're doing?"

T.J. groaned and sighed deeply. God help him, he was lost. He lowered his head to silence her indignant protestations.

"This" was all he said. He crushed his mouth hard against hers.

It struck her like a lightning bolt. What had happened and what was going to happen. As T.J. lowered his lips to hers, Robin recognized the danger she had been in. And was still in. *The near miss had not been an accident.* She clung to T.J.

His fierce kiss came as no surprise. And instead of fighting it, she melted into his protective embrace and yielded to his demanding lips. Her heart raced, and her breath caught again.

But not from fear.

* * *

They had to get out of the street, T.J. realized as he dragged his mouth away from Robin's trembling lips. She clung to him, trying to pull him back. God, he wanted to give in to her gentle demands. But they couldn't stay on the street. Not just because of his urgent desire for Robin, but because they were an easy target.

He hadn't seen him, but it had to have been the killer who was driving that blue compact car.

He looked around, but the speeding vehicle had disappeared.

"Robin, we have to go inside," he told her, his voice barely more than a hoarse whisper. He pushed himself up into a half crouch and looked around one more time, just to be sure.

"It's okay." T.J. rose carefully and offered his hand to Robin.

"That guy intentionally tried to run me down," Robin whimpered shakily as she scrambled to her feet.

"I think so, too," T.J. responded grimly. "Let's get inside. I don't like this. I don't like it at all."

"It was him, wasn't it? Should we report it?" Robin asked breathlessly as T.J. hustled her into the building.

The heavy door slammed behind them. "Yes. It's gone way too far now." T.J. took the steps to the second floor landing in two long strides, dragging Robin behind him. In another two strides, they were at the door.

"But which one? Digby seemed like such a nice man," Robin murmured as she followed T.J. inside. "He seemed so ordinary and quiet and agreeable at first. He lived in a nice house, on a nice street, in a nice neighborhood. I don't want to believe he could do this. He put flowers on her grave…. It was him, wasn't it? If Dub didn't do it, then who else but Herman Digby?

"But then Robbie Lee… I could really believe it was him. Heck, his school pictures could have been practice shots for the post office wall."

Realizing that Robin was babbling and on the verge of losing it, T.J. kicked the door firmly shut and turned the dead bolt. He knew he should call the police and report the incident. But he knew he had to calm Robin down first. He chose the only thing he could think of.

He kissed her again.

It seemed like the most natural thing in the world to be enfolded in T.J.'s warm embrace. Robin drew much needed strength from his. She hadn't had the time to be scared at first. She had gone from worry to anger to having the wind knocked out of her in five minutes.

Had it only been five? Probably less.

Then, as she followed T.J. up the stairs, the impact of what had happened walloped her almost as hard as T.J. had when he saved her life.

He had saved her life. A shiver of fear coursed through her. Or was it desire? The only thing that Robin was certain of was that at this moment, sheltered in T.J.'s strong arms, she felt safe. She didn't want to leave. She didn't want to stop kissing him.

She didn't want to stop with kissing.

T.J. felt his rising desire for Robin and knew he should stop. He had a phone call to make and a report to file. He knew he had to stop before it became impossible. He forced himself to relinquish his tight hold on the willing woman cradled in his arms. He reluctantly closed his hungry lips and pulled away. He rested his cheek against hers; it was as far as he could go.

"We have to stop," he protested. "We have to call…"

Robin's searching lips found him and pulled him under. "I don't want to," she murmured, as she worked her hands underneath his shirt.

"It's gone too far to keep it from the police now," T.J. protested, deliberately misunderstanding.

"I don't want to stop this," she whispered as she traced his belt line around to the rear and tugged his shirttails free.

T.J. tried to resist the gentle pressure of Robin's exploring fingers on the small of his back. He arched away to remove the sweet torture, but it only intensified as his aching groin pressed against her feminine softness as he tried to move away.

It was too late.

As Robin slid her fingers around to release the brass button that held his urgent need in check, he knew he was lost.

He swept her into his arms and carried her into the bedroom.

The thwarted attempt on her life seemed secondary to this all-consuming need she had. She needed to be filled by T.J. Completed. She felt as if she had to surrender to this or die. And the imminent danger imposed upon her by Robin Lee Digby's killer was inconsequential.

They fumbled with their fastenings, clumsy as a pair of teenagers afraid they would be caught. They tossed their clothing to the floor and fell to the mattress with fierce abandon. There was no rhyme or reason or sense in their flaming, urgent passion. Only need. If the world had come to an end at that moment, it would not have mattered.

T.J. laid her gently down, then fervently ripped the covers off the bed. Then he lay down beside her. He kissed the tender spot at the base of her neck, sending a series of small tremors down her boneless spine. Then he dotted a path of tiny kisses from there to the first of her twin mounds. He paused for a moment, fanning the fire within her with his hot, moist breath as he paused—to breathe, or to torture her?

Just when she was ready to weep impatient tears, he dipped his head again and teased first one breast to attention and then the other with his warm, searching tongue. Her hardened nipples acted as conduits carrying sensuous messages from him to deep inside her yearning core. There was no doubt that he wanted her as much as she wanted him.

"Please," she found herself begging. "Please." Stop this torment and make me rise above everything.

T.J. must have understood her half-whispered prayer, for he gathered her to him and slid one muscular leg across her. He fit himself to her and then pressed her thighs apart with his leg and knocked at the threshold of her very sanity. "If you don't stop teasing me now, I will surely die," she breathed, out of desperation and desire.

The whispered plea must have worked, for with those spoken words he thrust and entered her, sending her to the edge of an unseen precipice and beyond. Tendrils of fire and flame licked inside her, ignited by the smoldering embers she had long since banked away, forgotten. Or never known. She arched against him, raising herself to meet his each and every thrust.

As T.J. brought her soaring to heights she had never before imagined, Robin's only thoughts were of him. As she exploded with passionate release, she knew she loved him.

Sometime later, the warm glow of T.J.'s lovemaking started to fade in the cold truth of reality. Robin barely knew this man, yet she had given herself completely to him. Twice. She had given herself fully, with no reservations and no expectations.

Until now.

She'd been such a coward about talking to him. How should she deal with this? With him? They both had their own personal agendas. She had her five-year plan, with four years remaining, and she had no idea what kind of game plan T.J. might have. For that matter, was this wonderful feeling of love on her part nothing at all to him?

Robin remembered reading that sometimes the excitement of an intense life-or-death confrontation could stimulate sexual desire. Had this been one of those situations? Had T.J. made love to her, or had he simply given in to the excitement of the moment?

Another, more pressing thought struck her. Things had changed a lot in the past five or six years. During the time she was out of circulation, sex had changed. Once upon a time, unsafe sex could make you pregnant. Or sick. But now it could kill you.

Robin glanced at the man holding her in his sweet embrace. Should she ask him? They should have practiced safe sex. What would he say?

She rolled out of T.J.'s arms and squinted at the dimly illuminated clock on the bedside. It was only a little after ten. Why the time was important, Robin didn't know, but it was. They had never reported the incident with the car. They had been too sidetracked to think rationally. First because of the fright of the moment, then because of their sudden, overwhelming need.

T.J.'s breathing was slow and even. He hadn't protested when Robin vacated her comfortable place in his arms, so she assumed that he was asleep. Obviously, he wasn't tying his insides up in knots thinking about what had just happened between them. But Robin was definitely awake, with her thoughts speeding around her one-track mind a mile a minute.

Robin needed time to think this through. She did some rapid mental calculations; pregnancy was probably not an issue. But what should she do about the other matter? She needed to be alone.

There was no way to think about this rationally, with his naked body lying so close to hers. Then there was the matter of commitment. Maybe he had not taken this as seriously as she had. Could she accept this simply as what it was, or did she expect more?

Robin quietly shifted to the edge of the bed and worked

her legs over the side, to the floor. Holding her breath, she carefully pushed herself up.

"Don't go." T.J.'s voice was gentle and undemanding. But unsettling.

Robin clutched a corner of the bedsheet to her breast and answered. "I didn't think you were awake." She knew that her remark wasn't really an explanation for why she was creeping out of his bed, but she didn't know what else to say.

"I think we need to talk about this."

An icy shiver left a trail down Robin's spine that had nothing to do with the temperature in the darkened bedroom. Was this it? Was this the part where he told her that it had been nothing more than the heat of the moment? She had already told herself that. Would it sound any worse coming from him?

Chapter 18

Robin tried to bluff herself through it. If she acted tough, she might convince him it was okay. But who would convince her?

"Why talk about it? Stuff happens. I've read enough detective novels to know about the rush that comes from a dangerous situation. It wasn't me that turned you on." Robin wanted to charge bravely on, but she was afraid to continue. So far, she had managed to keep her voice even and nonchalant. She wasn't certain how long she could keep it up without losing her dispassionate tone.

The silence from T.J.'s side of the bed seemed to scream out an answer. *It was true.*

The mattress creaked and the linens rustled as T.J. pushed himself to a sitting position. He touched Robin's arm, caressing her as he trailed his fingers upward. "Do you believe that?" he whispered huskily.

"Yes," Robin answered firmly. She tried not to flinch at the touch of his fingers on her shoulder. She tried to look him evenly in the eye, but she couldn't.

"Do you want to believe it?" There was a pleading note in T.J.'s voice that gave Robin hope.

"No." Robin's voice betrayed her. It cracked on the simple word.

"I don't want to, either," T.J. whispered as he drew her into his arms.

He had lain there afterward, thinking, just as Robin must have. And the first thought had been that their impulsive action had been because of the rush, the danger.

Then he had thought of something else. It had been three years since Ginger died. For three years, he had gone without being with a woman. And all at once, there was a woman in his life, doing much the same things that Ginger had done. Doing everything except loving him. Had he somehow taken advantage of her to fill some long-dormant need?

God, he hoped not.

Then, when Robin tried to leave, he'd dared to speak. He'd read between the lines of her brave speech, read the message behind the proud words. *She cared for him.* Maybe even loved him. It was then that he'd known with certainty that what might have begun as a reaction to the old flight-or-fight instinct had become something more. He knew he cared about Robin, too.

T.J. cared about her because she had understood his panicked thoughts when they were trapped in the basement. She had understood his confusion about Ginger and Rusty and had not judged him or tried to talk him out of it. And he cared for her because, in spite of the curves Dub Doubleday had thrown her, she was trying to move on with her life.

And she had the best pair of legs this side of Radio City Music Hall.

It was a miracle how right it seemed to have her there in his embrace. T.J. wound his arms around her tighter and reveled in the velvety smoothness of her skin. He bent down and placed a kiss on top of her love-tousled hair.

Robin responded by tipping her mouth up to meet his. T.J. tasted the sweetness of her lips, savoring for the first time their delicate flavor. A low moan of pleasure surprised him. Had he done that?

A tiny nose nuzzled the hollow at the base of his throat, and Robin kissed a path up to his chin. Instead of continuing on to his mouth, she stopped.

"I know this is a heck of a time to mention this, but don't you think we should go ahead and call the police about what happened earlier?" Robin murmured from somewhere beneath T.J.'s chin.

"I'm sure they're not interested in what went on here," T.J. replied lazily, looking down at Robin and winking at her shocked reaction as she jerked her head up to stare at him.

She made an exasperated face, then laughed the tinkling laugh that came, so welcome, when he least expected it. "Not that. You know. The car."

"I know." Robin's reminder had intruded on the moment and completely destroyed the mood. "I guess we should."

T.J. relinquished his claim on Robin's willing body and began to dress.

If he had been an ordinary citizen, the police department would probably have put off their investigation until the morning. They'd have shrugged it off as an accident. Nobody was hurt, and the car was gone. But T.J. had been insistent and had quoted from the procedure manuals and had convinced or bullied the department into sending someone over. Robin finished dressing as T.J. paced, waiting for the patrol car to arrive.

The light in the bathroom seemed too bright as Robin tried to force her wayward hair into some semblance of order. She surveyed her face in the mirror and wondered how much an observant cop could tell about her just by looking. Would he see her bright eyes and flushed complexion and know what had occurred between her and T.J.? Or would he read her high color as due to the excitement of what had happened in the street?

Robin winced as she dabbed a damp cloth against the burning abrasion that nearly covered the right side of her face. She hadn't noticed it until she came into the bathroom to look, but now it burned like fire. Shrugging her shoulders, Robin tried to work out the stiffness in her body from the banging she had taken when T.J. threw her out of the path of the advancing car. In the time she had taken to dress, Robin had cataloged at least a dozen bruises.

She laughed. If this was how she looked after being rescued, imagine how she might have looked if she hadn't. The notion sobered her, and her brief smile faded. Her inconsequential bumps and bruises were nothing compared to what could have happened if he had been successful. She could have ended up dead. For real!

The doorbell chimed, announcing the arrival of the police investigator. Robin shrugged off the morbid thoughts and splashed a quick dash of cold water on her face. After giving herself a perfunctory blotting with the towel, she turned off the light and went to face the music.

T.J. was already talking to the officer by the time Robin joined them in the living room. They seemed to take no notice of her arrival, so Robin did not interrupt them. T.J. gesticulated with his hands, apparently describing what he had seen. The officer dutifully took notes as T.J. spoke.

Robin wasn't well-informed about police procedures, but T.J. seemed to be telling the officer exactly what he needed to know. The man didn't stop to ask questions, only scribbled the information on his pad, occasionally mumbling for T.J. to slow down.

Hovering nearby, in case either T.J. or the policeman

needed to consult with her, Robin listened avidly as he described what had happened. She was astonished by the detail with which he remembered the incident. How could he remember it all with such clarity? It had happened so quickly that to Robin it had been a high-speed smudge amid the details of her life.

T.J.'s description seemed so complete that Robin wondered what she could contribute to the report of what had transpired. Feeling useless and embarrassed about not being able to remember clearly, she edged toward the couch and sat. If she couldn't be useful, she could at least stay out of the way.

She had barely settled in when the blue-clad officer gestured in her direction.

"Is that Miss Digby?" The officer directed his question to T.J., not Robin.

Irritation edged the impotence Robin felt to the side. "She is capable of speaking for herself," she replied testily. She pushed herself to her feet and approached the spot where T.J. and the officer stood.

"Excuse me." The officer checked his notes and flipped to a fresh sheet in his notebook. Then he began to fire a volley of questions at Robin that, to her, seemed more like an interrogation than an information-gathering sequence.

Why was he making her feel guilty?

"Are you positive that the car was light blue, Miss Digby?" The officer had asked the same question in three different ways.

"No. I'm not sure of anything. It was dark, and everything happened too fast. All I have is an impression of blue as the car sped past me." Robin closed her eyes and tried to conjure up the image of the speeding car.

"What makes you think you knew who the driver is? Did you recognize the car?"

"I remember seeing a light blue car parked in front of Herman Digby's house earlier today. It was one of those old Japanese models. You know, before they got respectable. But I don't know if it was his. And we saw Robbie Lee getting out of a different blue car—old and beat-up, like the one at Digby's house—at his home the other night. Something like an old Pinto.'' Robin paused; her uncertainty hurt her even more than the raw spot on her cheek. "I guess this is going to sound stupid,'' she finally said. "Female intuition and all. But after T.J. picked me up off the ground, the first thing I thought of was Robin Digby's killer.''

She just wished she knew which one it was.

Robin looked uncomfortable as the detective went over the same questions with her again and again. It was the same information that he had already provided, and T.J. would have been willing to bet that Robin was certain that the detective was going over it again and again because he doubted her. T.J. hated that she was intimidated, but she was handling herself well. In spite of her lack of training, some of her perceptions were quite good. He wished there was some way he could reassure her.

The officer turned away from Robin. "Did the car hit either of you?''

"No. I managed to push Robin out of its path, and we rolled out of the way.''

"Then how did you get those bruises?'' This time the officer addressed Robin.

Shrugging, she replied. "T.J. tackled me as if he were a linebacker and I was the quarterback for the Green Bay Packers.'' Robin shrugged again. "I guess I landed pretty hard.''

"Did you seek medical treatment?''

T.J. interjected. "I've had some medical training, and I didn't think it was necessary. Robin had the wind knocked out of her, and I checked her for broken bones.'' Okay, so it wasn't exactly a clinical examination, but he had managed to run his hands over every inch of her body. If she had been hurt, they would know it by now. "I found no evidence of serious injury."

The officer flipped his notebook shut and eyed Robin skeptically. "You know you shouldn't have gone and tried to do our job for us. You could have been hurt."

"I know." Robin looked contrite, but T.J. noticed something mischievous lurking in her eyes. There was something about the way she had narrowed them.

"I'll get somebody to check for skid marks at first light. I'm done here." He flipped his notebook closed and fished in his shirt pocket and pulled out a couple of business cards. "You call me if you remember anything else."

"Yes, sir," Robin replied snappily as she accepted a card.

Was she resisting the urge to salute? T.J. could see laughter bubbling in the twinkling blue of her eyes.

He listened impatiently to the officer's final instructions as he walked him to the door and then closed it firmly behind him. As he twisted the bolt, Robin's giggles burst free.

She struggled to regain her composure. "'Yes, sir. I checked her for fractures,' he said brokenly," Robin managed to say before losing it again. She chortled as she resurrected the Tom Swifties she'd promised to forget.

"What was I supposed to tell him?" T.J. responded defensively. "That we got sidetracked on the way to the phone?" He crossed to where Robin stood by the hall door.

"Do you want to check for bruises again?" Robin looked up at T.J., an impish expression on her face.

Sweeping her into his arms, T.J. laughed. "Oh, yes. And for broken bones, too." He looked down at Robin's smiling mouth. "Maybe I'd better check out those lips."

Then caution slowed him. He grew serious. "Robin, we have to talk."

"Not now," she said as she ran a teasing finger across his lips.

"Yes, now." He brushed her hand away.

Robin's playful smile faded, and she turned away. She gnawed at her lip.

"Before we go into the bedroom, I need to say something." Damn, this is hard, T.J. thought. He cleared his throat. "Things have changed since I first met Ginger. Uh… Nowadays, people don't just jump into bed without asking questions. You'll have to admit that we sort of got the cart before the horse, and I need to make something clear…."

Robin looked up into his eyes. Light twinkled in hers. What was she thinking? And why was she grinning at a time like this?

"I've been trying to get up the nerve to broach this subject with you," she told him. "Look, T.J. You don't have to worry about me. I'm safe. After Dub, I had myself tested. Though he never showed any indication that he was fooling around when we were married, I had to be sure. I passed. One hundred, A-plus."

Relief flooded through T.J. How typical of Robin to try to make things easy for him. But it wasn't easy. The army training films had made it seem a whole lot easier.

"I was tested in the army." He sighed and went on. "I haven't been with anyone since…"

"I know. I believe you," Robin whispered. She looked as though a load had been lifted from her shoulders. She wrapped her arms around his waist.

"But what if—?" Why couldn't he complete a sentence tonight?

Robin understood his incoherence. "I think we're okay for now. But do you think in the future…?"

T.J. laughed and then finished her question. "…we should use protection?"

Robin nodded, and joy surged through T.J. Did her ques-

tion mean that there was going to be a future for them? He
drew a deep breath. "Whatever it takes. Now do you think
we can stop talking?"

Putting a finger to her lips, Robin pulled him into the
bedroom.

The phone, jingling insistently, woke them.

Robin rolled over, silently cursing Mr. Edwards's rule
that there be only one phone connection in the house, the
one that was in the living room. She swung her legs over
the edge of the bed in her haste to silence the ring. As she
reached for something to cover herself, T.J. passed her. She
found the polo shirt that he had discarded twice the evening
before and pulled it over her head.

"Yeah. Thanks. I'll tell her." T.J. hung up as Robin
reached the living room. He turned as she entered. "That
was Gardner Lightfoot. They've decided to bring Digby
and Lee in for questioning. They're sending cars out to pick
them up.

"It seems that Robert Charles Lee is a pretty sorry character. He's on parole on a weapons violation. He had no
business having so much as a peashooter in the house. No
wonder Dora sold the shotgun. Having it would have been
a parole violation."

"Good. Maybe then I can stop worrying about it. Once
they've got them in custody, I can breathe a whole lot easier." Robin crossed the short swatch of carpet and wound
her arms around T.J.'s neck, tangling her fingers in his
thick, unruly auburn hair.

She was surprised to find T.J. stiff and unresponsive to
her touch. "What's wrong?" she asked, alarmed. "Is there
something else you're not telling me?"

Concerned, warm eyes gazed soberly down into Robin's
upturned face. "They haven't issued arrest warrants," T.J.
told Robin gently. "They're just going to question them."

"Oh. But after they've talked to them, they'll know which one did it. Then they can hold him. Right?"

"Maybe. But I wouldn't count on it."

"Okay. I won't count." Robin changed the subject. "What're we doing today?" Her five-year plan had changed radically in the past twenty-four hours. All she was interested in right now was today. The next four years could work themselves out later.

"Robin, I've got some business to take care of in Birmingham. I can't do anything with you this morning." T.J.'s tone was apologetic, but the content was clear.

Robin felt as though he had slapped her in the face. Had he decided that last night was all he wanted? Was he trying to give her the brush-off? Robin released her fingers from T.J.'s hair and pulled away.

"I see," Robin said softly, lowering her head as she backed away. "I shouldn't have made any assumptions." She turned, ready to bolt toward her own room.

"Wait!" Warm, strong hands pulled her back and crushed her against T.J.'s chest. "You don't see." T.J. cupped Robin's chin with his hand and tipped her face up. Gentle lips pressed against hers, not taking, but simply offering assurance.

"It's not what you think," he told her. "I have to go to Birmingham to check with the caretaker at my house. It's a standing appointment, and it's too late to cancel. I go in once a month."

"You have a house?"

"Ginger's dream home," T.J. answered huskily. "We lived there just six months before…"

Sensing that it was difficult for him, Robin pressed her fingers across T.J.'s mouth. "You don't have to explain."

"I don't want to go until after those two are under restraint, but you'll be all right if you stay inside. Just don't open the door to anybody."

"Come on, T.J. I'll be fine. The cops'll pick them up."

T.J. sighed. "Okay. Make sure you know who it is before you open the door." He turned to go. "And stay away from the windows."

Maybe part of loving was knowing when not to cling. Robin waved him on. "Go on. Take care of your business. I'm a big girl. I'll be here when you get back." T.J. headed for the door, then he pivoted.

Robin watched, confused, as he searched the top shelf of his bedroom closet. "What are you looking for?" she asked, just as he dragged down a small metal strongbox.

He twisted and turned the combination lock. "This," T.J. muttered grimly as he withdrew a menacing-looking gun.

"Where did you get that?"

"It was my service weapon," he told her as he thrust the evil-looking thing in her direction. "Here."

Robin shrank back in horror, her hands raised as if to push him away. "You mean that thing has been here all along?" She backed away another step. "Is it loaded?"

"It is now," T.J. replied tersely, as he snapped the clip into place.

A sneaking suspicion crept into Robin's mind. He really expected her to use that if anybody threatening showed up. But surely they wouldn't be stupid enough to come here. She couldn't possibly use that thing; she didn't know how.

"Hold it with two hands and aim. Then all you have to do is release the safety, like this, and squeeze," T.J. told her.

"But what if I hit him?"

"I don't think you'll get to that point. Just firing ought to do the trick, and it'll alert Mr. Edwards."

"But T.J.... I can't... I won't..."

T.J. shrugged. "Look, Robin. I'll feel better if I know you have this. You probably won't need to use it." He put the gun on the top of the dresser.

"Okay," Robin agreed reluctantly. She'd have felt better

if T.J. stayed home and used the gun himself. Its presence in the house wasn't reassuring at all.

"I won't be long," T.J. told her as he turned again to leave.

"I just had to say goodbye," T.J. whispered softly to the empty room that still seemed to be filled with her. He knew Ginger would understand. Ginger would know that he was not erasing his past, but embracing his future. And he'd have bet she would approve.

Maybe that was what she'd been trying to tell him when he tried so hard to get himself killed. That he still had a future.

T.J. wandered through the empty house, remembering. He had tried to live there after Ginger and Rusty died, but the place had been too full of them. He hadn't been able to separate them from the place, and he knew he wouldn't be able to stay there again until he could.

He had finished the usual business with his next-door neighbor and sent her on her way. Now he strolled through the empty rooms, smiling and remembering. Now he was able to touch the things that they had touched, look at the things that they had seen, and not feel the overwhelming sense of loss that had sent him away from the place. Now he could remember and not hurt.

He would always love his first wife and child. Would always miss them and regret the future together that they hadn't gotten to have. But he could go on now—he saw that.

T.J. ran a finger over the thick layer of dust that covered the long-neglected furniture. He would have to do something about that. The place had been empty too long. It needed laughter, love and children. He'd have to let it go. It was time to let some other family build their dreams here.

It was time to move on.

He would call a Realtor when he got home and let her

list the house. One had been pestering him about it for months. Funny. Once he had thought of this place as home. Now home was the shabby, cramped apartment in Tuscaloosa that beckoned to him. And he wanted to be there. He switched off the lights and locked the past behind him.

Robin was his future now, and she was waiting for him.

Chapter 19

Robin tried to ignore the gun lying darkly on the top of T.J.'s dresser, but it kept drawing her gaze. How could he possibly think she could use that? Hoping that the weapon would soon leave her mind, she busied herself tidying the apartment.

How does that saying go? Robin asked herself as she stripped the rumpled sheets from the bed where she and T.J. had slept. And made love. Today is the first day…of a happy ending.

"No, that isn't it." Robin laughed. The saying wasn't the one she had been trying to remember, but this one was close enough. In fact, she liked it better, especially the part about the happy ending. Twelve months ago, she wouldn't have been sure that there would ever be another happy ending for her; Dub had seen to that. At least not the happily-ever-after kind.

Robin had figured she would have to carefully construct the rest of her life alone. And she'd been prepared to do it. Now, sharing a future seemed a real possibility. She laughed again.

It was funny how laughter always seemed to be bubbling just below the surface of her consciousness, ready to escape. It had been such a long time since Robin had been this carefree, and she had been long overdue for a change.

Her smile faded a little as she reminded herself that Robbie Lee or Herman Digby was still a problem. But not for long. The police had probably already picked them up for questioning and would decide to hold one of them. Robin breathed long and deep. Yes, things were definitely on the upswing.

Robin had even reworked her five-year plan. The timetable was essentially the same; however, the revised version allowed her not to be alone.

There were enough sheets and towels strewn around the room to allow for a load of wash. Robin filled up a plastic laundry basket and started for the laundry room. Humming a happy tune, she hoisted the basket to her hip and opened the apartment door.

The sharp scent of fresh paint assailed Robin as she pushed the door wide. There, in front of her, knelt Mr. Edwards, paintbrush in hand, painting the trim around the door. Robin sidestepped the man and rested the basket on the banister.

"What's up, Mr. E.?" Robin asked, greeting her landlord. It was apparent that Mr. Edwards was repairing the damage done by the intruder several nights before.

"Just trying to keep up my property values," Mr. Edwards responded, without looking up from his task. "I swear, you college folks can be rough on a building," he grumbled as he swabbed paint on the scarred wood.

The simmering laughter bubbled to the surface again. "I know, Mr. E. Isn't it a shame how we have all those wild parties and tear up everything in sight?"

"Ain't it just?" The old man laughed a wheezing laugh

that ended in a hoarse, rasping cough. He chuckled to himself, then got up to survey his handiwork. ''I reckon it's going to need another coat.''

There was still a hint of raw wood showing through, but the door looked presentable enough to Robin. ''It looks fine, Mr. E. Don't put yourself out.''

''It don't put me out none to keep my building looking nice.'' Mr. Edwards dipped his brush back into the can. ''Oh, I fixed the drain in the washroom,'' the elderly man continued as he wiped off the excess paint from the brush on the rim of the can. ''You won't have to sit there and watch to make sure it doesn't overrun.''

''Great. I can put my load in and come back upstairs and fix lunch. I'll be back up in a few minutes.''

The sun seemed to be shining brighter today than it had in a very long time, thought T.J. as he drove back to Tuscaloosa from his monthly pilgrimage. Was it really a brighter day? Or had the dark cloud that had hung over him for so long finally lifted? Whatever the cause, T.J. didn't care. All he knew was that he was going home.

Home to Tuscaloosa.

Home to Robin.

He grinned as he grabbed the paper bag from the drugstore and took the steps in front of the apartment two at a time. After all those empty months alone, he didn't want to waste a single minute. Or second. Every moment away from Robin was a memory lost. He'd learned his lesson the first time around. He wasn't going to squander his second chance at love.

Love. Yes, love. He'd already embraced the feeling, without naming it. Now that it had a name, it sounded more real than it had felt. He reached the top of the stairs.

The apartment door yawned wide, and the hairs stood at the back of his neck. This was all wrong. Robin knew better than to leave the door hanging open as long as Digby or

Lee could still be on the loose. Had he been caught? Or had he caught up with Robin?

Then he saw the traces of fresh paint and relaxed. Maybe the door was open to allow the paint to dry. He hurried inside, tossing the bag to the couch. Everything seemed as it should be.

T.J. called out Robin's name and waited for her welcoming answer.

It didn't come.

He made a quick check of the bedroom. The gun was on top of the dresser where he had left it, but Robin was nowhere to be seen.

He crossed to the front window and looked outside. T.J. saw no trace of Robin, but a flash of color drew him to look farther down the street. Digby! Why hadn't he noticed the light blue Honda parked near the corner when he drove up? Damn!

It had to be him. T.J. snatched the gun from the dresser, checked the clip and dashed down the stairs, nearly running over Mr. Edwards, who had just stepped out of his apartment. He stopped and hastily apologized.

"No harm done, boy. But where's the fire?"

"I can't find Robin. Have you seen her?"

Edwards chuckled. "Well, I reckon she's down in the washroom with her cousin, catching up on her summer away.

"I hoped you two'd get together. Guess this means it worked."

"Cousin? Did he tell you he was her cousin? What did he look like?" T.J. didn't have to wait for the particulars to know it was Digby, but Mr. Edwards's description matched what Robin had told him the night before.

"How long ago?" T.J.'s mind raced frantically as a list of possibilities—all bad—grew in his mind.

"Not long. Five minutes or so. I was just finishing upstairs when he come up lookin' for Robin. I sent him down to the washroom.'' Edwards looked confused. ''I ain't seen him come up. Is something wrong?''

T.J. drew in a long, deep breath and tried to slow his racing heart. He gulped in another lungful of air. ''Listen carefully, Mr. Edwards. I think that man is the man that killed that other woman. Robin figured out that he had done it, and now she's in trouble.''

He fumbled in his pocket for the card the policeman had given him the night before and gave it to Edwards. ''Call Detective Womble. Tell him what I told you and to get over here fast.''

He didn't have time to be polite. Without waiting for Mr. Edwards's response, T.J. hurtled down the stairs to the basement, slowing as he rounded the corner to the laundry room. He wasn't going to lose another woman he loved.

She sensed his presence in the dimly lit laundry room before she saw him. Robin tried to ignore the crawly feeling and finished loading the machine. She inserted two quarters into the slots and shoved in the starter as slowly as she dared. Trying to delay what she knew was inevitable, Robin measured the washing powders and dry bleach with exaggerated precision. The pouring water whipped the soap into a frothy liquid as she watched it do its job.

Unable to postpone any longer, Robin carefully lowered the lid of the machine. She took a deep, brave breath and turned around.

Herman Digby stood there, quietly watching her from his position at the laundry room door.

He looked harmless enough, leaning against the door frame, and Robin would have bet anything that the killer had been Robbie. Herman Digby looks more like an accountant than a wife-killer, thought Robin as she faced him. He hadn't said anything; should she greet him?

Robin decided to act as if she didn't know what was going on. ''Hi. Can I help you?'' It was more a stalling tactic than a greeting. She looked vastly different in her cutoff jeans and bleach-spotted T-shirt. Maybe he won't recognize me, Robin reasoned. She looked nothing like the carefully dressed cosmetic lady who had visited him the day before.

A flicker of indecision crossed Digby's bland face. Then it changed. Caspar Milquetoast was gone. In his place stood a frightening caricature of the former man.

Robin realized at that moment how people could have believed in demonic possession. If she hadn't seen it happen in front of her, she wouldn't have believed it possible. Digby's eyes had widened, his pupils had narrowed, and his soft form had tensed like a coiled serpent ready to spring. Robin knew she was in big trouble.

Digby still hadn't opened his mouth. He didn't have to. He just shifted slightly and let her see what had been hidden from her view. His right side had been propped comfortably against the door frame and had hidden the real threat.

What Robin saw resting lightly against Digby's side caused her to freeze where she stood. Leaning against the doorjamb, hidden until now, was a shotgun, ancient, but recently cleaned and oiled. Robin could smell the gun oil from her position across the small room.

"Yeah. You can help me." Digby's words snatched Robin's eyes away from the gun and to his face.

"What with?" Robin's voice was an almost inaudible croak. Her fingers opened and closed convulsively as she remembered the gun she'd left on the top of the dresser, the gun that T.J. had told her to use. Why hadn't she listened to him? Why hadn't she thought to bring it with her?

Because she hadn't really anticipated any threat in the laundry room of her own building.

Digby looked as if he were trying to formulate an answer, but couldn't come up with anything. Then his face crumpled, and he choked back a sob.

The unexpected response chilled Robin to her marrow. She stared at him.

"It can't be all that bad. Maybe I can help," Robin suggested with remarkable calm. If she could talk to him about it, maybe she could delay until help came. Hadn't she read somewhere that it was possible to talk some people out of bad intentions? It was worth a try. She sucked in a long, reviving breath and waited for what he had to say.

"You know, I almost didn't recognize you. Almost turned around." He looked at her shrewdly. "You look much better with all that makeup gone."

"Thanks," Robin mumbled. Anything to keep him from doing whatever it was he had planned.

"You can't bring my wife back. But you could replace her." Digby's twisted logic seemed eerily reasonable.

Hope surged through Robin. Maybe he wanted to kidnap her. If he only wanted her to go with him as a stand-in for his dead wife, there was still a chance to get away.

"If you still want your wife, why did you kill her?" That had been the wrong thing to say, Robin realized too late to call it back.

Now all she could do was hope that help would come. She watched Digby carefully, trying to guess his next move. Had he methodically set out to kill his wife, only to have his plan foiled when Dub claimed her? Robin groped for the correct response. Something to soften the harsh question she had asked.

A genuine expression of regret covered Digby's face. "I didn't mean to," he replied sadly. "It was an accident." He patted the gun in an oddly protective manner. "Robin found this old shotgun at a garage sale. She knew I had always wanted one. When we took it out into the woods to try it out on tin cans, I tripped over a tree root and fell. The gun went off. Robin was in the way." Digby gestured with the gun. "I thought it wasn't loaded then. I know it is now."

"Why didn't you just admit it to the police? They wouldn't have charged you if it was an accident." T.J.'s gun was seeming like a better idea all the time. Why hadn't she listened to him and kept it with her?

"I panicked. And Robin and I had been having some problems." He closed his eyes and sighed. "But we'd patched them up. We were talking about having kids...."

"I didn't think they would believe me." A catalog of emotions fluttered across Digby's face. "By the time I'd finally made up my mind to call them, somebody else had already found her. And they'd somehow got the idea that she was you. When your husband showed up and claimed the body, I figured I was in the clear. They couldn't blame me for killing my Robin if she wasn't really dead."

"Mr. Digby," Robin said, trying to reason with him, "so far, I think the only thing you've done wrong is to conceal your wife's death. Maybe if you stop now, they'd go easy on you. You could even avoid prosecution altogether."

The tortured look returned to Digby's face. "Maybe I need to be punished," he replied. "I did kill her."

"But you said it was an accident."

"I just want my Robin back."

"Then why do you want me? Just let me go. Turn yourself in. Admit it. You need help."

A slight movement in the dark hall behind Digby caught Robin's eye. A surge of hope flooded through her. T.J. was creeping carefully toward the door where Digby stood. He held the gun up, parallel to his body, ready to fire if the need arose. If Robin could just keep Digby distracted, maybe T.J. could ease on in and take the shotgun away from him.

Fortunately, the noise of the washing machine had covered T.J.'s headlong charge into the basement. If not for that, Digby would surely have heard him coming. He would have bet anything that Robbie Lee had been the killer, but Herman Digby's menacing stance erased any doubt he had.

T.J. chastised himself for being so careless. Damn, he was so out of practice. He could have put Robin in worse danger than she was already in. He raised a finger to his lips to signal quietly to Robin, but she apparently hadn't seen him.

Digby was still a good five feet away, and T.J. inched carefully forward. He knew he had to get Digby's shotgun before it discharged and hit Robin. T.J.'s only hope of subduing the man was surprise. His only advantage was the dark corridor in which he stood. He prayed that Robin would not inadvertently give him away.

"I don't want you," Digby told Robin, his voice filled with disgust. "You're not anything like my Robbie." He shook his head sadly. "As long as it was you who was dead, my Robin wasn't," he insisted illogically. He smiled. "She's off visiting her sister in Arizona, you know."

The impact of Digby's words stopped T.J.'s heartbeat and whammed the breath out of him as if he'd been gut-punched. The man had lost it. To his way of thinking, his wife was still alive. Robin was dead. Or soon would be. Did the man intend to create his own reality? The seconds seemed to tick into eternity as he watched for Digby's next move.

"She sure would be disappointed to find you in trouble when she came home," Robin replied with remarkable logic. Her eyes flickered toward the washing machine and back to Digby.

T.J. tried to analyze Robin's gesture. Had she seen him, and was she trying to tell him something? T.J. stared at the chugging washing machine. How long had it been running? A germ of a plan began to grow.

"You let me worry about that," Digby replied, with terrifying calm. He raised the shotgun and waved it toward Robin. "You just come with me."

Robin obeyed the order slowly, edging around the periphery of the room, instead of crossing directly to Digby. *Good girl,* T.J. congratulated her silently.

There was a nook between the three washers and the two tall industrial dryers. T.J. dared to hope that Robin would be able to see the safe haven and duck into it if she needed to. He nodded his head slightly toward the niche and hoped she'd get it.

Suddenly the fill cycle ended with a jarring thunk and the agitator began to churn. Startled, Digby swung the gun around toward the sound. It was the break they needed. As Robin ducked into the tiny, sheltering cranny, T.J. lunged.

The noise of the shotgun sounded like an explosion in the tiny, uninsulated basement room. Robin, tucked in her safe corner, didn't dare take her head out of the fetal crouch in which she was cowering. A shower of something—plaster from the ceiling, she supposed—rained down on her, and she buried her head deeper into her knees.

Debris continued falling for several long heartbeats. Robin tried to calm her racing heart and strained to hear anything that could tell her she was safe. There was a peculiar scrabbling sound that Robin couldn't identify. Then nothing but the humming washing machine.

"Robin, are you all right?" T.J.'s baritone was music to her ears.

She released the breath she hadn't realized she was holding. "Yes," Robin answered, her voice muffled by her protective crouch. "Can I come out?"

"No. Stay there. I have Digby under control, but I won't feel easy until he's in police custody." He was quiet for a brief moment, then added, "You don't have to curl up in a ball. Just stay out of the way."

Heart hammering furiously, Robin cautiously raised her head and peered through the narrow opening of her protective nook. The air was heavy with plaster dust, and a tardy chunk of drywall rattled down. The shotgun lay seemingly harmless on the concrete floor in front of her feet. From her angle, Robin couldn't see T.J. or Herman Digby.

There was little room to move in her tiny, cramped space, but Robin did what she could to see more. She scooted forward as far as she dared, stirring up a cloud of chalky dust. The powder found its way to her nose, and she sneezed.

"Bless you."

Was that Digby's voice? The seemingly innocuous remark, coming from him, sounded chillingly wrong.

The force of Robin's sneeze had carried her head forward, and when she opened her eyes, she could just see the edge of something, somebody. She pressed herself against the washer to her left and managed to widen her view. She could finally see.

T.J. crouched over Digby's inert form, one knee planted in the small of his back. T.J. had twisted the man's hands behind him and held him firmly. Only handcuffs would have made him more secure.

"Robin? Are you all right?"

"Yes. Can I come out now?" To Robin, her voice sounded shaky and weak.

T.J. seemed to think a moment, then answered. "All right. Be careful."

Squeezing out of the tight cranny was much harder than getting into it had been. Robin scrambled to her feet and dusted drywall powder from her backside. She took a tentative step forward, and her foot struck something solid.

Digby's shotgun.

"That's it, Robin. Kick it away." T.J. nodded toward the gun and jerked his head toward the open door. "Kick it there."

Swallowing her fear, Robin drew back her foot and kicked.

Once she had sent the evil thing skidding across the floor

to bounce against the cinder-block wall, she looked back
to T.J.

He nodded his approval. "It's all over, Robin. Now we
just have to wait for the cavalry to come to the rescue."

Digby lay there, still and unresisting. Did Robin detect
relief in his eyes? She tried to ignore him, but she couldn't
draw her eyes away from the little man who had caused
her so many problems. He was alert and appeared calm.
Did that bode well for T.J.? Could he relax, or were they
still in danger?

The washing machine that had been steadfastly going
about its business coughed its intention to change cycles
again. The drain cycle began as soapy water began to empty
from the tub. What was taking the police so long to come?
The draining tub seemed so normal, so ordinary, that Robin
was reassured. It seemed to tell her that life would go on
and the real world was still there outside.

Another noise came over the sound of the machine.

Someone else was in the hallway.

"Swift?" an unfamiliar voice called.

"Yeah. I got Digby subdued. Come and get him."

T.J. backed out of the way and let the squad of armed
officers do their jobs. He watched the milling men and regretted that they stood between him and the woman he
loved. Would they ever leave so he could tell her?

The rush of adrenaline that always coursed through him
after a particularly dangerous situation was curiously ab-
sent. And, more than that, so was the panic from delayed
stress. T.J. didn't miss either. It was another one of those
signs he needed. It told him that he was finally pulling free
of his past. He no longer wanted or needed to be a policeman. And maybe he could face the next storm—of any
kind—without fear.

His most consuming need now was Robin. All he wanted

was to make a future with the courageous woman backed against the washers across the tiny space from him.

One of the officers turned to her. "Are you all right, miss?"

Robin dusted herself off and smiled. "Yes, thank you. A little shaken, but all in one piece." She sounded teary to T.J. as she looked around the room, but when she eventually fixed her eyes on him, love seemed to radiate from her face, though tears streaked her dusty cheeks.

T.J. returned the bright smile with a wide grin of his own. Would the men ever be gone? He wanted to shout to the world what he felt for Robin, but he owed it to her to tell her first.

One of the officers read Digby his Miranda rights.

The man listened stoically.

"Do you understand these rights?"

Digby smiled—a weird, disconnected sort of smile. "Sure. I am a college graduate."

A man in plainclothes turned to T.J. as Digby, now handcuffed securely and flanked by two armed officers, was escorted out. "We'll need to get statements."

"I know the drill, Officer," T.J. answered. "Will you give us a few moments?" He looked pointedly at Robin, standing so far across the little room.

"I understand, sir," the young man replied, smiling. "I'll be waiting upstairs."

Robin stepped forward, grinning broadly. Even with tears muddying the plaster dust on her face and the huge scrape across her cheek, she was still the most beautiful woman in his world.

T.J. crossed the remaining space between them and crushed her into his arms. "I don't want to ever let you go," he whispered as he realized how close he had come to losing her. But he hadn't. He'd been there this time when the woman he loved needed him. Maybe that was why he'd been sent back.

T.J. brushed a tear away from Robin's lip and was rewarded with a smile. "You know, I'm really getting fond of seeing you with a dirty face." He lowered his head to her upturned face and found her soft, willing mouth.

She tasted wonderful, salty from the tears, and gritty and sweet at the same time. He kissed her hungrily until he had taken his fill. Satisfied, he pulled away.

"Don't stop," Robin murmured. She hooked her finger in a belt loop and pulled him back.

"No. I have something important to tell you," T.J. protested as he tried to resist Robin's gentle persuasion.

"I know," Robin said with a smile. "'I love you,' he said amorously," she teased. Then she laughed.

"You're slipping, Digby. That's not up to your usual standard." T.J. laughed, then he sobered. "I do love you, you know."

"I know," she replied, her voice husky with emotion. "I love you, too. I tried to resist, but I finally had to admit it."

T.J.'s chest swelled with joy. Too moved to speak, he wrapped his arms tightly around Robin's slender form and held her firmly against his heart. It was enough to hold her.

A rapid, rhythmic movement in Robin's slight form puzzled him. He looked down at Robin's strangely bobbing head. Could she be laughing? Robin confirmed it when she looked up, grinning.

"Listen," she told him.

T.J. knit his brows. "For what?"

Robin touched a finger to his lips. The washing machine chugged on. "Do you hear it now?"

"I can't hear anything but the machine."

"That's it." Robin laughed merrily. "Can't you hear it? It's telling us that life goes on."

T.J. cocked his head toward the sound. "I hear it."

He folded Robin tighter into his embrace. "I don't need a hunk of bolts and metal to tell me anything. All I need is you. I can't guarantee that I'm completely hang-up-free yet, but I'm getting there. In spite of my shortcomings, will you have me?''

Robin smiled impishly, her bright eyes sparkling. The next few years of her five-year plan would pass more quickly if she was not alone. There was nothing wrong with revision. ''Do you have to ask?'' she said challengingly as she looked up into his eyes.

''Oh,'' she added. ''About that platonic business... Do you think we could forget it?''

A chuckle rumbled from somewhere deep inside him. ''It never happened,'' he said. ''Now kiss me, and show me you mean it.''

She kissed him and erased all doubt.

* * * * *

SILHOUETTE *Romance*

Escape to a place where a kiss is still a kiss...
Feel the breathless connection...
Fall in love as though it were
the very first time...
Experience the power of love!

Come to where favorite authors—such as
Diana Palmer, Stella Bagwell,
Marie Ferrarella and many more—
deliver heart-warming romance and genuine
emotion, time after time after time....

Silhouette Romance—
stories straight from the heart!

Silhouette®
Where love comes alive™

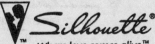

Where love comes alive™

From first love to forever, these love stories are
for today's woman with traditional values.

A highly passionate, emotionally powerful
and always provocative read.

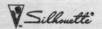

SPECIAL EDITION™

Emotional, compelling stories that capture the
intensity of living, loving and creating a family in
today's world.

Silhouette®

INTIMATE MOMENTS™

A roller-coaster read that delivers romantic thrills
in a world of suspense, adventure and more.

Visit Silhouette at www.eHarlequin.com